To Hal — Thanks for the lessons! Terry Dodd 7/21/97

Here's What People Are Saying About This Book . . .

"Terry Dodd has written a thought-provoking novel loaded with intriguing ideas about marketing and the power of subliminal suggestion."

—Bernard F. Sliger, President Emeritus
Florida State University

" . . . the first novel ever written that incorporates specialty advertising people and plots."

—Marvin Spike, MAS, President
Advertising Specialty Institute

" . . . excellent and refreshing!"

—Gail Hales, MAS, President
Gail Hales Advertising Promotions, Inc.

"Such a yarn. In *Uncommon Influence* the imaginative author has drawn on his promotion background to create a fast-paced mystery/adventure attempting to make believable the seemingly incredible sinister potential of the promotional products industry. And it works!"

—Richard G. Ebel, Director/Marketing Communications
Promotional Products Association International

"I got a real kick out of the concept and the story line."

—Gene Eherenfeldt, CAS, President
Eherenfeldt Company

" . . . read between the lines because you'll discover what may be the first primer on promotional products useable in a college classroom."

—Joel D. Schaffer, President
Downtime Broadcasting Company

" . . . to be commended for your creative effort."

—David M. Jones, Executive Vice President and Chief Economist, Aubrey G. Lanston & Co., Inc.

"You have a rich imagination and wealth of insights."

—Dan S. Bagley III, Ph.D.
Bagley & Associates

" . . . a talented writer who realizes that the reader wants to be educated as well as entertained . . . I like the short chapters and your clever use of words to describe the action and the characters."

—J.K. Osmond, Professor
Florida State University

Uncommon Influence

by Terry Dodd, M.A.S.

DCG Publishing
PO Box 767999
Roswell, Georgia 30076

First Printing 1994

ISBN 0-9641600-0-5

LCCN 94-72191

Design, typesetting, and printing services provided by About Books, Inc., 425 Cedar Street, Buena Vista, CO 81211, 800-548-1876.

Dedication

The industrialized world was yet again testing its ability to survive. In 1944, a young, small-town Iowa mother of three young boys struggled, waiting for her Marine husband to return from his nightmare in paradise. But their personal world war trial in the South Pacific wasn't enough. The eldest boy, barely seven, thrust his family into even deeper waters by dancing with a leaf fire.

The boy lay in his hospital bed, traumatized by third degree burns over nearly 10 percent of his body. His upcoming year-long rehabilitation, including relearning how to walk, would be made possible in great part because of his mother's untrained but calm initial emergency response. Under the doctor's phone directions, she cut away all the burned and still-smoldering skin of her son's right leg. That effort, and her subsequent tireless care guaranteed his complete recovery.

After five separate skin-graft operations had been performed, the doctor explained that unless the parents were willing to regularly and progressively stretch their son's leg—to the point of blood spurting from the freshly grafted skin—he would be crippled for life. The father's emotion-numbing experience of hand-to-hand combat on Guam and Guadalcanal had fortunately (in an ironic twist) steeled him to meet the task. A part of the overall price however, would be the family's heart rending endurance of the boy's cries of excruciating pain as the father faithfully executed the leg-strengthening regimen.

It is thus to the author's care-giving mother and his mentor father (who died before this work could be completed), that this book is dedicated.

Acknowledgment

To my loving wife, Judy, who unceasingly supported and encouraged me in this effort, and to my daughter, Wendi, who generously and ably served as my first editor, thank you, thank you . . . thank you. And to all the professionals at About Books, Inc., my sincere appreciation.

Prologue

All events have a traceable history leading to the happening itself, even if that backward running connection thins to unknown individuals and obscure beginnings. For the most part, however, such critical examination involves only those events which impact a great number of people in a most extraordinary fashion. That is precisely the case for the subject of our story. Its true birth can be laid at the doorstep of one Benjamin Walker, without whom the consequences of others' actions would surely have been far different for both man and commerce. You may find yourself forever marked by Walker's quest for the truth behind a most uncommon influence.

Part One

1

Phoenix, AZ—1973

"Chesser, how long do you think Sloann can continue to press Mirror Magic to his own greedy ends?" asked Gam'man. (Sloan himself had long ago dropped the final letter in his double-consonant surname.) The questioner stood staring out the picture window of the pair's home. The view framed a wondrously colorful portion of the impressive saguaro cactus forest. Practically overnight the late May landscape had turned fruit-red; even the smallest of the southwestern desert creatures feasted. It was time for the twosome's 300-mile bimonthly journey to the Las Vegas gaming tables. Gam'man and Chesser were both born of a special culture. It was one they had long departed yet one whose dictates drove its products to repeatedly test their individual abilities at influencing situations. This heritage wasn't as damning a curse for the two of them, however, as it was for the object of their conversation.

"Are you kidding?" replied Chesser as he sat playing and beating the odds at the solitary card game, Canfield, for the fifth straight time. He was much less judgmental than Gam'man. "He's already been at this self-appointed project for more than 25 years. He's not only shrewd but in my opinion he's ideally positioned to continue to pull off the masquerade indefinitely. Besides, what if he does fail? No real harm done, is there?"

"You're probably correct," Gam'man replied. His words were at odds with his expression as he turned to face his compatriot. "But you and I both know that under pressure Sloann tends to forget he is merely engaged in a game. If he should come to feel he can't win the greatest game of his life he would quickly disregard The Guidelines.

The two were neither related nor particularly drawn to each other out of personality or sexuality, although they were relatively compatible. Their time was spent primarily in each other's company for a single and overwhelming reason: there were only two of them left. Well, true that the third—Sloan—was loose in the mainstream, but they weren't yet overly concerned with his potential for disruption.

2

Atlanta, GA—1989

The razor's blade was poised by the left ear of its victim. An audio cassette had been caressing the early morning quiet with the pleasant, unassuming opening of Artie Shaw's "Begin The Beguine." Benjamin Walker waited an anxious moment for the downbeat that signalled the beginning of one of the swing tune's spiraling clarinet solos. With the razor held between his right thumb and the first three fingers, he pulled down smartly—squaring off the left sideburn. Following through with the stroke he raised both hands above his head, as if in celebration with his mirror image.

It was a mocking if humorous gesture he thought, and probably off his usual half-beat at that. As if to inspect his handiwork, Walker leaned forward on the bathroom sink. His eyes were of such a brilliant blue a waitress once asked him if he wore colored contact lenses. He supported himself on his knuckles and thumbs. He examined his A.M. beard. Unlike the stubble on his upper lip, he knew his beard would noticeably redden after two week's growth. He had seen enough of his own facial hair, however, to last his remaining lifetime. As far as he was concerned, a full beard was a societal disclaimer, not a fashion accessory. As he tilted his head and profiled his face, first the left side, then the right, he said, "Okay, who's behind there?"

He picked up his bathroom barber's comb and placed the narrow end to the surface of the mirror. He was a voracious reader and from his *Little Known Facts You Can Use* coffeetable book he had learned that if the reflection "touches" the comb end, the mirror is two-way.

If there's a distance of about ¼ of an inch between the actual point and the reflection, it's a one-way mirror. Satisfied that he wasn't under covert observation, he interviewed himself by addressing his mirror image. "What's your wonder-boy-geologist-turned-advertising-executive doing for adventure these days?" The reversed image lamely raised the left hand, signaling an answer. "Maybe screwing up yet another life path by playing part-time detective, your honor. Any other questions?" he added with calculated sarcasm.

The events which had brought Ben Walker to this very personal and increasingly regular trial-by-mirror hardly seemed likely. He was lost in a fleeting reconstruction of the past six years. The fateful memo launching his wild ride to date had arrived at the central Colorado post office a few miles from where his uranium exploration crew had been conducting field work for the past several months. It had read simply, "Important meeting tomorrow at headquarters, 2:00 P.M. sharp. Be here." Signed, "Kendall."

For nearly two years, Walker had been living a self-diagnosed 'near hermit's existence.' At least that was the way in which he had begun expressing his lifestyle to the occasional female he happened to meet on rare weekends away from crew camps. During these long two years he had worked himself half way through a third pair of field boots. Before that it had been two tiresome years in Santa Fe preceded by a challenging four-year stint near Flagstaff. Always with the same company. Through it all he had been earning excellent reviews and raises with National Nuclear for his work at interpreting and locating uranium-bearing rock strata.

It was a combination of physically exhausting and repetitive work—tromping around among rock-strewn, scrubby flora. His exploration assignments were dispatched to him accompanied by, in the words of his self-absorbed boss, Wyman Kendall, "a mosaic of two-dimensional symbols representing three-dimensional space."

"It's a frigging *map*, Wyman," Walker liked to chide.

If one wanted to make a human comparison to geology and its associated discontinuities, Wyman Kendall was the perfect example. His dress tended toward plaid ties, loosely knotted, and khaki shirts, the shade of which invariably mismatched his khaki trousers. His shirt sleeves were always rolled up three turns, exposing arms covered with an auburn jungle as dense as an orangutan's. His ever-present hard hat displayed an array of colorful decals that represented the seven different mines and mining companies at which he had labored.

The relatively enjoyable field work was always followed by increasingly tiresome labor back in the field labs. What had always made up for this downside of his occupation had to do with his own bumper-sticker description, “Geologists do it *outside*.” But even that purifying and offsetting attraction was fading. Ben Walker’s passion for doing his job these days could be summed up in the deliberately lapsed grammar he occasionally used when asked why he had chosen such a lonesome pursuit, “Because don’t nobody much mess with me.”

Walker, his hide cooked medium-well from long years under the western sun, wore his curly, brown hair short atop his lanky five-foot eleven-inch frame. He wore no visible jewelry. His ever-present pocket knife, an old, smallish, but sturdy, two-blade model to which he kept chained the keys to his apartment and pickup truck, resided in his right front pants pocket. Engraved on one stainless steel side was the logo and name of some long-ago advertiser. On the other side of the well-used tool was the still highly legible name of his father. The knife was probably the single most cherished artifact from his father’s estate.

What Walker didn’t yet realize was that he had begun simply putting in his time. He had reached into himself about all he could. That he had lost zest for his work could be easily read in any mirror had he only bothered to notice. That image would be sharpening for him any time now.

3

The next morning Walker had driven the 85 mountain secondary and interstate miles into Denver, including a short and amusingly-named stretch beneath the Rocky Mountains labelled "Beaucatcher Tunnel." Now that surely conjured a vision, except that one could see opposite-end daylight after only a few car lengths into the tunnel. That fact questioned the practicality of any young female passenger ever having had much of an opportunity for interesting a prospective beau, even if their chariot was being pulled by a slow-motion mule. Still, he liked the name.

By far, Ben Walker's most productive, creative time was spent in actual travel, whether by freeway or air. It tended to let his creative broth simmer. Mostly, he figured, it must be due to lack of distraction. At any rate, it seemed the best ideas of his life had been given birth, or at least nurtured, while he was either airborne or roadborne.

Ninety minutes had passed. As he exited I-70 into Arvada, Walker tapped off both his and the car's cruise control. As he entered the seventh floor National Nuclear offices he presented himself to the attractive, auburn-haired administrative assistant posted directly outside the stronghold of his sometime antagonist and full-time boss.

"Fair Jocelyn," he said, "I have been summoned by Kendall-the-Conqueror, probably to receive yet another Attaboy Button, certain to be accompanied by Mother Nuclear's promise of a raise any year now."

"Well, whether it's good news or bad, you won't be alone, Ben. The meeting is in the main conference room and the other five senior site geologists are already here. Tell you what," the petite, young redhead half-teased, half-promised, "if it's good news you can take me to dinner tonight. If it's bad you can come up to my condo for lasagna."

Jocelyn Raney, in her year-and-a-half as Wyman Kendall's gatekeeper had replaced her predecessor's 40-watt bulb-personality with a 400-mega-watt floodlamp, one that radiated empathy and wit as well as intelligence. On the half-dozen occasions when they had gone out together—the first time primarily because it was against Mother's office non-fraternization policy—they had found additional mutually interesting charms. But 170 miles was a long round-trip commute, so the relationship had remained casual.

Kendall, a National Nuclear v.p., characteristically communicated with all the touch of a rock hammer. He began no differently on this occasion. "Good morning, gentlemen. If you're surprised by the announcement I have to make today, you've been too absorbed in your own reports and not up on global news." Walker filed that one away for possible later use. He might want to quote Kendall his own words should the occasion arise when a site manager might actually be asked for an opinion relating to the three "P's"—Policy, Philosophy and Procedure.

The speaker continued, "The world energy supply, incredibly, is in excess; oil supplies are glutted and uranium demand has dropped off the charts. Energy supply and demand may never stabilize as long as dependence tends to place such an emphasis on natural resources and political control of fixed geographic yields. Now, after having exhausted all her other alternatives, Mother Nuclear . . ." Kendall paused. This was the first time Walker had ever heard him use the mock-affectionate company name employed even by most middle management people at National Nuclear. Maybe he had been wrong about Kendall having sprung from an injection mold.

The speaker caught Walker's eye and resumed his comments, correcting his wry slip, "National Nuclear is . . . downsizing." Kendall quickly recovered from the momentary change in the pitch of his voice. "You aren't the first people to be cashiered by the industry crunch, it's just personal this time. About all I have to offer you is advice. Ninety days severance will pass a bit faster than the Pleistocene Epoch. Get started today towards your future—maybe ground water—or even another field entirely. I'm sorry." No question about it, thought Walker. He had badly misjudged Kendall. The man had the makings of a real, live human being, however randomly assembled.

4

Back in his hotel room that evening, Walker thought about Jocelyn's invitation. He was momentarily torn between the opportunity for distracting R & R and the greater urge to take some sort of direct action to relieve the itch developing on his usually stress-resistant personality. The low coefficient of friction that normally allowed him to slip easily over life's everyday brushes and bruises was making a grinding sound. After all, this did represent a likely wash in his eight-year career investment in geology.

It turned out the ever-compassionate Kendall was at least intuitive in his outplacement comments. Walker had indeed sensed it was coming and all he had been waiting for was a shove. Only a few months ago he had phoned his best friend from undergraduate days at his alma mater in Tallahassee, just to kick around field-changing ideas. He didn't realize it until now, but he had been waiting for events to shape a personal decision, rather than the other way around.

It was time to phone again. "Can Flyn come out and play, Mrs. Bascom?" Walker asked in his best Archie Adolescent impression.

"Ben! When are you coming to see us?" she exclaimed.

"Maybe soon. I just turned in my compass, Janie. For the first time in years I'm not between a rock and a hard place."

She groaned. "I'll let you consult with the Doctor, poor soul," she said. Ben knew she was grinning and loving the brief *repartee*.

For years, both men had let a note scribbled at the bottom of a Christmas card serve as the renewing bond for the best-friends relationship they had long ago developed. Then, about two years ago when Walker had first begun to realize a vague but growing dissatisfaction with his lot in the uranium fields, he began initiating phone contact with the Bascoms three or four times a year. He had even spent a full weekend with them attending a geology symposium in Denver the past summer.

Dr. Flyn Bascom, as the keynote speaker at the Denver gathering, accomplished the unusual for an academic. Rather than offering up typical geology seminar fare with treatment something along the lines of "Uranium-Bearing Pitchblende Potential of the Green River Basin," his *déjà vu* title was, "Energy's Changing Times And What It Means To Geologists." A part of his focus had been on the growing potential for hydro geology. Bascom had further illustrated his talk by the use of colorful graphics about how the oil crunch of '73-'74 had been transformed into the glut of the late '70s. That, along with additional transparencies illustrating the concurrent rise of water pollution by industry, cities and private individuals, sharpened his focus.

His conclusion had been that regardless of where the energy situation might end up, ground water geology's needs would likely never dry up (Ben remembered Flyn's exact words; his ex-roomie loved to tinker with words). What Bascom had been telling him indirectly for the past two years was, go back to school today and learn tomorrow's geology. The potential lay in analyzing—on a consultant basis—a system's byproduct-polluted water in order to determine what metal and chemical pollutants were present. The payoff was in developing workable and profitable recommendations for clean-up in both the public and private sector. But Ben had lost his motivation to start over on a lateral course and had simply left things sitting on the shelf.

"Okay, Flyn," he said, "so I should have stayed on with you at Wild West U. and gotten those philosopher's initials. At least the bullets of energy economics can't hit you holed up in your quartz tower," he said. "But ground water just doesn't do it for me, partner."

It was easy for them to communicate with each other, though Flyn Bascom was a grind. He had plowed through undergraduate and graduate schools like a yoked ox. First, Florida State University for his B.S. Ditto Ben. Then, together, they entered the University of Wyoming for their Masters'. Divergence followed. Flyn married

Janie, a botanist-become-enthusiastic-housewife-and-mother. Ben got a real job while Flyn took his Ph.D. in metamorphic petrology. Then back to FSU, swift and prolific publication, and early tenure. Not without a cost, however; Bascom found it very difficult not to be working.

Raised by a set of upper-middle class parents in Washington, D.C.'s uniquely integrated government and teaching environment, Bascom had taken up golf both for the challenge of the sport, and because it ran counter to stereotyped minority interests. During high school he won many small-dollar, but powerful confidence-building, wagers with adult country club members. The premise was that he could beat them over nine holes of golf with only three clubs in his bag while they could resource the entire 14-club allotment. Ego always took that bet.

Golf took too much time to play, however, and when Flyn Bascom got to college he gave it up for tennis after having taken a single physical education course in the sport. Within three years he was playing well enough to earn a reserve spot on the university tennis team. But again, the need to compress exercise into an even briefer period without sacrificing the opportunity for one-on-one competition led him to substitute a shorter racquet and a smaller court. Racquetball captured his interest. The game had since become his only outlet beyond family and work. It pleased him to learn of Ben's subsequent interest in the sport.

"Nah, Ben," Bascom responded, "you wouldn't be happy lecturing and researching. All you ever wanted to do was think like a rock. Or, in your off time, maybe persuade others—usually co-eds—of some whimsical point of view. Has your dam burst or is it merely leaking?"

Walker laughed. "Flyn, the last few years have been real dam-flushers. As if I have to remind you. First came the mistake Susan and I made in confusing the nuances of simple physical attraction for the complexities of commitment, with the predictable result being divorce. The experts are right; the leading cause of divorce is marriage. Hah. At least we didn't have to fight over the custody of children. Now come the walking papers from National Nuke. Women and mining, two; Walker, zero. Trade me, Coach," he laughed.

"But seriously, the reason I phoned has to do with the seed you planted when I last called. Tell me more about that guy Baxter up in Atlanta. The one you said spoke to the faculty a few months ago on alumni donor recognition. Maybe I should go back to talking to people instead of rocks."

"Not much else to say, Ben, except that his subject reminded me of your having done so well selling your way through four and a half years of tuition and pizzas," Bascom joked. "I'll give you his number. Then if you should fly back to Atlanta for an interview you can zip on down to Tallahassee. Janie and I would very much like you to serve as an illustration for our kids on just how pizza can turn on you."

Those FSU times were indeed formative years, thought Walker. During his sophomore summer Ben had worked as a shipping and receiving clerk for Manley Promotional Advertising—MPA, as their telephone was answered. Manley was a successful and well-respected local businessman with an office located only a few short blocks from the east campus.

His business—as he would explain to university advertising and marketing classes at which he would occasionally guest-lecture—amounted to analyzing other businesses' promotional needs and opportunities. He would diagram the matching of target audiences and client budgets with imprinted promotional products. This constituted use of a very common, but commonly misunderstood, medium of advertising based on targeted distribution of relatively inexpensive but useful merchandise. This so-called specialty advertising ranged from such imprinted 'everythings' as balloons, coffee mugs, T-shirts, golf caps and calendars to more expensive, yet often imprinted, recognition gifts and awards such as clocks and leather goods.

Walker remembered those real-world activities in vivid detail, maybe because they were in such sharp contrast to the more mundane school year. Though he was thoroughly immersed in and committed to his geology, his interests in this newly-discovered fun business were broad and his questions of Manley were unending. Why would a client give away something for nothing? For what purpose? How would they distribute them? Is it important that the item be relevant in some way? How do you measure such promotion? You mean the buyer might purchase units by the hundreds or thousands, or even tens of thousands? And the questions didn't end there. How could simple one-on-one distribution of a certain quantity of an imprinted trinket be considered a true medium of advertising when each item apparently touched as few as two people—the person distributing the item and the recipient? These questions and others came to Ben in waves. He sought the answers on the job and off. What he kept hearing and appreciating as answers were two linchpin words: utility and repetition, the former allowing—or perhaps causing— the latter?

It certainly wasn't a mass medium. It could more aptly be called a niche medium. And why did most people, himself included—at least up to now—fail to appreciate the potential of such a common advertising vehicle, the only one that ingratiates? Heavy stuff to Benjamin Walker, apprentice.

Walt Manley was right of center in everything from business dress to his positions on personal and federal economic policy. He wore buttoned down, blue oxford-cloth shirts and a navy blazer over grey wool slacks as his business uniform. Their conservative symbolism represented his opinion on nearly everything about which he could be engaged in conversation.

He was more than simply successful at his business. He was also an astute judge of people—at least of potential salespeople. On more than one occasion he had lost a strong salesperson who longed for his or her own name on a business letterhead. The spin-off competition he thus fostered didn't really disturb him. They had their accounts and he had his. And most of his former business interns continued to look to him as their mentor, phoning him for an occasional lunch or asking for his opinions on whatever was giving them concern.

Manley had offered strong encouragement to Ben's obviously growing interest. Put in charge of the hundreds of industry manufacturers' and decorators' line catalogs and of keeping them current, Ben quickly absorbed the essence of the business. In less than a full year he had gained a working knowledge of general product specifications and pricing, as well as an understanding of many promotional applications and distribution ideas.

One day in late September of his Junior year, the full-time student and part-time salesman, had just arrived at the MPA offices per his daily afternoon work schedule. Walt Manley met him at the door with a somber look. "Ben, I have news for you and not all of it is good. I've just hired our bookkeeper's son to handle your back room work." For an instant, the young Walker felt sick at his stomach. It was just as quickly replaced with disbelief. He knew what an asset he had become and that Manley had often recognized his efforts.

His mentor turned quickly and motioned Walker to follow him down the hallway. Puzzled, Ben obeyed. In the larger room next to Manley's office, where the dizzying number of supplier catalogs were both displayed and filed along with dozens of carefully-marked plastic bins of samples from hundreds of lines, a little space had been carved from one corner. In it stood a three-quarter-size desk that had not been there the day before. On it sat an engraved name plate. The first line read "Ben Walker." The second line was in smaller type but carried much greater meaning for him. It read "Advertising Counselor." He turned and looked at Manley without speaking a word. But his grin was so broad it seemed the corners of his mouth would surely meet.

Manley assigned his protege a single medium-sized, but well-established account, training him how to service the client. Only then did he authorize Ben to begin soliciting and servicing new accounts. Of the many things the enthusiastic salesman Walker would learn from Walt Manley, the most poignant of all the lessons would be stated in barely more than a dozen words, "Selling is about neither product nor price, but about creative ideas and stellar service."

By the end of his two remaining years Ben's commissions were earning him five times the monthly gross of any of his student peers who worked for the prevailing part-time hourly rate. He stayed on full time at MPA for another very successful year and a half, in order to earn needed funds before heading to Wyoming to join Flyn Bascom and pursue graduate rock studies. It had been time to move forward into what both he and everyone else expected him to be doing with his degree and his life. It would be a sound—if misdirected—lesson in life.

5

Only seconds had actually passed as the ex-geologist traded simultaneous blinks with the mirrored wet-faced image in his suburban Atlanta bathroom. The suddenly disappearing pot of uranium beneath the National Nuclear rainbow six years ago had, almost as quickly, brought him to his subsequent job interview in Atlanta with Jonson Baxter. The details of that meeting were indelibly etched in his mind.

"What impresses me most about Baxter Products," Walker had said at the close of that mutually interesting session, "is the market potential for your particular product line of useful plastic promotional products, and your smaller line of mirrors. What challenges me is the competition for attention your line must endure—as must hundreds of other industry-competing lines. All of you have to depend on independent distributorships like Walt Manley's."

Ben had held only one job since completing his master's program in, as he still liked to phrase it, "WonderfulWyoming—that's one word," and although he was only 32 years old, he wasn't certain how much deference he should show at a job interview. He had decided to concentrate more on the opportunity than on the recruiter.

Jon Baxter spoke. "What impresses me most about you, Mr. Walker, is your success as an industry salesman at a very young age. That's no mean accomplishment. What challenges me—to use your phrasing—is your self-confidence at succeeding in a totally different perspective of the industry—the supplier side."

Walker correctly deduced that Flyn Bascom must have earlier told Baxter something of his experience with Walt Manley. In particular,

Flyn probably delighted in recounting Ben's first personal challenge at marrying politics and promotion. It had very nearly ended in an abrupt divorce. That chapter began in late May, a year after Walker's graduation. He recalled the events with a smile.

Manley had posted a note on the backrest of Ben's desk chair, asking to see him as soon as he came in that day. The Manley memo-on-a-chair technique. Walker's mentor routinely disdained conventionally placed memos—at least those requiring a direct response—feeling they were too easily put aside. As a result of that penchant, he employed a variety of strategic memo placements, from the simple chair back to desklamp shades to wall light switches, to his patented favorite—a piece of transparent tape suspended about two feet from the top center of the door jam of the office of the person being memoed. To this strip could be attached an entire series of notes. This ploy caused the object of the reminders—usually Manley himself, but by no means limited to him—to have to physically brush them aside thus jogging the memory. It was the time-worn string-around-the-finger concept elevated to an art form. Walker never got over it and he loved to tell the story.

"Ben," Manley had begun, "I have an invitation to attend an interesting business open house and dinner tomorrow night given by one of my clients who is toying with the idea of running for the recent opening for U.S. Representative. I have a conflicting family commitment and just can't make it. If you'll stand in for me I'll turn the account over to you. Buddy Jamison is only about ten years older than you and I think you'll get along fine."

"No, I couldn't do it, Walt. I'd have to have at least one additional account from you to make it worthwhile," Walker joked. He had come to feel quite comfortable in his business role. He smiled broadly. "Of course I'll cover for you, Walt. But I can't accept your turning the account over to me."

"No, I insist," said Manley. "I really think you can do a better job for him than I have." This characteristically unselfish justification continued to build his understudy's confidence. But Ben Walker had already progressed much further than Walt Manley suspected.

Walker attended Buddy Jamison's unusual open house. That year it wasn't being held as much to host a pre-Thanksgiving day dinner for foreign students as it was to show off the new office of his contracting business. Jamison enjoyed his alumnus big-business-brother role as much as anything he did. This third-year event was becoming a tradition for both him and for the foreign student community.

Also attending the dinner party was one of Walker's good friends, and fellow geology student, Nicholas Petrarkas—a Greek from Aeginia, a village on a small island near Athens. His wealthy family could afford not to live in the still-beautiful, but highly polluted, Athenian metropolis. Petrarkas would complete his graduation requirements by summer's end. The two of them and Flyn Bascom had shared many weekend afternoons boating on the Ochlockonee River, and had even triple-dated on several occasions. Since Nick Petrarkas knew Jamison from the previous year's dinner, he introduced Ben as an FSU graduate and added, "This is Walt Manley's star associate and heir-apparent."

Jamison shook his hand saying, "Good to meet you, Ben," then added a personal note, "I buy some promotional advertising and business gifts from Walt every now and then. He's always willing to do a little research to come up with the perfect item to fit both the situation and the budget. You can't go wrong learning from that man. As for Nick here, I think he's just cultivating American contacts before going back home to launch a few Greek oil tankers and then turn playboy." Petrarkas winced. For that jab he would extract a price.

They were all seated for dinner. The turkey and trimmings had been aggressively consumed by all but Petrarkas who, loudly professing never to consume fish, fowl or red meat, set about satisfying his hunger with salad and vegetables. Casually asked about his vegetarian diet by one of the other guests, Petrarkas launched enthusiastically into an explanation, winking at Walker as he began.

"Since I was a boy living near a very busy fishing village, the sight and smell of heaving, stinking and dying fish about to be gutted distressed me so much that even today I cannot eat fish. I was sickened even more as a child by watching headless chickens running around in nervous motor-response circles, spurting blood from raggedly severed parts as a result of my grandmother's hatchet labors."

Ben was rolling his eyes but Nick was having the time of his life, placing heavy emphasis on the more graphic descriptions, and at the same time, using his hands to grasp his nose, throat and stomach. His presentation usually led to a mass offering by others of their untouched desserts. He concluded with a wrinkle new to Walker.

"Even today I have been able to overcome the notion of eating meat from long dead cattle only through my requirement that it be 'burned to blackness.' You see, by ordering that particular entree in such a manner—intellectually at least—I can somehow push past the notion of its redness stemming from the sticky, putrid blood of a decaying animal."

Jamison shook his head and looked at Petrarkas with amused tolerance. "May we count on this being your chief contribution to dinner this evening, Nicholas?"

But Petrarkas wanted to go one-up on his host who, after all, he reasoned, had landed the first good-natured but challenging jab. "Speaking of speeches, Mr. Jamison, would you care to enlighten us about your rumored interest in the local U.S. Representative's district seat? And further, how you would manage both a full-time political office and a business that sooner or later might well involve a conflict of interest in your district?"

The 'light' conversation had crossed a threshold but Buddy Jamison barely paused for a breath before responding, "Well, as some of you already know, my two brothers and I grew up in our father's business and took it over when he died prematurely several years ago. If necessary I could readily sell out to my brothers. Now, as for actually running for political office, I have always felt strongly about getting involved and working within a system in order to better it. In fact, if I could find a solid campaign manager, I would go for it. How about you, Nick? You always seem to have something to say." The host was enjoying himself also.

Benjamin Walker had been enjoying the evening as well, including the interesting people, the conversation and the delicious food and wine served by Jamison. But if ever he had been witness to a classic poker bluff, this was it. He knew Nick had only banter to offer in response to Jamison's hand. Maybe it was the second glass of Beaujolais prompting Ben but he not only wanted to call the bet, he was pondering a raise.

From the opposite end of the table he opened his remarks forcefully. "That's no step for a dancer, Mr. Jamison. If you truly had a mind to do what you say, I believe you could not only win the seat but you could do so without a budget for mass media."

As if seated at a tennis match, all heads had suddenly swiveled from Jamison to Walker and now back to their host. Walker waited impatiently for the expected return shot. He suddenly felt inspired. The fingers of his left hand gripped the tablecloth beneath them like a vise while with the right hand, he picked up his wineglass and rapidly drained the last of the Beaujolais. He was eager to charge past the baseline and attack the ball he knew Jamison would be sending his way in another two seconds. Patience. It might just as likely be a lob as a missile. Easy.

Buddy Jamison absolutely loved a challenge and his success in business had not come without testing the convictions of others. "Very interesting remark, Mr. Walker. Would you care to elaborate on that point?" he said, firing a dust-sucking screamer low over the net and squarely into the court of Benjamin Walker.

Ben paused and took in a little air, but nothing anyone would notice. "Let me put it very simply," he responded calmly. "I believe my medium of advertising could get the job done." His was a high lob, calculated to put his opponent into the position of having to put Walker on the spot.

Jamison sat back in his chair, only half-smiling, trying to assess Walker's play and at the same time sensing an opportunity to—at the very least—turn a passing comment into lively dinner conversation. "Wait a minute, young man. Are you trying to tell me that emery boards, calendar cards and bumper stickers could get me elected to the U.S. House of Representatives?"

"No, sir, I didn't say that. What I am saying is that if your positions are mainstream: if you haven't boxed up a sick aunt somewhere in an attic, and if you can raise the proper funds and attract the proper support, then with a solid campaign platform and theme, election to this office could be successfully executed through my advertising medium—the most common one in America." The only sound in the room was that of the ball tearing its way back across the net to touch down two steps in front of Jamison.

Just as quickly as the brash Walker had decided upon his tactic, so did the veteran. "Ben, my young friend, I don't think you know what you're talking about, but if you really believe what you're saying, and you think you can back up your statements with action I'll make a full and complete commitment right now to run—

providing you take on my campaign, beginning tonight and right on up to the November election. You gonna hold 'em or fold 'em?"

For Christ's sake, thought Walker. You've done it again. He looked at Nick, who returned his glance with a "What the Hell?" expression. Jamison thought he had served an ace. Ben returned his gaze to the smiling Jamison and raised his wine glass, saying, "To the uncommon candidate with common sense. I not only accept your offer but I challenge every one of your friends in this room to actively support your campaign in every way possible."

Walt Manley not only thought Ben had acted rashly but was as yet too inexperienced to follow through, since he—Ben—had never been involved in any political campaign except for student body elections. However, after hearing reports of meetings, study and preliminary planning between Jamison, Ben, and a handful of surprisingly easily-recruited, capable and highly enthusiastic supporters, Manley dropped his earlier negative estimate and actually jumped aboard to contribute his own support.

The memory of how things developed from that point would never be forgotten by Ben. He had immediately decided to stick with his initial gut instinct for a personal-appeal campaign. He took Jamison's straightforward, if middle-of-the-road positions, in a time of abating civil rights activism, Asian oil ploys and military involvement—and packaged them, presenting his 'common sense from the uncommon candidate' to the public. In fact, the presentation practically became a second campaign theme in itself, brought to local Americans through America's most common medium.

Jamison had seriously questioned Walker's tactics only once during that planning period, asking, "Ben, how am I going to get my message and name across, even in this relatively small-population district, without using at least some mass print and electronic media? Even if we alternately mail or press tens of thousands of inexpensive cleverly imprinted doodads into people's hands, we still need far greater coverage."

"Buddy, I didn't say we wouldn't use mass media. I said we wouldn't have to buy it. Remember when I used the cliche, 'the medium will be the message?' What I meant was exactly because of the relatively minor position in the overall advertising media occupied by promotional products, we will get air and print coverage. Whoever heard of a serious political campaign being waged exclusively in the common person's medium?" If Walker was correct, well before the final poll-taking, this unusual political campaign—which had purchased zero mass media advertising—would of itself become news.

Practically on cue the various local news media seized upon the candidate's and the campaign's novel, limited exposure methods with the result that both the campaign and the candidate began receiving daily play in district newspapers, on radio talk shows, and on local nightly newscasts. On more than one occasion its human interest perspective even made for a mention on various network news programs and a few nationally-read newspaper dailies. Buddy Jamison's visibility and popularity peaked with election day. He never once had to look back.

Ben Walker could obviously do no wrong in his successful candidate's eyes and Jamison tried his best to persuade him to join either his brothers' construction business; in which Jamison would soon be selling his interest—or much better, the staff he was assembling in Washington, D.C.

Ben would have none of it. In fact, the greater difficulty lay in leaving Walt Manley. He still had his sights set resolutely on his geology career and he had managed to contribute to his resumé a well-orchestrated point as to both his creative and management capabilities. It was a print claim that concluded with the ultimate punctuation—success!

All this was brought into focus for Walker as his Atlanta interview with Jon Baxter concluded. The subject of their common interest, specialty advertising, brought Ben's previous industry experience to mind. For Baxter's part, he had no specific middle management opening within his organization at the time. He did have a high regard for Flyn Bascom, however, and thus Bascom's recommendation to interview this goal-oriented young man who brought to the table both an unusually early and successful background in the industry.

For some time the founder, CEO and majority stockholder of privately held Baxter Products had lamented the fact that one or both of his children had not come into the company business. His oft-estranged but successful son had defined his interest in Baxter products more than once, describing it as, "never, in any capacity." It was a classical clash between a father's expectations and a son's rebellion. Unfortunately neither had the will to give the slightest bit of ground.

Baxter's daughter, Muriel, was much more interested in the business but she had married and her husband had strong professional interests of his own, with the result that she didn't have the geographical latitude to permit her involvement. All this had delayed the internal development of people within Baxter Products who might well be capable of top management back-up. Finally, after careful review and intensive self-examination of just why he didn't feel confident with elevating someone from within, Baxter concluded that he simply had no one who could move far up the ladder without tripping on a rung and leaving Baxter Products even more vulnerable than they already were.

And there was one other factor. For more than four years Jon Baxter had beaten lung cancer into remission—if not submission. His primary physician frankly discussed with him the concept of a disease's outcome sometimes having more to do with what goes on in the patient's mind than in his body. Baxter had given his mind the ultimate and successful role in that decision. Now he had this decision to make.

He was much impressed with this people-oriented scientist-salesman (if that didn't sound like a contradiction-in-description, he had never heard one), and the management issue seemed ever greater. Jon Baxter was only impressed by performance, however. As a result of that characteristic he had coincidentally become a better judge of people's abilities to get along with others than he would have ever imagined. Ben Walker, it seemed to him was the person for the position or at least for the opportunity. No guarantees. He would have to earn every—in fact, any—rung, and this point was made as clearly as the potential. As for Walker, he was no less enthusiastic—or wary—than Baxter.

6

In their comfortable mountain-side home on the north side of Phoenix, Gam'man and Chesser sat across from each other at a glass patio table. Chesser was in the middle of a game of his own, a new and more difficult version of Canfield. He had just broken open a new deck, a promotional token from one of the many casinos frequented by the pair. Gam'man was gazing at an 8½" x 11" document, which he was holding. It had a simple two-word heading which read, The Guidelines.

Gam'man spoke, "What are we to make of Sloann's only written communication with us in 16 years? His fax message of last night read simply, 'So that you know, I hereby revoke any and all responsibility for Guidelines covenants.'"

"Who can tell?" said Chesser. "He is simply stating the obvious. There is no longer any link between us. So what?"

"Still," objected Gam'man, "something caused him to go to the trouble of breaking his self-imposed black-out with us. Maybe it was a need to rationalize yet another decision. I wonder which Guideline he has broken this time?" he mused as he glanced down at the paper he'd just retrieved from their wall safe. It was not typed, just carefully hand-printed in a curiously elaborate style. It was quite legible, however.

The Guidelines

1. The Game is only a game.
2. The Game shall not interfere with local customs.
3. The Game shall not exceed its initial objective.
4. The Game shall not be confrontational.
5. The Game shall immediately terminate in the event of violence.

If this pair of friends were bookends, as the few who knew them usually thought, then Gam'man took the weight pressing on him far differently than did Chesser. Gam'man was keenly observant and speculative by nature, curious about much, and given to aggressively resolving that curiosity. At least he would try to do so within the low profile constraints placed upon them by unique circumstances. Gam'man, the analyst.

Chesser, on the other hand, was much more conservative. The modifying aspect of his normally retiring personality was his creative flair, his sense of expression, and his anticipation of reactions to those broadly varied forms. Chesser, the provocateur.

All three had radical histories. Sloan, however, was obsessed. Sloan, the menace.

7

Two more rapid eye blinks in the mirror served to remind Walker that his six short years with Baxter products found him still working with samples—not of earth, but of plastic and glass. These particular commodities were disguised as useful articles of merchandise, which coincidentally carried an advertiser's message. Had he come home or what? He had moved up quickly, from customer service to product manager, to national sales manager and finally his year-old appointment as sales and marketing vice president. Baxter Products was a company with nearly thirty million dollars in annual sales, and maintained a top-20 industry position. It was only in the past six months that Ben Walker's high-speed ride had left the pavement for loose gravel.

He finished his shave and swatted at his unruly hair before selecting a shirt he could live with. For work, Walker favored white, short-sleeved dress shirts and a never-buttoned, single-breasted suit jacket; although he would prefer the absence of any uniform at all. His only concession to dress-consciousness was incidental. For all of his considerable interpretive abilities, he was not usually well tuned to personal observations and judgements of his or others' dress or personal appearance. He usually and randomly stuffed the same red silk kerchief into his chest coat pocket. "My urban bandanna," as he referred to it.

Walker had a naturally inquisitive nature, as might be expected of someone who had spent eight years looking at the fabric of solid rock and seeing something of intense interest. He loved puzzles in nearly any form: from crosswords, to Ludlum spy thrillers, to genetic interpretation of rock structures.

Two things in particular during recent months had piqued his interest in closing loops. First, the incidental, but totally surprising revelation by Jon Baxter that their major competitor, Mirror Magic, and BP had a common beginning! MM was well known in the trade; it was the industry's runaway sales leader, more than three times BP's size, and not a conglomerate division.

The second was the firing of Mirror Magic's assistant marketing director and Jon Baxter's immediate recruiting of her without consultation with Ben. That was a surprising move for J.B., and it had rankled Walker a little, although Baxter had explained it somewhat apologetically as, "a spontaneous judgement call."

As Ben reflected on his first meeting with Amanda Booth he recalled how she had charged into his life. "I've been looking forward to meeting you, Ben," she had said. "Jon says you're the best thing to happen to Baxter Products in the last ten years. What are you holding over him?"

"I bought him a pair of black lizard cowboy boots for his birthday and turned him into putty," he joked. "As a matter of fact, Ms. Booth (uncharacteristically, he wanted her to know who was boss), it's just the other way around. Although he's not a full generation older than me he's related to me as much like a father as an employer/trainer. Funny thing, I've been blessed with two non-family mentors in my adult life and both of them have been in this industry rather than the one in which I studied formally." Directly contrary to his intent, with only three sentences Ben had managed to speak more casually about some of his feelings than he had with any new acquaintance since college days.

"Tell me about Mirror Magic," he said as they both sat down in Walker's office.

"I really began my fall from favor with Phil Sloan when my application to join the industry's national association public relations committee was accepted. Then, later on, to compound matters I semi-innocently committed 'The Sin' at Mirror Magic; I invited my fellow committee members to visit the MM factory. Sloan was so livid over that he axed me the same day," she related with some embarrassment.

"Well, don't let it bother you. I've been spit out by bigger fish," said Ben. "I'm not surprised about his reaction to your little plant tour, though. You had to be a bit naive there. As a matter of fact, I had just agreed to serve on the same committee. I would have canceled any plans to make that visit to Mirror Magic. Here we are, two major competitors located in the same city, and in nearly six years I have never been able to get a single invitation to visit his factory. At the same time I've given half a dozen opportunities to Phil Sloan to tour our facility. Apparently he doesn't let any of his staff participate for fear of expected reciprocity. He has to be the most secretive son-of-a-bitch in the industry," said Ben with obvious but surprising dislike for a man he had never met.

"It's very curious," Amanda picked up on the point. "For being in the sales promotion business he certainly goes out of his way to avoid positive publicity. You know the figures, Ben, Double M has twice the sales volume of the second largest corporation in the industry, yet it contributes no leadership beyond that."

Walker added the most telling observation of all. "The most amazing thing to me is that all their eggs remain unbroken in one basket. They're in the advertising mirror business. Period. You must know that Baxter Products, and virtually every other advertising mirror manufacturer, has found it economically necessary to diversify—most, more than twenty years ago. Well, I'll be looking forward to your report on mirror products and marketing strategy recommendations, Amanda. We need to beef up our new C.P.S. introductions for next winter's Dallas show."

She smiled, suddenly realizing that she had been dismissed. She stood up, commenting, "Over here you probably refer to the acronym C.P.S. as 'creative plastic specialties.' If you'll pardon my French, at Double M it was 'cheap plastic shit.'"

Well, she obviously hadn't led too sheltered a life, thought Walker. If Baxter hadn't just dumped her onto him he probably would have been his usual gracious self at their first meeting, rather than being somewhat distant. Too bad, he thought, which was to say to his subconscious mind, "Who is this person fascinating me against my will?"

Amanda Booth was innocently stunning, and not in some subjective fashion. She was Miss World material. He wasn't yet aware of it due to his initial bias from his run-in with her fiery will.

The high cheekbones of her four-times removed Iroquois ancestors contrasted nicely with her strawberry-blonde, curly hair, green eyes and porcelain complexion.

8

A final glance at his bathroom mirror to determine his suitability for public presentation brought Ben Walker back to real-time and the early 'o-dark-hundred' hour in his brightly-lit ready room. He had an eight A.M. meeting with Jon Baxter.

Walker was punctual almost to a fault, a trait which he considered important for himself but, to his credit, easily tolerated as a shortcoming in others. He had once laughingly told Jon Baxter that he was, "stress-avoidance programmed for on-time arrival." This he disclosed to a man to whom appointment times were more likely to be measured in plus-or-minus twenty-minute intervals—when he remembered to mark his desk diary in the first place. He stood waiting in Baxter's unlocked office, looking around the over-displayed room. Several plaques proclaimed Jonson Baxter to have done well in several out-of-town member-guest golf tournaments.

One engraved marble-base clock evidenced the single hole-in-one of his 45-year golf affair. The sport first blossomed for him when he was a ten-year-old caddie for his father. Golf was the one outlet which afforded Baxter the needed opportunity to combine physical and mental competition. To do so in an outdoor environment truly made the game a sheer delight for him. The sensory contributions of freshly cut fairway grass and long, late afternoon shadows falling across a favorite green would fill him with enough after-work inspiration to carry him through the toughest of his business challenges. Or at least until the next of his three-a-week appointments with his persimmon woods and a tee time. He was as much a traditionalist in golf as in management.

Walker had been in Jon Baxter's office many times, but until this morning had never taken the time to closely observe more than a few of the hundreds of imprinted samples from Baxter Products' customer orders which lined the shelves along two full walls. They included items as diverse as plastic rain gauges, multiple versions of plastic key rings and desk items of every description, plus various sizes and models of glass mirrors. In one corner hung a sample of the major competition's product, a jumbo mirror nearly a foot wide by two feet in height, which was imprinted in two locations. Near the top, the mirror read, "Look Into Mirror Magic," along with the MM logo. At the bottom of the mirror the occasion was highlighted, "1939—Looking Good for Forty Years—1979."

"I picked that up at double M's only open house on record, more than ten years ago," said Baxter as he appeared at the office door. "It was the rarest of occasions. Phil Sloan actually stooped to socialize with a few customers. But if I hadn't insisted on tagging along with a local banker friend I would never have gotten inside the general offices; although no one was allowed to tour the factory itself. Frankly, I don't know what possessed 'Paranoid Phil' to make even that gesture," said Baxter.

"And that's exactly what I want to discuss with you, Ben. You know this is both Baxter Products' and Mirror Magic's fiftieth anniversary. You've been harassing me about the industry's declining market for advertising mirrors—except for the anomaly of Double M—and our two companies' common start-up ever since I mentioned our origin to you."

At Baxter's gesture, Walker sat down opposite him across a small glass-topped coffee table. It reminded Ben of the difference in style between J.B. and his previous superior, Wyman Kendall. Whenever Walker had been granted an audience in order to defend or petition something at National Nuclear, Kendall invariably positioned himself in the superior-to-inferior seating arrangement. Whereas Kendall had preferred to seat a subordinate on the visitor's side of the desk, Baxter always came out from behind the throne to seat himself as an equal.

Both men were about the same height and both were within 10 or so pounds of the weight their doctors felt they should be, although Jon Baxter tended to discount even that number when reporting it to anyone presumptuous enough to ask. But aside from their 15-year age differential, the similarities between them didn't advance beyond these physical parameters. Baxter sat in a chair at a meeting like he might in front of his television set—'draped' would most accurately describe it. Walker, on the other hand, treated any office chair but a straight-backed one as an interruption. He was anxious to be out of it because he expected little to be accomplished while in it. This was the result of spending too many years walking around beneath a broad-brimmed hat and a bright sun.

Walker opened his end of the conversation. "I'm glad you're willing to discuss it, finally, Jon. It isn't that I give a damn about Mirror Magic even though it is the industry's most enviable market-share holder. It has much more to do with why Baxter Products can only maintain mirrors as a token line within our now mainstream plastic products line, while MM continues to fly its glass flag in the face of everyone else in the industry. It doesn't make sense.

"Jon, you scooped up Amanda Booth for the express purpose of reevaluating both the market and the marketing strategy for advertising mirrors. I just read the report you assigned her to develop some weeks ago; I simply don't agree with her assessment. I don't refute her facts, just her denial of potential."

"What's to dispute?" said Baxter. "As far back as the early '60s and even late '50s, plastics technology had begun to undercut the appeal of more expensive advertising mirrors Most ad specialties were used at that time to generate simple goodwill with a small, targeted market." Baxter loved to bait his analysis-oriented executive.

"I understand that, Jon," objected Ben, "but that's yesterday's news. Furthermore, that's precisely why we need to make some type of adaptation to the times—as has Mirror Magic. MM's own success defines both their existing and our potential market. Jon, it's time we mounted a serious challenge to Double M's obscene share of the market." Walker's inflection was becoming more pronounced.

"And until we are able to deal with this particular problem I suggest we make some changes in our marketing strategy. I want to raise prices on the glass mirror line. We can position ourselves a bit differently than MM by taking a high profile with our commitment to recycle both our glass and plastic waste. Now that's something Phil Sloan would find totally counterproductive. He isn't into adding man hours and procedural changes simply to be responsive to alarmist environmental needs."

Baxter took a deep breath, his fuse flaring. "Who called this meeting, Ben? You or me? For Christ's sake, whoever said, 'surround yourself with people with talent greater than yours' should have added, 'but make damned certain they don't know it.' Used to be nobody around here could hit themselves in the butt with their left hand. Now everybody thinks they can work themselves up to take over my job. I don't know which costs me more aggravation in this business," he frowned, "the problems or the solutions. What we really need around here is a little less self-confidence and lecture and a little more overtime."

His tirade finished, Baxter sighed and sat down. In fact, he took immense pride in his reshaped staff, both with Walker, and the promise held by Amanda Booth. But he found it difficult to verbalize recognition. Ben, however, read him like a book.

"Yassuh, boss, that's no step for a dancer," Walker sassed.

Seriousness returned. "Okay, Ben, we're tuned to the same wavelength. I'm as frustrated as you. I do want you to tackle this. Find the answer to why Mirror Magic can and we can't. You're free to do whatever it takes. Of course it goes without saying that you can't neglect your regular responsibilities," added Baxter, only half-serious but always with an economic bias to his thinking.

"Naturally, Lord. I'll simply add an eighth day to the week," Ben dismissed the qualifier. "But I'm going to start with you, Jon. Amanda tells me that MM only provided her with a figure as a cost base, not the elements from which it was derived. In other words, her department, and presumably others at MM, worked in considerable darkness. Obviously they took their cue from the man at the top. In fact, she didn't know of MM's and Baxter Products' common beginning. Until now I've really only given it cursory thought, simply because you attached no importance to it. All I know about it is that your father and old Alexander Sloan were partners until they both died in the late 1940s. Give me a few more pieces of the puzzle, Jon."

"It's just personal stuff, Ben." Baxter shrugged. "Not much in the way of a clue, I'm afraid. It all has to do with feelings of personal tragedy borne by my father. He, Alex Sloan, Phil Sloan and my uncle were on a deer and elk hunting trip in the Wind River Range in western Wyoming in 1949. They hunted on horseback and I remember Dad telling me that the November snow was two feet deep at their mountain top altitudes of 9,000 to 12,000 feet—very close to timber line."

Even 40 years later it was clear it was not easy for Baxter to recall events told to him by his father and uncle. "The terrible accident happened near dusk just as heavy snow had begun falling. Dad was hunting with a scoped .270 Winchester and he was tired by the day's hunt. He got in one last shot at a fuzzy target. Alex Sloan was shot and killed by Dad—mistaken for an elk. They had been the closest of friends and my father never forgave himself for his tragic carelessness. Dad died unexpectedly within a year of the accident. The doctor said unresolved guilt and the attendant stress brought on heart failure."

"I'm sorry, Jon. I didn't know about your father. But how did Phil Sloan enter the picture?" Ben persisted.

"That's a bit odd, but explainable. Young Sloan was the Mirror Magic controller at the time. He had only been hired two years before. Sort of appeared out of the blue, and within a year had married my cousin—a girl much younger than himself. The Sloan in his name was merely a coincidence. Common-enough name. They used to joke about it, that my cousin was the outsider. But it was just as tough a year for the Baxters as for the Sloans. Phil Sloan's wife died the same year as the hunting accident and only six months after their wedding.

"Whoa, Jon. Those are quite the revelations. I don't know if they're significant with respect to our problem but the facts are certainly interesting." Walker loved to find a fit for a puzzle piece even if it was the first of a thousand-piece time-soaker.

"Well, Phil Sloan became much more involved in the business and before long he convinced the board of directors, by virtue of his inherited interest, to dissolve the partnership and split the assets in half. He retained the Mirror Magic name, and my uncle formed Baxter Products. End of story. I know nothing else about Phil Sloan except that he lives in his own world relying on a few close subordinates for operation. They're as secretive about MM as Sloan himself," concluded Baxter.

9

Later that same day Walker found himself at the ten year old, eight-story, central Atlanta-Fulton Public Library on Margaret Mitchell Square. A dozen reference books sat, mostly opened, on a cheap, wood-laminate study table in an alcove he had selected for a little one-on-one with the latest facts of his business life. In the past, whenever he had been presented with a formidable project, whether in academia or in business, he had usually found his beginning by reviewing the givens and then researching the subject at some length. This method had served him well when he had first come into the industry years ago under Walt Manley's tutelage, then again six years ago as a novice on the manufacturing side. He had immediately gained the basis for his current expertise by first analyzing and then attacking his objective. This approach had applied not only to his desire to understand the manufacturing and decorating processes, but also to his direct responsibility in sales and marketing—particularly as applied to plastics. Since the mirror portion of the line was apparently more of an anachronism within the future plans of Baxter Products, he hadn't previously pursued that division with any zeal.

It didn't take him long, however, to find a fascination with mirrors. People naturally take them for granted; yet Walker began to perceive that their simple purpose somehow contributed to something more profound. He read from an encyclopedia, "Most mirrors are made of a pane of glass which is coated on the back so that light cannot pass through, but is reflected. Standing three feet away from a flat mirror, your image seems six feet distant, due to light rays having to travel three feet to—and then another three feet from—the mirror surface."

Walker recalled having once read in a freshman humanities course about Louis XIV and how he had strived to create the ultimate reflection in his Versailles Palace's Hall of Mirrors. Modern manufacturing techniques offered vast improvements for common use. He noted that today's highly polished mirror surfaces can reflect more than 90 percent of the visible light.

As he read from the more detailed references on the subject, the chemical composition notations brought a rush of Mineralogy 301 to mind, but he set nostalgia aside with his usual single-mindedness. He absent-mindedly spoke aloud, to reinforce his purpose, "Not relevant, Walker." A librarian, re-shelving books only a few feet in front of him, turned her head slightly and reproached him with a look over her half-glasses. He smiled to himself as he burrowed his head deeper in glass, coughing twice.

His *World Book Encyclopedia* article appeared to be playing Abbott to his Costello ad lib: "The first four centuries of the Christian era has been called the First Golden Age of Glass. The Second Age of Glass began with the 1200s," he read, then added in a medium whisper for the librarian's benefit, "And yes, glass lovers, the Third Golden Age of Glass was brought to you in the mid 1900s by Mirror Magic."

The only direct benefit from his six hours spent in the library that day was the curiosity generated by the term 'silvering.' He decided he was now sufficiently qualified to direct additional questions to specialists. He would attend to that as soon as he could break loose to fly or drive down to Tallahassee to see a few old Florida State friends.

10

The next morning Walker had not even had his second cup of coffee before Amanda Booth pushed open his partly closed office door. She stood framed in the doorway, feet apart, directly facing him at his desk, one hand on a hip, the other clutching her report. She glared at her boss as if he were a rock she had just stubbed her toe against and was about to kick out of the way.

In spite of his initial negative reaction to Jon Baxter's semi-end run with her, his conscious mind finally caught up with his subconscious and she struck him as quite stunning as she stood there. He ignored her body language. "Good morning, 'Manda," he opened. "What brings you to the bear's lair so early in the day? Perhaps to share some fresh berries?" No reaction. "Okay, then how about coffee and half of a moon pie?" This time he waited for her to answer.

Amanda wore her hair and clothes smartly, professionally. Her nails were carefully polished but subtly colored. She was partial to stylishly-draped silk scarves. Still, her most stunning physical characteristic was the perfectly synchronized features of her face.

Having earlier taken careful measure of what she might encounter during her sortie at confrontation, an unusual tactic for her when she was in such a base state of agitation, she was prepared. The weekend had allowed her time to assemble her plan of attack. She paced her barrage.

"I see you haven't entirely forgotten your geology training. You did a first rate sabotage job in my first week, undermining me with Jon." She advanced to his bunker "I don't think you even read it. I stand by my situation analysis and recommendations. And I'm touched by your support, Mr. Walker."

Ben set his defense realistically, quickly assessing the situation. He would apologize, then briefly state the facts, and finally make an appeal to her emotions. He liked the plan. "You're right, Amanda. I was dead wrong. I did read the report, but I should have reviewed it with you first before passing on my comments to Jon." So far, so good. Her stance softened a bit, if not her expression.

He continued. "Although you have spent time in the enemy camp, I have the advantage of greater experience in the industry, including some just-completed research of my own. I had then, and have now, reason to take exception to your conclusions." He gestured her to a chair. She took it, frowning, still challenging.

"Then why did Jon assign this project to me when you obviously could have done it better?" she asked.

He had survived the assault and quieted his attacker. Why he was going to this trouble he wasn't sure. Women know why they flirt, or at least that it's in their nature. Men don't have a clue. "Amanda, you left Mirror Magic because you didn't share Phil Sloan's philosophies about business and people. And of course because of your attraction to me." He knew instantly by her flinch that flanking move would have to be recalled.

"Well, kidding, of course," he said. "But, seriously, who better for another assessment to balance Jon's and my own analyses? He didn't point that out at the time because it might have influenced your effort. Anyway, that's done. Both Jon and I feel you did an outstanding job on the assignment. It has reinforced our own suspicions about Mirror Magic."

"So what's next?" She understood what Walker was saying, even accepted it. But still, she did not appreciate his style.

He laid it out. "Amanda, we're going after the reason for MM's unwarranted niche success; and once we learn that, we're going to take them on, head-up. We very much need your help on the project."

Placated, if still not entirely pleased, Amanda acknowledged her surrender in this battle. She hoped it would not become war because she was attracted to Ben Walker. "Okay, Major. You've sold me, but now that I know you're capable of blind-siding, I'll be more on my guard in the future."

Ben winced. A draw, at best, he thought. “Tell you what,” he said, “I have some research to do today but let’s schedule an hour tomorrow morning to review and discuss several key aspects of your report. That should give us a basis for the next step in Plan A.”

11

The next morning at precisely nine A.M., Amanda Booth was again framed in Ben's office doorway, this time in a neutral if not conciliatory pose. She responded to Walker's questions about the conclusions she had drawn in her report.

"The paradox begins," she said, "with the appeal of the advertising mirror relative to its greater cost than other industry products available on the market to perform essentially the same function. The industry looks for economy of cost, elimination of waste distribution and products with a personal appeal that, through utility, insures repetition of message. Glass wall mirrors, are very expensive. Mirror Magic's inordinately large market share simply does not square with the facts, effective merchandising aside."

"Well, now that sort of ignores the reality of the situation doesn't it, Amanda?"

"Ben, you aren't paying attention. The facts themselves don't make sense. It's as if Mirror Magic's distributors, the same network used by Baxter Products, are saying, 'we know all mirror suppliers' products are functionally the same but we can sell MM mirrors and not yours.'"

"But you just said yourself that it's a generic product, Amanda," argued Walker. He understood her point but he wanted to play devil's advocate a little longer. "The appeal of the graphics and the service alone don't make the difference. We have, or more correctly, had, as many variations on mirror size and models as MM. And as for customer service, why is it we were the recipient of the Sudden Service Golden Pyramid award from the national association last year? It wasn't recognition for Excellence on Sports Day! We need to take a look at this from the perspective of alternatives. What do we do about this disparity? That's what I was speaking of yesterday."

She didn't walk out but she was having a hard time with Walker's presentation. Was it merely misdirected competition? Amanda Booth suffered from an occasional preoccupation with what she felt was the norm for most adult males, at least those with whom she had worked, that they tended to discount offhand, otherwise-qualified female opinions and positions in areas of traditional male dominance. Fortunately for her, she benefitted from her challenging attitude. Her actual performance in the corporate arena supported her outspokenness.

At 29 she was very confident of her own abilities and expressed them with common sense. Her values had been nurtured through her very positive early home life and four years and top-honors recognition for her marketing degree at a no-nonsense midwestern state university.

For Ben's part, he was already beginning to sense a latent attraction for Amanda Booth. Was it perfectly normal Carter-lust? He could probably control such feelings, of course, but he had already failed a true-false test once and he was cautious, especially since the object in this case also happened to be a subordinate. "Okay, Amanda." He adjusted his thinking before she could do it for him. "I just wanted to see if you would really stand behind your position. You did, and as a result, I'm beginning to buy into it myself."

12

Walker went to his regular Saturday morning racquetball session and alternated doubles-play with six to eight other B-level players who regularly met three times a week. They had become his closest friends outside his growing but less-personal industry circle of acquaintances. "What's the matter today, Walker? Are all your partners playing poorly for you?" asked his final partner after the last of Ben's teams' three successive losing games.

"I've been brooding over a female I've never even dated," he mumbled to Gene Ellison as they walked off the court. Ellison reminded Walker of the bulldog of Gene's alma mater, the University of Georgia. He was short, barrel-chested, even a little bowlegged. He was relentless in going for tough 'gets,' which made up for a lesser talent than Ben's intuitive game strategy and generally better shot selection. As a result, the competition between them was fierce enough to cause either one of them to risk a sprawling 'save' on a hard floor for the sake of a two-dollar wager.

"Gene, I'm having trouble concentrating on a very important project I've been working on for the past month because one Amanda Booth is in the same office and working for me. I think I should fire her and then make a move on her. How does that strike you?"

"About like your play today: poorly," said Ellison as he juggled two racquetballs and his racquet while they sat cooling down on the locker room bench. Ben always tended to ignore this casual ego-display even though he thought it a unique method of self-expression and relaxation. He knew his typical omission of comment irritated

Ellison, and in itself was a form of entertainment for Walker. Ellison said simply, "Give her a transfer."

"To where? Our only factory is in Atlanta."

"To field sales, putz. Didn't you tell me earlier that Baxter Products needed to focus more on distributor relations? Put her on the road and let her work with your reps and some key accounts. Like you used to do before you got caught up with your titles. That way you won't be working with her on a regular basis. And you can have her report directly to Baxter."

Walker rolled his eyes at the simplicity of the solution. "Of course. She already knows a lot of distributors anyway, having met them at tradeshows, and she actually enjoys travelling. Then, in that capacity she could also support me in various ways on the project I mentioned," Walker reasoned. "Good job, Counselor. Bill me!"

Ben made excuses to the others for not participating in the ritual Saturday lunch, the group's profane protests falling on deaf ears. He wanted to work out the details while they were fresh in his mind so he could present the concept to Amanda on Monday. He knew Jon would have no problem with it.

Neither did Amanda. In fact, she was relieved. She had likewise been experiencing varying reactions to a series of mixed signals, both on the sending and receiving end. She wasn't as acutely aware of it as Ben.

Over the next three months things between them went smoothly. In fact, Ben began seeing her outside the office. At first only for an occasional dinner, a play or a baseball game. Then it was most weekends. She was in the office for a few days every other week. When they sat in meetings they interacted mostly on a subtle grinning level, which soon began to border on embarrassment for them both.

They needed to talk. Rather than fly to Tallahassee as earlier intended to follow up on his previous glass research, Walker decided to invite Amanda to make the six-hour drive with him, making a long weekend of it. "I want you to meet Flyn and Janie, Amanda," he had said. She thought it a wonderful idea.

Once on the road he began to open up on everything from the Bascoms to his current Baxter Products agenda. "Flyn and Janie and I used to spend weekends together water-skiing on the Ochlochonee River south of Tallahassee, near where it empties into the Gulf of

Mexico. As a matter of fact, Flyn taught me to ski in record beginner-to-veteran time. The second time up on the skis, with me savagely hanging onto the rope with both hands, he steered me toward a six-foot surface-swimming rattlesnake. I saw it only a few yards before I was about to intercept its course. I began shaking my head at about 4,000 rpms when I suddenly found new confidence in staying upright. Flyn said all I had needed was a little motivation. What a pal."

"So that's what it takes with you, snakes. I'll remember that. But I'm just as anxious to meet Janie, Ben. And then what about this 'expert' you mentioned?" asked Amanda.

"He's a chemical engineer and new faculty member. Apparently he's also been doing consulting work for some sort of glass association. Flyn thinks I might be able to learn something of value."

That night after the foursome had returned to the Bascom home following a laugh-filled dinner 'out,' Ben and Amanda found themselves retiring to a single guest room.

"I'm having serious doubts about this new hybrid marketing and sales role, Ben. I like the work and I appreciate both the challenge and the contribution I'm making, but I'm not certain we can properly develop our relationship. I mean, with me being a travelling saleswoman and you moonlighting at running a business while working full time as a private detective. Maybe one of us should give up something."

"Of course it'll work!" said Walker. "We have weekends together and we aren't actually mixing business with pleasure," he grinned and worked his eyebrows up and down two or three times. "But you're right, and if it doesn't work I'll just go back to eating berries in the wild and you can do light cave-work."

He knew how easy it was to set her up with a simple sexist jab. They had both begun playing off that theme on occasion, each to his or her own particular advantage. There was no question he fully respected the accomplishments she had made on her own, and she appreciated his respect. They both implicitly understood these ad lib innuendoes had great potential for developing into foreplay. Amanda had even confided to her mother recently that she liked to think of the whole scenario as 'enwrapment.'

"Enough talk," he half-joked. "Either put up or shut up."

"Ben, this is your best friend's house. It's like being in a parent's home. No. I'm not comfortable."

"It's okay, 'Manda. I checked with Flyn right after dinner and he said it would be all right if we didn't make too much noise."

"You what?" she protested in a loud whisper as she made a mock attempt to inflict damage to his just-bared chest. He caught her small fist in his right hand as his left hand slipped under her blouse. Together they circled the wagons.

13

Flyn Bascom had arranged for a meeting between Walker and one Ernest Kobsavich, a chemical engineering professor at FSU. They were to meet in Bascom's office in the Carraway Building, which housed all the faculty offices, labs and classrooms for the Department of Geology. Ben arrived a few minutes early as usual and, as he dawdled along the familiar first floor hallway and then up to the second and third floors, he was struck by a flood of mini-memories triggered by the glass display cabinets. It had been 16 years. Exhibits arranged by geologists tend neither to change with time nor do their arrangements reflect geologists' creative nature.

He noticed an exam grade list posted by student number just outside the invertebrate paleontology lab and instinctively looked it over. The exhibit area, just outside another formerly favorite room, the sedimentation lab, still served as a display cabinet for tubular earth cores. Here he was forced to pause, smiling. It took him back to a moment years ago with Flyn Bascom and a dinghy in Alligator Harbor, thirty miles due south of Tallahassee and directly on the Gulf. The gist of that particular day's field lab conversation flashed as if it were yesterday.

"Here we are," Walker had begun, "a burning sun, hard bread and cold beer, and not another soul within hailing distance. The geologists sit easy in a breeze-washed rowboat, garnering yet another handful of university credits."

Bascom had expanded on the narrative. "And get this, students. The day's methodology is to periodically slip over the side of the boat into this disgustingly refreshing body of water, take quick and easy samples of bottom sediment and sea water, then clamber back aboard to record the water temperature, salinity and visual make-up of cool mud. Name a better occupation."

Walker had then hoisted a mock salute to their sedimentation professor, adding, "Yeah, and here's to the poor bastards laboring at this very moment to identify pre-Cambrian scum-sucking fossils in paleontology lab!"

Recovering quickly from his reverie, Walker found himself standing in front of Flyn's small third floor office, about to be introduced to the bearded and obligatory elbow-patch jacketed Ernie Kobsavich. He was always at least 18 pounds overweight. At the obligatory weigh-in during his annual physical check-up, his doctor told him his current weight had taken up residence for so long in his file it had become his baseline figure. Ernie's invariable response to such chiding was rooted in defensiveness but always manifested in humor, "You call it 'portly,' doc. I call it 'portable.'"

Introductions completed, they sat down and Bascom restated the purpose of the meeting. "Dr. Kobsavich, my former co-adventurer is trying to understand some of the intricacies of mirror manufacture. Go slowly with him and above all, humor him. He operates in the corporate world these days and his grasp of things conceptual has naturally narrowed to those producing a quick economic return for the effort." Walker shot him an 'up yours' look and silently vowed to verbally cut Flyn off at the knees at the first opportunity.

"Never mind the mad doctor, Doctor." Walker demurred. "I certainly appreciate your time. Ben says you are an expert on mirrors and silvering. Do you know Phil Sloan of Mirror Magic Corporation?"

Ernie Kobsavich nodded at mention of both names, a slight frown fixed on his face. "Well, yes, I met Sloan once. A very unusual individual and quite a strange situation at Mirror Magic." Kobsavich didn't seem reluctant to discuss the subject, in fact he was signalling his willingness to entertain questions.

"I hear he runs a quality shop and that you could picnic on the floor of his factory," said Walker as he cast his line onto the waters.

"That may be so, Mr. Walker, but more interestingly his company continues to prosper at a rate well ahead of the industry's small, but steady annual growth. What's even more astonishing is that this success comes without the benefit of much more than token promotion. It's even absent the typically obligatory incoming 800 lines. And they have absolutely no field representative network. Yet it isn't that they simply convert those unspent dollars to support a no argument customer complaint and service program. These guys just have no significant competition!"

Bingo! Ben Walker could scarcely believe Kobsavich's summation. He thought he was listening to one of his own exhortation speeches to Jon Baxter. "How is it that you're so familiar with their market position, Dr. Kobsavich?"

"These are points of interest for my consulting clients in the wholesale mirror business. They fear the possible expansion of Mirror Magic into their own industry, which often involves contracts with the government and private sector furniture and automotive industries. I don't think they have any worries since MM's expertise lies in producing advertising mirrors. It is my personal contention, however, that Sloan must either work under the table or else he markets what amounts to a cult product."

"I appreciate your candor on the subject, Doctor, but to the basics. What could possibly be different about Mirror Magic's mirrored glass product that would account for this marketing anomaly?" asked Walker.

"Absolutely nothing," replied Kobsavich. "Glass is one of man's most useful materials. Yet few products are made of such inexpensive raw materials, mainly consisting of sand, soda and lime. As you know, there are many different kinds of glass: plate glass, bullet-resisting glass, glass building blocks, fiberglass, polarized glass and the police and voyeur's delight, two-way glass. Most mirrors are simply plate or "float" glass that has been carefully ground and polished to smooth the surface."

Walker made no attempt to get Kobsavich to abbreviate his remarks. On the contrary, he wanted the benefit of anything the man had to offer on the subject. "Interesting," he said. "Tell me more."

"Well, first they grind and clean the glass and then sensitize it with a bonding agent for the adhesion of the silver, which is applied in a solution form," Kobsavich explained, a shade condescendingly. Walker was absorbed, never having anticipated that the meeting might also shed light on the object of the hunt itself.

Kobsavich continued, this time without direct encouragement. "Following that process, a layer of copper is galvanized to the silver coating for reinforcement, you see. Then the surface is painted for additional protection. Finally, the glass is baked in order to cure the treatment and the surface is cleaned once again. It's a standard manufacturing process, Mr. Walker, although Mirror Magic does make a big fuss about continually flushing the mirror surfaces with deionized water which keeps the product chemically clean. But that really isn't unusual either," Kobsavich ended his technical explanation with a shrug.

Walker added a finishing touch to the narrative. "From what I know about our own in-house screening process, Dr. Kobsavich, we lay down the ink for the graphics prior to the silvering operation itself. Of course that's what makes for customization of the mirror for advertising purposes. That is certainly the same process MM must use, which brings us back to my earlier point that 'a mirror is a mirror,' by definition."

"There is one curious thing about the Mirror Magic process, however," interjected Kobsavich. "They go to the expense and effort to individually register each wall mirror, and then they guarantee it indefinitely." The mirror expert leaned back in his chair, his lips slightly pursed.

"Translate that for me, Doctor," said Walker, obligingly.

"Of course. The market for advertising mirrors within the specialty advertising industry, is a declining one, witnessed by your own firm's long-ago retrenchment."

Walker prompted him again and Kobsavich responded. "Why go to the expense of adding the cost of a feature not really needed by the end user?"

"Purely as a marketing tool?" suggested Walker.

"Possibly, but is such a feature really even value-added? For example, if they wanted to tout the fact that each individual mirror comes pre-registered, why wouldn't they just consecutively number the mirror backing instead of embedding a costly, numbered metal plate? I doubt if they're asked to replace more than one in ten thousand pieces, one one-hundredth of a percent potential replacement. There's considerable cost to implant the plate. The result is an insignificant, but expensive competitive distinction. What's your best guess for this ploy, Mr. Walker?"

A germ of an idea burrowed its way into Walker's mind. "Partly because it's useful as a marketing tool and partly attributable to their finding it expedient to combine the registration plate with a hanging bracket." Walker then abruptly almost rudely ended the meeting. "I hope I may contact you again should additional questions arise, Ernie, if I may call you that."

"By all means, Mr. Walker. I do earn a substantial portion of my income from such consulting work," said Kobsavich, a little miffed at his short dismissal. He made certain it was understood that further discussions would not be without a fee.

Ben was sometimes given to intuition. It hadn't helped him much in working with the inanimate objects of his former field, but he had often followed its lead in dealing with people. He said to Bascom as they left the office, "Flyn, something just nibbled at my line. My bobber made only the smallest ripple, but I have to play it out. Thanks for the help and the hospitality. I'll be back in touch."

"Whenever you're hungry or thirsty, Ben. And I'm glad I could be of so much help at this critical meeting," Bascom winced. Walker smirked at the wince. Bascom laughed at the smirk.

Halfway back to Atlanta Amanda said to her usually conversational driver, "Well, aside from an exotic getaway weekend with yet another beautiful, blonde seductress, did the mild-mannered 'Walkman' benefit from his interview with the Glassman?" She spoke over his oblivious finger-tapping accompaniment to another of Ben's swing period favorites, Harry James' "Jalousie." The refrain always reminded him of his father's own trumpet scale-tripping delights.

Suddenly realizing he had been keeping all his thoughts to himself, he apologized, adding, "Amanda, we need to talk with some Mirror Magic customers. Not end-users, mind you, but distributors." He glanced up from the interstate at a billboard, then invited her to dinner. "How about dining at the Catfish Cottage, my discerning and delightful companion; all-you-can-eat-easy-off-easy-on-exit-now," he grinned.

14

"Walt, it's great to see you again," said Walker, genuinely glad to see his old friend and mentor, Walt Manley. "Once a year at the winter show is simply not enough. As I mentioned when I called a few days ago when I was in Tallahassee, I couldn't come by then, but I'm back. I want to see and hear how things are going for you, and of course I want to update you on the BP line. But I also have another mission."

Manley was always happy to see Ben whom he considered nearly a son. "Fire away. I won't hold back, you know that."

Walker took that statement as his cue. "While you do a first rate job of selling our line overall, you don't even send us a token order for our wall mirrors. Are you selling anyone's advertising mirrors, Walt?" He was asking The Question of the man for whom he had more respect than any other one person—save possibly for Jon Baxter.

"As a matter of fact, Ben, we sell a hell of a lot of 'em, but they're all Magic's mirrors. Funny thing is I'm not even sure why. We've *tried* to switch to Baxter but our customers tell us there's a difference, though damned if I know what it is."

"Then what accounts for the fact, Walt?"

"Here's all I can tell you," confided Manley. "We would certainly have no switch-over problem with the ultimate recipient of the mirror. The resistance to switching from MM to a Baxter mirror comes from our accounts, the advertisers who selectively give the mirrors to the ultimate recipients. Follow me on this, Ben: our customers tell us that their name awareness, and thus the success of their business, is unusually influenced over a significant period of time following distribution of the advertising mirrors bought from us. I mean well beyond the simple preference-building that comes with the specialty advertising medium itself. Some of our larger and more sophisticated accounts have even quantified their results."

"Please elaborate, Walt. I'm not sure I follow you," said Walker.

"What I do know is that we get far more repeat business with relatively expensive mirrors from 'Magic' than we do even with much less expensive wall calendars which have built-in obsolescence. Now, why would that be?"

That was Walker's question! Everyone was asking it of him these days. He loved the challenge of solving a puzzle, but he was still searching for only the first matching piece of this thousand-part monster.

15

Jon Baxter was approaching his own office when he heard the sound of breaking glass, common enough out in the factory during the two days a month when they could justify running the silvering and screening equipment for mirror orders. He had been advised countless times by his accounting people to drop the mirror line altogether. Unjustifiable pride had apparently taken up permanent lodging in his mind on this subject was how his CPA had put it last week. The time had come to move decisively in this regard. And while Ben Walker was making some progress, Baxter's itch required more strenuous scratching.

As Baxter entered his office, Walker stood over what was left of the souvenir double M mirror which had formerly hung on J.B.'s display wall. It lay flat but broken in a number of pieces, still held in position by its frame.

Walker looked up at Baxter and then back at their multi-cracked reflections staring up at them from the desk. "Mirror, mirror, off the wall, who is the most curious of them all?"

The intermingled images of the two men leaning side-by-side over the desk offered a silent, appropriate commentary on their closeness. That link had developed initially out of pure compatibility, mutual trust and respect. It had grown to something approaching a familial relationship, due primarily to common interests. They cultivated the challenge of mutually beneficial growth.

Baxter began the dialogue with a quip. "You have one syllable too many in that rhyme Ben," he laughed. "Is this display an expression of frustration on your project's progress or do you simply resent the way I've decorated my office?"

Walker uncharacteristically ignored the opening salvo. He was absorbed with his own thoughts. "Neither, Jon. You know mirrors like no one else. What's different about this one?"

Baxter thought for a second, not about Walker's question, but how he might bank the fires of whatever train of thought Walker might be trying to fuel. He knew Walker resented questions being answered with questions. "What possible difference could there be? Two suppliers sell advertising mirrors. Both still manufacture and decorate them. At best, one might be more highly polished, but the advertising imprint would be perceived no differently except for the nature of the graphics. Nothing technical justifies what distributors have been telling you about end-user preference for MM performance, Ben."

"All right, then don't you find this warranty-registration plate curious, Jon?" He carefully lifted the back-plate from the broken glass and inspected it from multiple angles. "If we decided to offer an end user product registration program like MM's, how would you do it?"

"I'd use consecutive-numbering equipment and either stamp each piece or imprint a pressure-sensitive decal and slap it onto the back of the mirror. Uh, huh, I see what you're saying. I certainly wouldn't bother with an added-cost metal plate, regardless of it's size," said Baxter.

"What about as an attachment for a hanging-cord or wall-mounting bracket?" Walker pursued an earlier thought.

"Why do it any differently? We either staple the cord to the heavy paper stock on the back of the mirror surface itself, or attach the hanging-bracket to it." Baxter sat even further back in his chair, his hands interlocked behind an uplifted head. "The plate seems superfluous, but I see no connection whatever between that and our problem, Ben. I think we need to push from some other angles. And one may have just jumped up in our faces.

"I took a phone call at home from Amanda just before I came in. As you know, she's in Chicago working with our rep. This morning she learned from an early local newscast that a Chicago-schooled plant engineer with Mirror Magic died last night in a private flying accident. She used to work with him and intends to come back for his funeral. You want to go with her, maybe learn something?"

16

"Jon says you're into buying bad luck these days," said Amanda as she and Walker left the graveside service.

"He's closer to the truth than he realizes. I told him I broke the mirror to better-examine a double M product but the plain fact is I'm frustrated with the lack of significant leads in my quest of Mighty Mirror. By the way, what caused your friend's plane accident, 'Manda?"

"Freak weather, apparently. But it wasn't an airplane; it was an ultra-light aircraft. I think Frank referred to it as a gyroplane—a sort of mini-helicopter. I only saw it once and it looked like a giant insect. He flew it for recreation, but it's all he ever talked about to anyone who would listen."

"Um," Walker answered absent-mindedly, distracted by another thought. "Amanda, I have to fly to Miami to do a table-top show this Thursday. Why don't you take a few days off from the midwest March weather and go with me. It's only a one-day show. If you can switch your schedule around we can make a long weekend out of it—a mini-vacation."

"Now, of course you'll want me to help you at the show while I'm on my 'vacation,'" she said matter-of-factly.

"Great idea! I hadn't thought of that," he smiled. "In fact, you can also help me conduct a little informal survey while we're at it. I want to find out what a few more distributors have to say about the state of the advertising mirror business."

17

Ben had traveled to Miami many times. It was the same to him whether winter or summer—delightful. The temperature might vary from warm to hot but the high humidity was usually offset by the breeze blowing in off the ocean. There were other constants of course; the evocative smell of sea air and the constant hum of traffic on the concrete ribbons that bind the city. Miami's traffic was far worse than Atlanta's, but at least familiarity with the city wasn't required to get around. A street map and a little fortitude allowed almost anyone to navigate since the metro area was divided into a strict grid.

Miami, and all of southern Florida is flat, flatter and flattest. The entire city barely lifts itself above sea level and, unlike Atlanta, isn't carved into irregular segments by a forest or a snaking river. Any elevation without windows can be assumed to be a landfill overlaid with layers of dirt, refuse and grass seed, topped with constantly turning, wheeling sea gulls attracted by an irresistible but inaccessible smorgasbord.

Walker loved the area in spite of its violent reputation. What city of major magnetic draw was without it? He was especially fond of the indigenous birdsong, the palmed flora and the wonderful myriad of boats—from bass, sail and junker to yachts and cruise ships.

After they had settled into their rooms and then set up their tabletop display, Amanda struck gold in the show's opening minutes.

"Mr. Allejandro," she asked of one of the very successful Miami-headquartered distributors attending the show, "you say most of the business you do in South America and around the Caribbean is with the less expensive items available to you. Nevertheless you do substantial business with various wall mirror products. This is curious considering the obviously greater freight costs on top of the significantly more expensive unit price. Why is this?"

"I don't understand it either, Miss Baxter," he said, confusing her name with the company name. "For twenty years I have been selling my mirrors to good businesses in the islands and many South American countries, and even my customers do not know why the 'magic mirrors' seem to do so well for them," shrugged the interviewee. "As you say, the transportation charges are horrible, but still they reorder. I think it is better I spend my time selling than spelling, if you know what I mean. I'm sorry about your Baxter mirrors but I must sell my customers the 'magic' or my competition will. We like your plastic products very much, however. We give you some business, no?"

On the plane back to Atlanta following a weekend spent in the sun, poolside, but working on new fiscal year budgets, Amanda said, "The next time you offer me a fun-filled getaway to an exotic clime, Mr. Walker, I think I shall point out that thee, me and a laptop computer are a crowd."

"Hey, not so fast," Ben rebutted. "Delightful dining, meal after meal. You should be so lucky."

"Yeah, *one* dinner out, one pizza delivery to my poolside work table, and two continental breakfasts in the lobby," she pursed her lips and skewed them sideways sarcastically.

Determined to come out of the competition with no worse than a draw, Walker winked and said "Well, what about dessert? You said that was sweet."

"Bitter-sweetener, at best," she said, breaking up with her own clever humor.

Walker's accompanying laughter quickly degenerated from sincere to forced. It was certainly more fun to dish out zingers that to catch them full in the face. He squeezed her hand. He was, at the least, in like, if not in love. And she no less than he, but something else was also on her mind as a result of the trade show.

"Follow me on this, Ben," Amanda sobered. "Every single person I spoke with at the show who regularly presents mirrors as a part of their primary product mix stated categorically that Magic Mirrors repeat more like a supply item than a one-time business gift or promotional item. How can that be? It isn't even a dated product. Just how many wall mirrors can a recipient use? I mean it isn't like they're going to wear out or be misplaced or something."

"So what do you make of that, Watson?" encouraged Walker.

She attempted to analyze it further, "Either the advertising copy itself must be so well crafted as to exert an exceptional influence—unlikely. Or, crazy as it seems, the mirror itself somehow impacts the viewer in an abnormal fashion. An advertiser's dream, huh? Well, that's illogical. Where do we go from here, Holmes?"

"To the files," he responded in a thoughtful tone.

"Which files?"

A tripwire had triggered somewhere in Walker's mind and presented him with a cryptic clue. He looked at Amanda quizzically, saying, "Maybe the answer lies with history, back in the Baxter & Sloan partnership days. I wonder if there just might be some original files somewhere in Baxter Products archives that would provide us with a lead."

"Well, if so," observed Amanda, "Jon Baxter is certainly not aware of it or he wouldn't have so belatedly joined your crusade. A reversal of position which, ironically, has now become the Corporate Obsession for him.

"I understand, but nothing is to be lost by following through. If we don't turn up anything we can always commission a covert detail to investigate Mirror Magic's own files. Any volunteers from former MM employee ranks, Ms. Booth?"

"You mean you want me to take the fall in Mirrorgate? No thanks. I think I'll stick to 'woman's work.' By the way, of late it's been accounting for the solid sales increases of Baxter Products, which in turn is providing the financing for top management's adventuring." Amanda winked as she offered that assessment.

18

"Bingo," yelled Jon Baxter into the New York-Kennedy airport pay phone. "On your archives hunch, while I'm up here speaking to a regional association I called the office of Bramble, Cohen and Callow, the mega law firm which handled the original legal work for my father and the elder Sloan. I knew the attorney firm had merged years ago and the corporate offices were moved from Atlanta to somewhere in New York. They were in the phone book!"

"Did you see them?"

"Of course, although they weren't much interested in helping me with what I wanted. I prevailed upon the newest junior partner to assign a first-year intern to examine the Baxter & Sloan account files for anything pertaining to manufacturing processes. I privately presented the overworked intern one of our Person-Of-The-Year executive mirrors for his office and told him how much we appreciated his trouble and that we naturally expected to be properly billed for all of his time. I think one of the partners had already told him this project was a favor and to make superficial work of it, implying there was nothing to find. I went back to see him two days later."

As enthusiastic and effective as Jon Baxter was with anything he took on he still had to be coached to get to the point. He would normally have spent another 10 minutes with a detail-by-detail account of particulars. But this time he did neither, concluding the phone call with, "I made an interesting discovery, but I can't explain things to you over the phone, Ben. I'm only now beginning to understand the implications of what I've read. The operative elements, however, have to do with an incredible concept concerning subliminal advertising.

"Be thinking about how that might apply to advertising mirrors. I'll see you tomorrow morning before you've had your second cup of coffee. Pick me up at Hartsfield on Delta's 8:30 A.M. arrival from Kennedy. This is what we've been looking for, partner."

At two A.M. Ben had been lying awake in bed for nearly an hour and a half, wrestling with 'subliminal.' What possible connection could exist between that and an advertising imprint on a mirror? It was crazy. He just couldn't share Jon's apparent elation. Only anxiety. Seven years prior to this, Ben Walker had been provided a very important vehicle with which to turn a crucial career path. He valued the man who had given him the opportunity more than the opportunity itself.

This wasn't the first time he had thought about the paternal aspect but he had only partially succeeded in ever telling Baxter as much. He had stopped short on several occasions, not being quite able to put it into so many words, although he felt Jon knew. In fact it had occurred to Walker that perhaps Baxter might well have been experiencing a similar difficulty of expression. They had a strong bond made even stronger of late—courtesy of their absorbing common cause.

All of this bothered Walker, particularly in light of their renewed fervor in tilting with mirror shadows. He, Ben Walker, not Jon Baxter, should be doing the leg work on this particular trail. Oh, well, J. Baxter was tough. Walker only hoped Jon knew what he was doing.

Neither of them did.

19

The flight arrived without Jon Baxter. The airline verified for Walker that his employer had been ticketed for the flight. "I'm sorry, sir. He was a 'no-show.' We get a lot of them," the service agent shrugged.

Not by a man on a mission, thought Ben. He was uneasy and immediately went to the concourse's nearest bank of pay phones. A check with the New York central police department revealed more than a half-a-dozen automobile accidents in the vicinity of Kennedy airport during the past twelve hours, but no listing of a Jon Baxter.

Walker took a deep and somewhat relieved breath, fearing to think past the few facts at his disposal. "Begin again, Finnigan," he said to himself as he redialed the same police station number. "Could you give me the names of the hospitals nearest Kennedy airport, ma'am? I have reason to believe an accident victim may have been taken to one of them."

The fourth call located a hospital administrator relieved to hear from someone with the firm or family of Jon Baxter. Part of her job was to expeditiously unite unaccompanied emergency admissions with responsible parties. She had been unsuccessful in reaching anyone at Baxter Products since it was still early morning. She factually, but compassionately, explained that the patient had been brought in several hours ago from an automobile accident. So much for police efficiency, Ben cursed.

"Mr. Walker, apparently, two paramedics responding to a cardiac arrest call at the same building your friend was visiting had just arrived on the scene as Mr. Baxter's vehicle was struck. His car was hit broad-side by a speeding car just as he was exiting an underground Manhattan hotel garage. An explosion resulted and his condition is critical. Mr. Walker, I'm sorry. Will you or someone be coming in immediately?"

She went on to explain. Baxter's rental car had erupted into a furnace of blazing steel practically before the eyes of the paramedics as they were arriving on the other call. Within seconds they had radioed for a second ambulance and had themselves rushed to Baxter's aid.

Within 45 minutes of the phone call Ben had booked himself onto a flight, boarded, and found his plane taxiing down the runway for takeoff.

At Parkway Trauma Center's fifth floor ICU information desk he was told the on-call doctor would be with him in a moment. Yes, he could see the patient if the doctor okayed it. He sat down, his emotions and thoughts intermixing. Muriel Baxter-Bennett was on her way from California. He had called Jon's daughter from the Atlanta airport just before he took off. There was no one else to call.

Walker recalled that Baxter's mother had followed his father in death more than 20 years ago. Jon's own wife had been sadly successful in her second attempt at overdosing on drugs after chemotherapy had produced no remission of her cancers. She had not yet turned 50. The Baxter family did not have depth of numbers, either in longevity or in family members. Muriel would make contact with her lone sibling; communication lines between her bachelor brother and her father had long been down. Concerning the lone occupant of the other vehicle, Walker learned that his death had apparently been instant.

Dr. Julien Townsend entered the waiting room and introduced himself to Ben. "Mr. Walker, your friend is in serious condition. With a strong heart and exceptional motivation, he has only the slimmest of hopes."

Of the latter personal characteristic, Ben had no doubt whatsoever. More than that, Walker knew of Jon Baxter's fervent belief in the inherent abilities of the mind to channel healing. If he could be given the chance, J.B. would apply the cure to which more and more physicians had begun to lend credence—'patient, *help* heal thyself.'

"Call me, Ben, Doctor. Talk to me."

"Mr. Baxter has third degree burns over 90 percent of his body—almost everywhere but his hands, feet and lower legs; he was apparently wearing driving gloves and cowboy boots. We have stabilized him for the time being and have already removed some of the burned skin. It will require three more operations just to complete that procedure. The greater problem, however, is dehydration and infection. If we get past that, and let me say I have no confidence he will ever survive to that point, we would normally graft skin from undamaged areas of his body. Unfortunately, not nearly enough exists."

The specialist's eyes were more sympathetic than Walker would have expected, given that he must see this sort of thing on a regular basis. He had twice now been impressed with this hospital's personnel. Ben was still not focused on his point but he was able to take comfort in the doctor's manner, if not his words.

"Then he has no hope whatever?" Ben interpreted.

The primary care physician motioned for him to sit, and he did likewise. "Not necessarily. I have explained the facts, now consider this. I share a medical belief with many other, far more brilliant minds than mine: Osler, Bernard and Hippocrates. The outcome of even such an ordeal as awaits Jon Baxter has more to do with what sort of person he is than the nature of the physical problem itself. The very best that surgeons can do in a situation like this is to buy time to allow a patient the opportunity to begin healing himself."

"Well, you've got your man in Jon Baxter, doctor. Are you saying there is hope?" Ben raised his head and eyes level with the attending physician. Walker didn't know if he could buy into this holistic approach wholesale, but he was for anything that might advance his friend's chances.

"Let me explain. For a few years now this hospital and a very few others have been doing successful but experimental work on culture cells from a patient's own outer layer of skin. The cells grow into transplantable sheets of skin for permanent wound coverage. You can call it cloning. It has been performed less than a hundred times before—anywhere. But it's his only chance under such an extreme circumstance. If he can survive the initial devastation to his systems, then the nature of this individual will play a greater role than we."

"I appreciate that, doctor. Thank you for your candor and for that thread of hope. His family will be here within a few hours. I am here for him now."

It would be too late. The irony of it all was that the strongest link, the physical one, had failed when the often less dependable mental, emotional and spiritual links might well have aided this particular patient in challenging death's encroachments. Ben could not know that Jon Baxter had fought tenaciously for unconscious hours the tendering of welcoming hands on the other side. Touching had been inevitable.

20

The day following Jon's funeral Ben sat staring vacantly at the stacks of mail his secretary had opened and placed in carefully labeled categories. Margaret was not only a sweetheart, she was efficient.

For the first time in five days his mind was in a state other than the sadness-continuum which had begun on his flight to New York. For distraction he forced himself to puzzle over some particulars.

"A garage parking lot," he said to himself in a barely audible tone. That was bizarre. What's the probability of a fatal accident happening there versus out on the open road with five million crazies on their way to or from work? No witnesses had come forward other than the paramedics, perhaps because of the early hour; it must have happened not much before six A.M.

He dialed the New York hospital and got the paramedics' names. By chance, one of them happened to be in the hospital at that very moment.

"Yes, Mr. Walker. My partner and I did get the license number of the other car. I thought you knew the police had identified it as stolen."

"No, this is the first I've known. He must have been speeding. Did Mr. Baxter say anything between when you pulled him from his car and your arrival at the hospital? Oh, I'm sorry, my manners are inexcusable. I haven't even thanked you and your partner for the heroic efforts on your part. I had asked for you several times when I was at the hospital but they said you only came there on emergency runs. If you hadn't been there when you were and did what you did, he wouldn't have had even the barest chance given him, Mr. Pachecki. Please accept my thanks and those of his family."

"It's all right, Mr. Walker. We were just doin' our job. As for Mr. Baxter, he only moaned. He was goin' into shock. I was drivin', but my partner said he sort of gurgled a word Lonnie didn't understand. He said it was something like factory. Sorry I can't help you more."

"Factory. Fact-o-ry. Fact, facts, *fax!*" Could Jon have sent him something concerning the report he had so enthusiastically phoned him about the night before? If so, where would it be? Where else? Lying on his desk in the pile Margaret had marked "facsimile messages!" He moved some papers. Jesus, there it was!

Before he could finish reading, however, Walker broke down. For the last time, he vowed. He resolved at that moment to replace the emotion of his loss with commitment to finish the job he and Jon Baxter had begun.

Complications had already set in, however. The responsibility for running Baxter Products had just been placed squarely on his shoulders by J.B.'s will, backed up by Muriel Baxter and the unanimous wishes of the board. Well, never mind that. He read the incredible contents of the fax for a second time and then noted the date. It had been received the morning after Walker had gone to the airport. The day following. How could that be? Sent by whom?

"Someone has the answers," he said aloud.

"Bramble, Cohen and Callow," said the receptionist. "Yes, sir, I know the Baxter Products account name. Is this Mr. Baxter?" She remembered having met Jon Baxter because he had given her a little stand-up desk mirror when he had first come in about a week ago. When Walker identified himself as Baxter's colleague she told him as much, mentioning that the desk mirror he had given her was still sitting there. "It has your company name on it, Mr. Walker."

Irony. Jon was forever lamenting that the industry should make more of an effort to practice what it preached.

"I wonder if you could assist me, ma'am, by checking our file to see if you have a copy of a document that was being prepared for him by an intern that day."

"Of course, sir, he's the nicest gentleman. Checking. No, I'm afraid there is nothing in your file for the entire month. Could I help you with anything else or do you wish to speak with a partner?"

"Oh, no, thank you," he said. "Well, yes, one thing. Could you give me the name of the clerk who has been doing the research for Baxter Products?" Walker took a swing, hoping.

"I'll have to transfer you to the office manager, Mr. Walker. Please hold," she said.

A full 30 seconds elapsed before the office manager came on the line. "Yes, Mr. Walker, this is Marjorie Robertson. I'm sorry to say that there is really nothing in your file other than reference to a brief consultation, for which no billing was made. I'm sorry but we don't currently have any interns in our employ, either. If we can be of further help, please let us know."

21

The next day Ben met Amanda for lunch at his favorite watering hole. The recent events diluted the normal charm and character of Kelley's. The staff danced attendance upon him as always, however, including the best table and immediate seating. He seldom came in without some little imprinted trinket which he high-spiritedly handed anyone with whom he came in contact, from hostess to cashier. It wasn't the value of the simple items themselves, but the value of the gesture. Both Walt Manley and Jon Baxter had taught him the fun and benefit of such a philosophy. But not today.

He had told Amanda about everything except what was actually contained in the fax by the time the waiter had brought their light entrees. "My best guess," he said, "is that the missing law clerk completed his assignment and put the results on paper and into the out fax file. A pool secretary probably saw to its routine dispatch the next morning."

"But why would there be no record of it in the law office's file?" asked Amanda. "And just where is this law clerk, Ben?"

"First of all, we only know what we've been told. The only explanation I have fits with a bizarre and maybe even murderous scenario," he said, looking straight into her eyes and taking her hand in his.

She was silent for a moment. Then, "Ben, are you suggesting that Jon Baxter's death wasn't an accident? All of what you've told me so far holds no justification for such an accusation."

"Yes, I know," he sighed, "but I haven't yet shared with you the contents of the fax. It's a copy of an old Sloan and Baxter report.

Get a grip on yourself 'Manda, and listen. First, consider the paper's title: 'Synopsis of the Research Report on the Effects of Subliminal Mirrored Advertising.' Now, it isn't dated, or at least the date isn't reflected on the fax, but the report itself must predate the demise of the former Baxter and Sloan partnership. Here's how it begins:

"'Exhaustive and private testing by B&S has attempted to determine if programmed subliminal messages presented to viewers via specialty advertising mirrors would have an effect benefitting the advertiser.'" Walker looked up and swallowed. "Amanda, I don't think this sort of thing is possible now, let alone pre-1950, but if Mirror Magic's business is involved in any way with something as unethical and illegal as this document suggests, then there is also probable reason to suspect that Jon's death was not accidental. Here, read the rest of it for yourself."

Amanda took the paper from him, still a skeptic, and very aware that Ben was yet suffering, not only from severe heartache, but also with a bias towards MM. She read to herself, "Fundamentally, consciously received messages viewed on silk-screen imprinted mirrors have the same effect as other imprinted specialty advertising products, i.e., the utility of the item itself contributes to message visibility and therefore to repetitive exposure of that message, whether a symbol, logo, a name or some slogan. In different words, with this repetition comes increased brand or name familiarity, whether conscious or subconscious, and thus is the viewer more greatly influenced with respect to this brand or name consideration."

Amanda continued reading, familiar with the boring definitions, but assuming that Ben's point would quickly make itself evident. "Unlike mass advertising media, with specialty advertising the greater the utility of the product carrying the message the greater the exposure to that message. The mirror for example, whose value is as a looking glass to satisfy the personal vanity universal to man, could be adapted very effectively.

If a normally visible and tolerated advertising message is rendered invisible to the conscious eye, there exists no natural filtering defense for the subconscious. This built-in conscious-awareness filter is what protects people, to a degree, from the thousands of printed and audible messages that daily bombard our overt senses."

Amanda's expression was one of fading amusement as she finished reading the first page of the two page treatise. It went on,

"A lingering or even brief glance into such a treated mirror by anyone seeking the mirror's inherent utility, is without the built-in partial defense to consciously perceived advertising messages. As a result, an advertiser's subconscious message to those people innocently using the mirror's image-reflecting qualities yields far greater impact than what the medium's normal visual message would be able to deliver."

She looked up at Ben as she turned the page, an expression of revulsion now beginning to spread over her face. Ben prodded her to read the report's closing summary. "Research and extrapolation offers reasonably conclusive evidence that this project can be successfully implemented, given that the technology is (exclusively) available to us. The empirical nature of advertising is repetition of message begets familiarity which tends to yield heightened trust and ultimately increases the potential for a favorable reaction on the part of the recipient of the advertising message. This axiom is multiplied by a factor of approximately one hundred through subliminal application. In our opinion this would hold true whether the intended viewer response is a simple predisposition towards trying a branded product or service or some simple choice of action. Overall results would, of course, be directly proportional to the number of products distributed."

Aloud, Amanda added her own conclusion, "Where would one stop with such an advertising advantage?"

Walker answered the rhetorical question. "Certainly not with niche market share. Irrespective of current scientific studies and conclusions that are locked in debate over the power of messages directed to the subconscious mind, someone has apparently not only concluded that the mind *can* register information outside of awareness, but has both developed and applied the technology for doing so."

22

Tersa Ver Meer parked her nails-red BMW in a Mirror Magic 'reserved' slot, entered the administration building, and strode purposefully to Philip Sloan's office.

"Good morning, Ms. Ver Meer," greeted Sloan's secretary, not attempting to conceal her dislike for her boss's untitled and mysterious sometime-assistant. "We haven't seen you for quite a while."

"That is correct, Ms. Powers. A true traveller knows no home," she responded without a trace of warmth but with a slight accent Pauline Powers mistook for German. "Mr. Sloan is expecting me. I'll see myself in."

Without formal greeting of any kind, Philip Sloan waved her to a chair as he closed the office's massive wooden door. Returning to his desk he stood looking down at her and bluntly inquired, "Without the details, did you think of every possible element in making Baxter's death look like an accident?"

Ver Meer stared back at him, pausing for a moment before replying. "That is the challenge; perfect execution." It was not an intended pun. "Just as with the engineer," she said, "the plastique explosive was detonated by a jarring contact, in this case violent collision with another vehicle. Absolutely no telling evidence remains, including the fool I hired to hit-and-run."

"What of the law clerk?" Sloan continued his grilling.

"He knew nothing, suspected nothing. But as a safeguard he has been quickly and quietly recruited by and relocated to our attorney's Seattle office."

Tersa Ver Meer was of Dutch origin. She emigrated to the United States with her foster parents when she was barely a teenager. Her superior intelligence, competence and physical beauty were subordinate, but extremely complementary to her bitter ambition. Sloan had recruited her from among the 20 or so high-priced call girls he had interviewed in the course of personal indulgence.

Contributing to her sensuous appearance and haughty demeanor was Tersa Ver Meer's only indispensable accessory—spike-heeled shoes. They were available to her in any one of six dozen versions and colors she typically kept closeted. She had long ago observed that most men would interrupt any conversation or other pursuit whenever their culture-conditioned hearing detected the tell-tale sharp tap of a high heel striking a hard surface. In her own case their knee-jerk glances were never disappointed. She was never without such enhancements in the presence of men, whether in public or in the boudoir.

She paid a price, however. Her tightly-packed 120 pounds hammered more than 700 unforgiving tons onto her heels each normal five-mile walking day. That translated, through three, four and even five-inch heeled shoes, into gruesome claw toes, ugly bunions and lower back pain. To her they were simply trade-offs. Ver Meer's philosophy concerning relationships with men was a simple one born of her own early conditioning; any man might rent the body, if she were so inclined and he had the fancy price, but no one could buy the franchise.

Had Sloan not been completely devoid of anything even resembling a sense of humor, he might easily have referred to his assistant as his henchperson. As it was he hardly thought of her at all. For her part, she carried out her assignments with minimal feedback. She made no effort to satisfy even her perceived nominal self-recognition need. As a result, time would exact a terrible emotional toll.

Sloan's initial proposition was to double her best year's earnings as a prostitute. She countered by quoting him a doubling of that already impressive figure, barely curious as to what the work itself would entail. She made no objection to his job description, "Whatever I require."

Sloan had read her perfectly in that respect. He closed accordingly, offering three months' advance salary on the spot, but with one caveat, "Mistakes on your part which reflect negatively on either me or Mirror Magic, will cost you dearly." She did not wince; it was simply another rental contract with some fine print.

That was 10 years ago. She continued her report, "Ben Walker and his sometime live-in assistant perceive the competition with Mirror Magic with minor frustration and major helplessness. I have tracked them extensively and for their inquiries they have gained nothing substantive."

"Good," Sloan grunted, totally uninterested in any attempt at personalizing their conversation. "Continue your surveillance of both Walker and Amanda Booth, and from now on report to me weekly and in person."

This was the Sloan of the former circle completed with Gam'man and Chesser. Since he had long ago willfully deserted their once continuous line of personal interdependence, Sloan considered the pair to be superfluous. He was totally uninterested in either them or their former relationship. If they got in his way, historical connections would carry absolutely no weight in his decisions. He was singly and unalterably interested in his version of The Game.

23

"Amanda, what we're dealing with here is a competitive situation that is not only totally unethical and absolutely illegal but incomprehensible in the bargain," Walker summarized for her in his Baxter Products office.

"Not to mention the probable direct role in Jon Baxter's death," she added.

"The real question," Ben said, "is what we're going to do about it. We have nothing concrete to take to the police. And if we went to the FTC, or whatever other federal regulating body that deals with trade restraints or monopolistic positions, with only a single, unsigned and undated memo on a long-defunct corporation letterhead, we wouldn't even rate a comment on the weather. We can't follow suit, Amanda. We need a trump card. Got any?"

"Come on, Benjamin," she rebuked him. "You want me to coax it out of you, right? I know you. You're an ordered individual and you probably have a plan of action already in mind, but you like to visualize the logic. First, you bounce the set-up off your foil, the role I get whenever your friend Flyn can't come out to play, and then you flash your hand. So, tell me, what'll it be?"

"Lay out our hand. That's it!" said Walker, suddenly animated. "What a marvel you are, A.B. Okay, how does this play? I'll press Flyn Bascom to see if he'll plant the idea of an interview with Phil Sloan. He can tell Sloan he's thinking of a university journal article about unusual southeastern businesses that illustrate a successful marriage of manufacturing and distribution. He can say the American Glass Association suggested he contact Mirror Magic."

"Ben, if you're just trying to bait him," said Amanda, "it ought to work beautifully, but if you hope to actually get anything out of him it will be a waste of time."

"Well, I want to establish a position with him before we go public, but do you really know him so well?"

Amanda cocked her head, nodding twice with that by now familiar expression that meant, "Yes, and here's why."

"Remember the Mirror Magic employee whose funeral you attended with me—the engineering/PR friend, Jack Petersma? Well, I recall him telling me just before I left MM that he about had it out with Sloan over his reaction to an idea for a simple 50th anniversary 'how-it-all-started' piece for an industry trade journal. Jack was so upset over Sloan's irrational and near-violent reaction to his presentation that he lost it for a moment and implied that he just might leave and take what he knew with him."

"What did he have on Sloan?" asked Walker.

"Nothing. I mean, I don't know," she said. "At the time Jack mentioned it I didn't think anything of it except that at worst double M might have committed an OSHA violation or something. I do know this: Jack Petersma was an engineer first, and a public relations man second."

She caught herself in mid-sentence and stared at Walker, furrowing her brow as if trying to remember something. Then it came to her. "Ben, Jack was not only a fine engineer and someone who respected equipment, but he was thorough. I recall him once describing the gyroplane that he supposedly crashed as being docile, 'and absolutely the safest form of aircraft flying today.' I remember so precisely because I had never before heard anyone use the word docile in describing an aircraft. And when I asked him what made it so he went into great detail, explaining why a gyroplane could not stall or spin, and in fact could land at very slow speeds with little or no ground roll."

Walker was about to comment but she continued before he could wedge in a word. "He bought that aircraft because of its unique reliability, Ben. What's the likelihood of such a combination of cautious engineer and super-safe equipment resulting in a fatal accident? Puny! Now factor in a paranoid Phil Sloan and see what that does for your equation, Mr. Scientist." Amanda had succeeded in working herself into a visible state of emotion, her inflection becoming more marked with each sentence.

Walker thought about it. "Amanda, this just might lead to some hard evidence. I'm already presuming motive and opportunity for Sloan and company. As for means, we need help. We have to find out exactly how Baxter Products and this entire industry is being victimized by Mirror Magic. Once we have those answers we'll have a shot at seeing Phil Sloan salted away, and double M put on the griddle." He paused. "Now, speaking of that, when did I last take you to dinner and dancing, my fair lady?"

"Last night, but I guess I could be seen with you in public two nights in a row, if you promise not to wear the same gravy-stained tie." They both laughed for the first time that day.

24

The next evening, after racquetball with the three other 'Off The Wall' gang members who showed up at the club for two hours of fast-paced exercise and trading of verbal insults, Walker and Gene Ellison sat cooling off in front of the glass courts. Ellison spared Walker his usual post-play juggling routine. They each ordered a banana-fruit drink and Ellison offered to pay.

Receiving change for his $20, he carefully melded the bills with others he pulled from his pocket. Ben noticed with idle interest that Ellison not only rearranged all of them so they were in descending order of denomination but also with the darker side facing up and the faces turned in the same direction. Finally, they were carefully folded in half with the face side out and returned to a front pants pocket.

"What's that all about?" Ben asked. He knew by Ellison's own admission that Gene was a world class nitpicker. In the course of a typical visit almost anywhere, for any purpose, he would tend to straighten, pick at, rub, tighten or otherwise correct or adjust almost any object appearing to be the slightest bit out of synch with his perception of how it ought to look.

Once, they were late leaving his office for an appointment when Ellison's eye noticed a potted plant on his doorstep. It had the barest droop to its leaves. He stopped in mid-track, unlocked the door and went back inside for a sprinkler can. He watered the plant and before they could finally leave, he rotated the planter first a quarter turn, reversed that, and turned it 180 degrees in the original direction, all the while cocking his head like a dog watching curious behavior. World class, no question.

Ellison laughed at Walker's question. "Well, partly because it lessens the chances of mistaking a larger bill for a smaller one," he sighed. "But mostly because I'm driven to do it. It's involuntary, not like your own elective and wimpy pinch shots on the front court when power passing shots are called for." He grinned broadly at Ben. "So how goes the battle for control of the advertising universe?"

"Glad you asked. I need your professional help with a couple of items, barrister. Number one involves finding a mysteriously misplaced law clerk. I'll give you all I have on him later. Just finding out who caused his disappearance will probably tell me more than the clerk himself knows. Item number two concerns an equally mysterious ultralight aircraft accident by a former double M employee. Any connection you come up with between the two would be more corroboration than surprise, but don't let that influence your approach."

Ellison feigned mock indignation. "Look here, Mr. Walker, I'm a respected member of the bar, not a sleazy private eye. Besides, you can't afford me unless you happen to know the precise route of that new ambulance service." This time Ellison grinned broadly.

Walker tossed Ellison the ball they had been using as they both stood up from the table, ready for the showers. He said, "Remember, we trade out services. No dirty cash or embarrassing checks to mar this relationship. What I will do, my man, is call my supplier counterpart and order you another 100 of your favorite client pass-out. You know, the decks of poker cards imprinted with your firm's name and your business slogan—'Here's The Deal—Sue The Bastard!'"

"Make it 250," laughed Ellison. "I have to say this though, 'boss,' you're talking about some pretty secure folks. I doubt your friend Sloan leaves much in the way of fingerprints or footprints."

25

"Mr. Sloan, this is Dr. Flynton Bascom of the marketing department at Florida State University. Your secretary said you received my letter of a week ago about my interest in doing an article concerning advertising mirrors in general and your company in particular." Bascom read from a script he had worked out based on what Walker had described as the objective.

"I don't have a lot of time for this sort of thing, Bascom. My secretary will send you something." Sloan had no intention of asking her to do so and thought that would be the end of the conversation.

Flyn had learned a few things from Ben over the past few years about salesmanship. He persisted, addressing his remarks to a specific interest of Sloan's. "Sir, in having done some marketing research for the Glass Association of America we note that your firm, alone among the promotional product industry's manufacturers and decorators, has succeeded remarkably well with a seemingly generic product. Somehow you entertain no serious competition. We would be interested in printing your comments on such a notable accomplishment." He paused.

"You don't hear very well, friend," said Philip Sloan. "I told you my secretary would send you something. You just lost that!"

Bascom now understood some of the reasons why Sloan and his underlings made every effort to keep this particular CEO out of the front line of public relations. Here was an anomaly of the first order. Even when it would surely serve the man and his company well to express a simple if only superficial courtesy, he instead exhibited a curious and total lack of civility.

"But Mr. Sloan," pressed Bascom, "surely you know that if you refuse to comment in any form, well, that fact combined with your remarkable success will only serve to intensify inquiries into your story. Let the university journal's non-sensational, but professional approach work to your advantage." He closed with a calculated request. "Could I send someone up to interview you yet this week, sir?"

Sloan's response was equally calculated, but with venomous delivery. "Screw you, Flint!" No further qualifier preceded the line's going dead.

Bascom pondered the unambiguous rejection. It was the first time since his undergraduate days that his name, even an understandably corrupted version of it, had been used with that street cliche with such obvious sincerity. Well, at any rate, mission accomplished. He had set the stage for the local television news interview Ben wanted to arrange in Atlanta. Now at least, if it became necessary for him to do so, Walker could casually and fairly comment on the unsuccessful attempt to raise a dialogue with the 'bad guys' of his intended personal 'state of the industry' PR release.

26

The local television channel's "Seven-Come-Eleven" ace news anchor walked through Ben Walker's office door on time and on-camera. Lynn Michelson turned to her cameraman and said, "Okay, Duane, cut. I just wanted to get some local color for the opening."

Addressing Walker, the attractive, hard-punching local media celebrity quickly revealed her own opinion along with the station's interest in the assignment that had brought her there. "Mr. Walker, my general manager thinks you have something to add to our current "Inside Advertising" series.

"Well, I hope you'll also share that opinion by the time we've finished, Ms. Michelson," Walker replied.

"Please, call me Lynn." She might as well make it pleasant since it was certain to be light. She could be charming, she could be hostile. She could certainly be indifferent. It depended upon her mood as much as her subject, but arrogance usually found its niche at some point in her dealings with others.

Her job, and to a fair extent her station's ratings, were intertwined. Both were primarily influenced by her skill as an interviewer, but empathy was not in her job description. She did, however, add a degree of entertainment to her presentation which the other local anchors either could not command or were prohibited from using. As a result, an increasingly fickle, channel-flipping public was currently settling for her brand of nightly delivery at least as often as the other two major network affiliates combined.

"We begin," she commanded. A pair of symbolic red, dice-shaped lights lit atop the "Seven-Come-Eleven" camera. "Mr. Walker, most people are very familiar with the products of your industry." She looked at her notes and continued with a list she had made, "Advertising-imprinted novelties such as pens and pencils, calendars, coffee mugs, caps, decals, folders and folios, even knitted blankets I understand. And the many types of plastic gimmicks such as your firm, Baxter Products, manufactures. Frankly, however, most people do not really think of them in connection with advertising, at least not in the sense this is a true medium. Tell us about that."

"You are absolutely correct, Ms. Michelson," he began in a sure, even tone, wanting to properly lay the foundation for the thunder-bolt close. He hoped it would be the impetus for the interview tape to be picked up by the news services and relayed around the country.

"Most advertisers themselves tend not to think of specialty or promotional product advertising as a separate medium, such as they would about television, radio, newspaper, or even for some of the other, similarly smaller media like magazines or billboards. All of these tend to be much more readily definable than specialty advertising, and are essentially single product media. But perhaps most critical to the public perception of the considerable role played by promotional products in our society and business is that ours is not a mass medium. Rather, it's a personal or targeted medium, and involves distribution of imprinted items such as those which you have already described, Ms. Michelson.

"When creatively applied, these items can indeed support marketing or promotional strategies, even if that ambition is merely to express token goodwill or recognition for individual performance." The camera focussed on Ben Walker but the anchor was glancing around, thinly disguising a near yawn. Walker was undeterred. His geology training suggested that an eruption is most dramatic when it rises from an otherwise undisturbed setting.

Michelson returned her attention to him to ask another obligatory question. "Mr. Walker, agreed that your medium is quite small, give us an idea of how much money advertisers spend on promotional products."

"Well, I can't argue that ours is indeed dwarfed when compared with the television or newspaper advertising revenues. It is quite significant, however, with billings that exceed five billion dollars a year. As to individual business expenditures, since many buyers consider specialty advertising a support medium, they often tend not to distinguish us in their media mix and budgets. Major corporate users many times have no idea as to the amounts they actually spend in this area.

"One thing is certain, however," He paused for effect and caught Michelson's eye as he did. He deliberately slowed his delivery while increasing his inflection as he continued, "Serious players overlook nothing that will help them gain a share of their advertising target's awareness of name or message; be it that of the consumer, employee, dealer, distributor or voter."

Ben paused and brought a coffee mug into view. He had deliberately chosen a product from a competitor. It would be less likely to detract from his accusatory closing remarks. "Let me give you a simple example of how promotional products are more and more being sold not as mere commodities, but as part of the total media mix. A firm specializing in placing temporary secretaries in professional and corporate America recently gave each temporary who achieved a certain level of competence a ceramic coffee mug with the firm's logo colorfully imprinted on it along with boldly proclaiming the user to be a 'Top Temp.' This was the same theme used in the firm's national and local advertising campaign. So here was each qualified secretary proudly carrying her 'billboard' coffee mug from one temporary job to the next, prominently and repetitively positioning the company's campaign message in the actual offices of both new and established clients.

"As to cost per impression—something the mass media uses to reinforce value—the CPI for a mug seen as often as ten times a day works out to be less than three-tenths of a cent. This is based on a $2.50 mug with an average life span of one-and-a-half years."

Walker made his point while gesturing with the mug. "Make no mistake, Ms. Michelson, this medium works, regardless of what you call it or how well or poorly defined it is by the practitioner, the end user or targeted recipient—or what form the message might take."

Walker stared for a long moment into the anchor's eyes, catching her off guard. Was he somehow trying to one-up her in her own *milieu*? If so, she could only benefit. But she doubted that was the case. No, no such luck. Well, that was the end of it. She shrugged it off and made a tentative move to wrap up the interview, but then hesitated when he authoritatively raised his right forefinger to his lips in a contemplative gesture. She blinked and he continued on-camera.

"Please listen very carefully to what I say next, Ms. Michelson. Jonson Baxter, a former close friend, my superior, and the CEO of Baxter Products recently died in a mysterious automobile explosion—which I believe was no accident."

Michelson's eyes widened as they leveled on Walker, her lips touching and then her tongue slightly parting them in an involuntary response. Would this be the lead-in to a chance on-air sensationalist remark by a credible interviewee?

Walker spoke in a steady, measured tone. "It so happens that at the time of his death he was following up on hard evidence in my company's possession that points to a tightly controlled and insidious scheme to influence the public through totally unethical and surely illegal advertising practices. It involves, unfortunately, the very medium about which I have been interviewed. I make this public accusation without naming names because I am as yet unprepared to file suit against the perpetrator, which happens to be a major force within my industry. I have chosen to go public because by so doing I may be able to protect lives I believe are endangered.

"A part of my own company's business is that of manufacturing advertising mirrors. Ours is a quality product but I want to be on record as saying," he paused for the close, "There is absolutely no 'magic' to advertising mirrors." Walker handed the lapel microphone to the beaming anchor, then turned and exited.

Persistent efforts on the part of Michelson to elicit elaboration from him, were to no avail. She was left instead to offer a game, two-sentence wrap-up about her exclusive news report. She alluded to follow-up on the next edition of "Seven-Come-Eleven's" exciting "Inside Advertising" series.

27

"All right, Ben-O," said the always upbeat Flyn Bascom, "I had to come to 'Hotlanta' for a few days anyway to earn my keep for one of the corporate boards by which I am handsomely paid, so you didn't have to spring for the air fare in order to get some moral support for your latest *exposé*. You really made the station's day. Of course in Peoria they'll think you're trying to play poker with a pinochle deck, but you surely must have gotten Phil Sloan-and-company's attention."

"I know. Mirror Magic will instantly be on the media's short list of 'potential sensationals,' and then when they discover double M's past history of playing off the news media, they'll be about as bashful as a vulture circling a road kill. Sloan doesn't dare screw with us right now for fear of giving the story credence and causing a flock of Woodward-and-Bernstein type stakeouts. We have two 'gotchas.' I've already used one on the interview, but Sloan has no idea when I'll use the other. As long as I don't we should be able to keep him off balance. That will give us more time to find out exactly what the hell is going on. Now, professor, give me your thoughts on this can of subliminal advertising worms we've opened."

"Well, first of all," responded Bascom, "I resent the 'we' implication. You have drug my reluctant ass much further down this path than I ever intended. I'm a geologist, remember, Ben? No, of course, you don't. But I will say this subliminal mirror scam, however it's accomplished, must certainly be beneficial for everyone in the manufacturing-to-distribution-to-advertiser chain. Now, I certainly can't believe collaboration extends to distribution, let alone to the end user, in spite of the very real benefits which have accrued to advertisers for their 'astute' purchases."

Walker ignored the personal complaint portion of Bascom's commentary.

"Flyn, I took the question of 'how' crosstown to several engineering department heads at Georgia Tech last week, along with a couple of MM's mirrors. They examined them and the registration plates very carefully, and while they couldn't give me all the answers I wanted, I got a few breath-takers. Get this. Those plates contain micro-circuits of an unbelievably complex nature, miniaturized to the thickness of a few coats of paint." The nature of this disclosure made Walker uneasy. He feared where all this might be taking them, having no earthly idea just where that might be.

"Who possesses the technology for such a product, Ben?"

"That I can't answer," said Walker. "But as for the physical result, let me make a close analogy. A supplier friend of mine makes advertising playing cards. They custom imprint some of their playing card orders by impressing foil ad copy through the plastic coated card stock, just to the point where the metallic foil is flush with the plastic coating itself, effectively embedding the imprint. Now, in the case of Mirror Magic's treatment with back-plates, their process similarly inserts the plate directly through the already applied paint, copper and silvered layers to a point where it doesn't quite break the surface of the mirror itself."

Flyn nodded, "H'mm. Then we could suppose the purpose for the three-eighths of an inch, five-sided protrusion from the backside is not really for the decoy registration and hanger at all. In fact it could be some sort of super sensitive solar-charging power pack, using whatever faint light would nevertheless penetrate around the back of a typically hung wall mirror."

"Bingo! Now, since you're on a roll, what do you think the engineers at Tech theorize would be the method for subliminally pulsing a message or image through the face of the mirror itself?"

Bascom didn't hesitate. "A laser," he said.

"Keerect again, professor, although they claim, as you suggested a moment ago, the technology is unknown."

Bascom dug in, "But what I don't understand at all are the dynamics of the process from the perspective of distribution. Surely MM's distributors, in many cases the same firms selling Baxter

Products, can't be in on the scam; such a widespread thing couldn't possibly be kept secret, Ben."

"I believe you're correct in that assumption," said Walker. "The distributor only knows that the MM product *sells*. And by virtue of repeat orders he also knows that the advertiser or promotional buyer is more than satisfied. Therefore, someone, some few highly trusted or otherwise restricted individuals at MM, must duplicate each incoming distributor order's ad copy in the programming of the subliminal plate which is then implanted during the normal production sequence. And as we have already deduced, the subliminal implant is effectively camouflaged by the registration plate. The finished product, then, Dr. Bascom, amounts to advertising's most invasive consumer manipulation since the sliver screen's infamous subliminal flap over 'Eat popcorn, drink cola.'" Walker uncharacteristically slumped into his chair, more emotionally taxed than physically tired.

"Brilliant, my boy!" Bascom clapped his hands three times in a muted fashion, then extended Walker's logic, "And if the mirror should accidentally be broken in the business place or at home, and in the equally unlikely event the actual user should desire to take advantage of the warranty imprinted on the plate, replacement of the mirror and its message is simple enough. And even if the plate were accidentally separated from the mirror itself, nothing is revealed. Who, besides another renaissance man like yourself, would be motivated or qualified enough to dissect a random and innocuous looking wafer-thin metal plate, even if he were to spot the nearly invisible seam? It would seem that all their bases are covered."

"The only problem with all this deduction, Flyn, is that it is mostly conjecture. How do we go about obtaining proof in order to hang both Sloan and double M?"

"You need a little insider trading, so to speak," suggested Bascom. "Someone at Mirror Magic obviously knows something. Someone besides Philip Sloan. It seems to me that Amanda might have a handle on who could be approached. At any rate, you've made remarkable progress, Ben-boy. Fascinating as all this is, however, I have to be getting back to Tallahassee. Let me know if I can be of more help. And by the way, you and I still haven't gotten in that game of racquetball. I'd really like to kick your tail in front of your friends!"

28

"A name is about the only information I could get from the formerly mysterious law clerk," said Gene Ellison over the phone. "A 'T. Ver Meer.' That was his contact in New York just prior to his hurried move. He turned up in Seattle on my computer interconnect with various network-subscribing attorneys from across the country. One item on the program menu is a list of registered recent law school graduates. The clerk was a pawn. I talked with him. He said he did a short internship stint with MM's law firm, but then he was suddenly offered a potential junior partnership in a branch office, if he could move immediately."

"Oh, by the way," added Ellison. "He did acknowledge transmitting to Jon Baxter some sort of report he had ferreted out the afternoon before the accident. He said he gave it to a pool secretary to fax to J.B.'s office. He remembers because he had been hitting on her at the time and he made a comment about her work load as he dropped the report into her ASAP basket. He said he doesn't recall anything of it, only that it referenced Baxter and Sloan."

Gene Ellison was a student of observation and as a result, claimed most people answered initial questions superficially. He was convinced secondary questioning was the only way to get substantive response. He knew how to probe and had done so with the law clerk; in the process he had made some judgements. "Ben, I don't think this guy really knows anything of consequence. Forget him. But get this, our Ver Meer character phoned the same clerk just a few days prior to my call, asking if anyone else had contacted him about his work in New York. And our new player is a female! He said she had a slight German accent and that confirms what we had already learned. Howd'ya like them apples, Jonathan?"

"Great, Gene," said an appreciative Walker. "I can use this. Amanda just may know that name. Now, what did you find out about Jack Petersma, Amanda's all-American gyro-plane pilot?"

"You'll be as proud of your racquetball idol as you are of your girl friend, Benjamin. Amanda was right on target about Petersma having had a falling out with Sloan. Only I don't think it was just over a lack of PR cooperation from our pissant friend. It seems old Jack had coincidentally taken a few turns with the same call girl that Sloan apparently favors with occasional assignments of one sort or another."

29

Three days later, after Amanda had returned from a week on the road, she and Ben met at Kelley's for lunch. "What a week. Reps are funny," she said. "They kept me booked every day with appointments right through the lunch hour, but you can't tell me those guys have missed many meals. I guess it's the equivalent of bringing the teacher an apple."

"You and Ellison are both into apples these days, Amanda," said Walker. "Maybe I should get you drunk on cider and play right into your hands," he joked.

Amanda Booth was into a different discourse today and chose to ignore the invitational opening. "I'm beginning to see why you like Kelley's so much, Ben," she said. "The library setting with random hardback books on shelves in each of the dining rooms is relaxing, although you have to admit that some of the decor is a bit cornball."

"What!" Walker responded in exaggerated amazement. "You mean just because the wall clock is done in small-town '50s, with outdated insurance and funeral home advertising boards flipping one after the other every ten seconds, you label my place 'Oh Shucks?'"

"Oh, no, of course not. I like the clock. It has style. I'm referring to the sign hanging below it that reads, 'This clock will never be stolen. Our employees are always watching it.'"

"Sophisticated lady, huh?" he said. But the smiles Amanda had coaxed from the frown Ben came in with were short-lived. "Here's what's happening, Amanda. Ellison dug up a few things that brightens the light on the likelihood of Jack Petersma's death being more than just another simple accident. Did you know someone at double M by the name of Ver Meer? First initial, 'T?'

"Ver Meer? That doesn't sound familiar and I'm certain I would remember such an unusual name. Why?"

"She may or may not have had something to do with Petersma but she definitely figures somewhere with Jon Baxter's inquiries of the old Baxter & Sloan law firm," he said.

She tilted her head slightly for an instant, "Well, now, wait a minute. I once saw a very striking brunette leave Sloan's office. Phil Sloan's secretary was in the hallway with me when she passed us and I idly asked her about the woman. All she said was that her name was 'Tersa,' and that she did some sort of consulting or PR work for the firm. I even remember asking her if she didn't mean 'Teresa,' because I had never before heard the other name. I don't think Pauline, that's Sloan's secretary, much liked her from the way she placed the emphasis on 'PR.' If that's the same person, Ben, what's the connection?"

"I have no idea. Do you think you could learn anything from the secretary?" Walker hated to ask her. This was the first request he had made of her to become directly involved in his chase. He told himself he could certainly spare her a little time for such a follow-up because the store was being properly minded. Just this morning he had met with the department heads and was confident that 98 percent of day-to-day business was being competently seen to. Was his current role in this company down to only a two percent function? Well, hell, as a matter of fact he really wasn't on top of much of anything these days.

He did have mixed feeling about involving Amanda in what was an increasingly greater risk situation. He felt more strongly attracted to her with each passing week. Employer, shame on thee, he thought. Then he rationalized. It was better to direct a limited involvement in the situation toward her than to have her pursuing some things independently, which she would be inclined to do. Amanda strongly shared Walker's interest in Jon Baxter's untimely death, as well as the mystery of Mirror Magic.

"I'll see what I can get, Ben," she said. "Now, are we going to order or are you, too, trying to impress me by working through lunch?"

30

"Pauline, this is Amanda Booth. How are you? That's good. Look, I know Mr. Sloan wasn't happy with me before I left, but you know how those things happen. Anyway, the reason I called is because I haven't received my earnings statement from last year, for tax purposes, and I don't know with whom I should speak to check on it."

"I don't know, Amanda. Would you like me to transfer you to accounting?" she said with a trace of empathy in her voice, but still very much aware that Amanda Booth was on her boss's persona non grata list. She had no idea why.

"Yes, please, Pauline. I appreciate your help. Oh, by the way, I think I saw Tersa Ver Meer at Hartsfield last week. She might even have been on the same plane with me from Chicago, but I'm not sure. I know she travels a great deal," said Amanda, and then paused, hoping.

Ego and dislike for her perceived competition as 'most valued assistant' title kicked in, "Detroit, not Chicago." Then she added, "And I doubt if she's a stranger to any auto worker."

"Oh, of course, Detroit. She's MM's liaison with the U.A.W. as well as with the Big Three, isn't she"? Booth pushed.

"Look, Amanda, I have work to do," said the secretary, "and Mr. Sloan wouldn't like me talking with you. I'll switch you now."

When Amanda relayed this information to Ben, his eyes narrowed. "She's our man."

Interesting about the U.A.W., a major end user of promotional products—just as the vehicle manufacturers and dealers themselves.

Imports and other factors have conspired to require that Detroit review their efforts about making their mark even more decisively on their audiences. If Ver Meer was courting the account on behalf of a distributor, then the contact was understandable. But he didn't think her low profile responsibilities ran to sales. Could there be broader implications?

31

Walker and Gene Ellison were changing in the locker room when Flyn Bascom arrived at the racquetball club with Ernie Kobsavich, the glass industry consultant and Bascom's fellow professor at FSU. Bascom opened with, "I can only hope this is going to be as much recreation as business, Ben, but since you're footing the tab for two days, I guess it'll be your call, boss."

"That's the way it's going to start out, partner. You and I are going to turn these two into whimpering, whining, air-sucking, runners-up in a best two-of-three doubles match. Hitch up your jockstrap, Dr. B. Later we can talk about how to get into Mirror Magic through the back door."

Walker and Bascom won the lob for serve, then proceeded to win the first game handily, the former's surprisingly quick front court game complementing the latter's back court power and confounding passing game. Then Ellison switched court positions with Kobsavich. The new combination of the Pole's maddeningly disconcerting ceiling game and their opponents' overconfidence was all Ellison needed for his keen coaching and steady play to pay off with an equally big win for them in the second game.

The rubber game was on. The score had been knotted by Kobsavich at 13-all in a 15-point game. Kobsavich was his team's first server on the next point. He missed an easy return off the back wall, at which Walker loudly intoned, "Next man!" Ellison's thin skinned partner had been bridling all evening at such calculated and taunting remarks by Walker, who was having the time of his life. Kobsavich subsequently let Ben know of his lack of appreciation for such needling. Ellison quickly defused the flare-up, saying, "Forget it, Ernie, that's just Ben's way of compensating for an acute lack of talent. Come on, let's close 'em out."

Ellison and Kobsavich then won the final two game points with a hard fought rally. Ellison twice let out loud, Neanderthal-type 'Yeahs!' Then, upon taking the game and match point, they nearly hurt themselves high-fiving one another in post-game congratulations. Ben winked at Bascom as they shook sweaty hands all around.

During a break at dinner in the clubhouse and while the two winners were in the men's room, Flyn Bascom said with a feigned look of resignation on his face, "Partner, you didn't go into the tank on those last two points, did you?"

"No, but it couldn't have worked out better," said Walker. "I want Kobsavich to do a little grunt work, for which I'm certain he'll grossly overcharge me. He'll feel better about the job though if he gets to stick the needle into me from time to time. Flyn, it was great playing with you but you're out of our league."

"Yeah, I enjoyed it too. Like old times on the harbor sedimentation project. Only problem today is that I was rowing with the anchor thrown out," chuckled Bascom. "But seriously, Ben, you know I want to help with this Mirror Magic thing. I thought a great deal of Jon Baxter."

"Thanks for the vote of confidence," said Walker. "I continue to have good reason to suspect that Phil Sloan's subliminal mirrors may be 'magic' well beyond the accepted convention. The scholarly Dr. Kobsavich may soon be able to back up my suspicion on that count. I'm going to ask him to fly to Detroit to interview some automakers on the pretext of doing a glass association article. Since you know the dodge by now, maybe you can provide Ernie with a little guidance and even certify his purpose should someone check him out with the university.

Their dinner guests rejoined them, their faces still fixed on grin. Walker couldn't refrain from the final verbal counterpunch. "A toast," he said as he raised his wine glass, "to the champions who today discovered their true calling—a life dedicated to the rare sporting defeat of their personal idols!" Ellison and Kobsavich looked at each other and gagged in unison, then all four of them fell to laughter.

32

Kobsavich was more energized by this short consult (He was thinking of it as a caper.) than any in the past five years. He was doing so well with the project he looked forward to the phone report to Ben. He wondered idly if he could earn as much money being a private investigator as he was as an academician and consultant. Maybe he could moonlight for awhile. He'd lose a few pounds, borrow some start-up financing and . . . Hey! Wait a minute; he wouldn't mind investing the time, but as for the other two, well, tenure was certainly a less risky goal and far less strenuous. Reality bites.

"Ben," said an excited Ernie Kobsavich over his motel room telephone, "I may have something for you. The first automaker headquarters office I called gave me an immediate appointment to interview them. But when I arrived all I could get was a plant tour and a dealer's hype booklet about their newest model's features. Concerning my real interest in how and who makes their glass and mirrors, they just patted me on the head and fed me 'glass is glass.'"

"But let me guess, Ernie, you took a different approach on the next call," Walker primed his sleuthing 'temp.'

"Kee-rect. I've learned a little something from you sales-promotion types. I was first told that the manager I wanted to see would not be back until the next day. I went to the PR office anyway. Once there, I handed the receptionist-gatekeeper one of your Baxter Product's overpriced, if moderately appealing little stand-up desk mirrors; the very same item bought this year for our glass association's annual election meeting, I might add. She loved it. I told her I was scheduled to meet with the director the next day, but that I was going to have to break the appointment for a family emergency. Would it be possible to talk for a few minutes with one of the director's assistants before I had to leave town? It was and I did. What disproportionate return-on-investment this 'adcentive' medium of yours offers, Walker! I was able to ingratiate myself to the receptionist, and as a result she found a way to reciprocate."

Walker smiled to himself. "You know, Ernie, for a university-type, you have a lot of common sense; I confess when I first met you I didn't peg you for a people person."

"Well, now that's before the underdog team whipped the Lone Ranger and Tonto in a horse race. I have a new perspective on you marketing types; the more one accomplishes, the more one can charge."

"I now regret the earlier compliment," Ben retorted. "But what did you actually learn?"

"Well, I told the assistant that I really had pretty much all I needed for my article on the changes in glass use within the auto industry, but that I could use some comments by their glass suppliers. I asked if she knew of anyone they worked with at Mirror Magic other than Tersa Ver Meer. She checked her little black computer and confirmed only that name. *Voilà*! Now, what next, benefactor?" added Kobsavich.

"Good job, Ernie. Now go home and turn off the meter. Don't call us, we'll call you." Walker's thoughts only left him more perplexed than before, which was also to say more determined than ever to solve this puzzle. How could Mirror Magic be selling unimprinted mirrors out the back door to such a huge concern as this? All MM had to offer them was a commodity since the normal value-added custom imprint was totally absent.

Wait a second. That thought triggered another, maybe that was the answer! Advertising specialties were more and more being positioned not as pure product, but as a part of the buyer's promotional and communications mix. With the marketing edge owned by Mirror Magic, perhaps they had decided to no longer bother hiding their nearly exclusive and ultimate industry niche behind the medium itself. What were the direct outlets for such a franchise? And why had Sloan even bothered with subverting the medium in the first place? Questions without answers. Maybe it was showtime.

33

At the third meeting in as many days concerning the rapidly upcoming annual industry winter show in Dallas, Walker had finally delegated coordination of the company's eight booths to the recently appointed national sales manager, the veteran manufacturing vice president and a full complement of staff. Ben felt he would be free to talk to distributor accounts away from the booths. Amanda would be on hand for most of each day to assist in the booth PR effort. It was she who knew most of their larger accounts by both name and face.

Mostly though, Ben needed time to prepare for his upcoming meeting with the national association's suppliers committee. He wanted to filet and package Mirror Magic so he could then put Sloan on the ethics scales for the committee's oversight.

On a Sunday morning three weeks later in Dallas, Walker located the meeting facilitator and bent his ear. "But, Ben, it's not on the agenda," protested the committee chairman. "And besides, it would be poor publicity for Baxter Products to spearhead a 'get double M' campaign. And if that weren't enough, you know better than I it isn't even legal. We're a trade association, not a sanctioning group. My suggestion is to recruit a few key people you know and trust who could advise you of anything they might learn concerning Phantom Phil and this subliminal mirror scam you're so worked up about."

"You're right, Hal. No point in expecting the association to take any sort of position on something as petty as messing with people's minds. After all, you and I and our distributors and end-users do it every day. But there's one big difference between us and Mirror Magic. We use warning labels."

Walker's sarcasm was lost on Hal Freeman. The committee chairman was the principal of a wearables supplier. Partly because of the tremendous competition for the nearly 20 percent of the more than five billion dollar industry claimed by all wearables products, he was not overly sympathetic to a complaint by another supplier whose business involved a single, wildly successful product category with so few competitive makers or decorators. Walker's 'subliminal criminal' story was a little thin to say the least and Freeman had no stomach for stoking yet another inside-the-industry flap. Things still hadn't cooled from the 'invisible public image' cry as analyzed by every other practitioner who took the time to write the editor of one of the several industry trade journals. Freeman changed the subject. "Is Phil Sloan at the show, Ben?"

"Of course not," said Walker. "But double M has an army of staff on hand, as always, and by far the biggest block of booths of any supplier in the show. I'm telling you, Hal, Sloan has a crooked handle on becoming *the* major advertising influence in and out of our medium. In another ten years he could even be bigger than any ad agency in New York or Tokyo. He's one serious asshole!"

Freeman had his own agenda. "Well, I personally think you're exaggerating by a factor of 100. It'll all shake out. But, look, I've been saving something. A maxi-sensuous brunette with a way of looking at you with her entire body asked me at the association information booth if I knew you. If you care to trade badges for a few days I'll be happy to see to Tersa Ver Meer's needs, old friend."

Walker's eyes widened perceptibly, unable to completely mask his astonishment. "From Mirror Magic? She's here at the show? Asking for me? Hal, that's Sloan's hit lady! At least from all I've learned."

"Well, I don't know if she's an MM'er or not," said Freeman. "I missed her badge due to other distractions. I assumed she was someone's staffer, looking to resume a tryst from last winter's show. Look, Ben, I'm having a little trouble with the front side of this conversation. Personally, I think you've been reading too much Ludlum or Spillane. But if you need any help with 'The Temptress' I'll be in the old booth."

34

Ben Walker sat at the small cocktail table in one of the main floor lounges at convention hotel headquarters. It was only one of the dozen hotels on the convention shuttle route for the 12,000 or so attending exhibitors, distributors and sales staffs. With pre-exhibit national committee meetings, continuing-education day, evenings spent entertaining key distributor accounts and multi-line reps—all this before exhibit set-up and actual show days were counted—the week-long national winter show was as exhausting as it was beneficial.

He could not fathom why Sloan's 'wicked witch,' as Amanda had labelled Ver Meer would deliberately seek him out at the show. It was unnerving. She must at least know of his suspicions. He had attempted to respond to this overt act with one of his own by going directly to the Mirror Magic booth.

He had nearly forgotten the physical presence MM had at the industry's biggest show of the year. For all of Sloan's reticence in other promotional matters, he did not come up short when it came to putting double M on display for its flocking distributor hordes. It occupied both sides of a mid-floor aisle and took in a total of 40 booths. The Mirror Magic Floor as some called it.

Special effects mirrors were everywhere. It looked like a circus and drew as if it were. People could see themselves in almost any mirrored proportion; including disconnected angles like the magician's head-on-a-plate delight, in checkered reflection, and even in pseudo-hologrammatic projection. Recognized distributor customers certainly were not permitted to leave without having a handsome wall-sized mirror sample thrust upon them which read, "Look into Mirror Magic." The irony of MM's slogan had not been lost on Walker even during his first year at Baxter Products, when he had begun to perceive questionable competitive disparities.

But Tersa Ver Meer was not to be found in the MM booth. He left her a message to meet him at six 'o clock that evening at the hotel lounge whose name he wrote on his business card. He did not know what to expect.

Never having met Walker, his adversary nevertheless walked directly up to his table upon entering the bar. A half-smile barely parted her full lips, so red-rich and flaming that it seemed to Ben they might actually mirror his tie. If what Hal Freeman had described her as wearing on the floor was hardly demure for the business day, it had not deterred her from changing into something even more revealing. The disturbance caused by heads whipping violently in the direction of her flow to the back of the room where Walker sat, drew uncomfortable attention to him—exactly the opposite of his intention. In spite of himself he had to agree with old Hal that the proof of the pudding certainly was in the filling.

"Hello, Ben, I'm Tersa Ver Meer. It's a pleasure to meet you."

"I guessed as much, Ms. Ver Meer. Please, have a seat," he said as he stood and then re-seated himself, unable to avoid a momentary frozen glance at cleavage that would have embarrassed a strip joint bouncer. "Would you care for a drink?" he managed to say.

He immediately knew he had to dispense with the small talk he had been preparing for the ten minutes she had kept him waiting. Otherwise she would have him at a distinct disadvantage.

"In spite of the fact that you must already know that I hardly hold your boss in high esteem, you asked for this meeting. I doubt it's for the 'how's business' conversation we'll be engaging in for the rest of the week." Then deliberately opening with the cliche he considered above all others to be the single most impersonal, if disguised, form of address between two people, he asked, "How can I help you?" Now, they would surely talk at some length so he could take his mind off the dazzling display fronting him.

"Ben, let's don't talk shop. We are competitors after all, and we aren't going to share anything of value—in the business sense, anyway. And I know you don't like Phil Sloan, but all of us at Mirror Magic aren't ogres. I wanted to meet you because for such a relatively short time in the industry you have an enviable reputation. I also suspect you were responsible for persuading one of our talented employees to leave double M."

She cocked her head slightly to one side and allowed her eyes to fasten first on his, then at the lapels of his beribboned jacket and back again to his eyes, communicating in exaggerated sign language that she approved of his measure.

"I wanted to meet the man behind the deeds. Now, what sort of exciting new things do you, Mr. Walker, have to offer this year's show for someone who is, so far, bored with the usual show makeup?" She brushed his leg with her foot and in an embarrassingly open fashion moistened her upper lip with her tongue. There was no mistaking her intentions.

Ignoring his involuntary blood rush at pants-pocket level, Walker knew this was a woman who would overlook no potential brought within her very lethal range. "I can't say I'm flattered by your attention, Ms. Ver Meer. I know full well there is more to you than meets the eye (well, that was brilliantly stated). No less can be said for Mirror Magic," he recovered.

He attempted his own bit of deception. "If I hadn't Jon Baxter's business legacy to occupy all of my time, I would vigorously pursue answers to the enigmas presented by both you and MM. If you'll excuse me, I have work to do."

Tersa Ver Meer had no more believed she would be successful in seducing Ben Walker than she would accept his statement about walking away from the greatest personal puzzle of his life. She did, however, believe she had somehow made a net gain as a result of their meeting. Know thy adversary.

35

It was to be a late winter drive from Atlanta, through the Carolinas, to Raleigh. Amanda, true to her practical, realistic nature, had checked the weather forecast before they departed. Amanda was midwestern born and bred; she not only dressed carefully for social circumstances but for the weather as well. Ben's announced casual day trip dictated Amanda's selection of black wool slacks and a red wool blazer over a cream- colored cashmere sweater. Based on the weather report she took no overcoat. Yankee by birth, Southerner by influence.

"Ben, why didn't we just fly to Raleigh instead of having to make this all-day drive?" complained Amanda as she studied the North Carolina road map from the navigator's seat. "And what's wrong with my plotting the shortest distance between two points?"

"Who wants to make short work of time away from the office with a gorgeous roadie?" he jokingly patronized her, already benefitting from the clear-headed thinking such multi-hour freeway drives always provided him.

"Business as usual for me," she said. "But remember the Baxter Products employee no-fraternization policy." She exaggerated her slide away from him as she simultaneously tightened her shoulder harness.

Walker glanced at her and smiled, concluding their little interplay with, "Lady, I ain't takin' you to no opera. I come to pick you up for a fraternity party!"

"All right, cut the comedy, Ben. Something is up beyond the regional table-top show we left for a day ahead of time. What is it?" she asked, curiosity taking over her thoughts.

"Well, we need to participate in the newly formed Carolinas Association's first official event," said Walker. "But you're exactly right, Amanda. We're going to knock on another door en route. Remember your having mentioned to me shortly after you came to work at BP that while you were at Mirror Magic you once noticed an unusually large number of shipments in the same year to a single location for a customer not listed as an industry distributor?"

"I do," she said. "It was Piedmont Furniture. What about it?"

"Well, I thought you might like to see how furniture is made. We're going to visit the factory, which is even now only a few miles from us. No stop too inconvenient for this tour, Ms. Booth."

36

"Mr. Wilkins, my wife and I are interested in picking up some furniture lines for our independent store in Atlanta. We have good financing and are traveling to several manufacturers around the state. I know it's near closing time and we don't have an appointment, but frankly it was one of your road signs that stopped us. You do sell wholesale as well as through your local outlet store, don't you?" Walker inquired of the sales manager who appeared most eager at the prospect of picking up a rare walk-in account.

"Why, yes, Mr. Walker, that's our business. Most of our lines are sold under private label for the major department store chains, but we welcome qualified independent outlets as well. Would you and your wife care to tour the facility?"

They were assigned a factory engineer as their guide, As Ben engaged him in answering questions about both manufacturing and marketing, Amanda dawdled behind as if intrigued by certain operations, designs or fabric cover. She was looking for something—anything—that might throw some light on the Piedmont connection to Mirror Magic. She just didn't know what to expect.

Finally, in desperation and nearing the end of the tour, she put the point directly. "Could you show us your mirrored furniture? I've always been fascinated by vanity dressers. Do you use a variety of suppliers for different styles of mirrors?"

Walker shot her a hard side glance but then relaxed with their guide's reply.

"Well, yes, ma'am, to both questions.

"As a matter of fact we used to work with various mirror manufacturers, like most every other Carolina furniture manufacturer does today. But over the past ten years or so we've somehow ended up with mostly a single source, Mirror Magic.

"As a matter of fact," the engineer continued, "they're considering building a plant only 40 miles from here. As a matter of fact, their sales rep is here right now; maybe he would have time to meet with you and tell you more about the line. I don't think the boss would mind."

Ben looked at Amanda as if to consult her, then spoke to the engineer, borrowing his trite and overused phrase, "As a matter of fact, we really don't have time. Thank you. You've been very helpful."

37

Two hours later and a good hundred and thirty miles down the interstate from Piedmont Furniture, they decided to stop for the night. It was dark and well past seven o' clock. They would have plenty of time in the morning to make it into Raleigh for show set-up. Walker pulled in, registered, then drove the company mini-van around in back of the mid-range budget hotel. As Amanda was collecting a few things from the back seat, Ben made one trip to the room and returned. As he was about to close the mini-van's rear lift-up door, he thought he saw shadowy form near a dark-colored foreign-made sedan.

In a moment the form was a figure within two feet of Ben. At that uncomfortably close proximity he could easily see a bulky man who gripped a full sized wooden baseball bat which he slapped lightly against his huge left hand. The thug growled in a decidedly non-southern accent, "You and the broad find any good furniture buys lately?"

It didn't require much analysis to figure the stranger's connection or intent. In all his years, Walker had never actually been in a fist fight. He couldn't count encounters with brothers, boyhood rivals or even a college scuffle on a geology field trip to New Mexico's Sangre de Cristo mountain range. He had on occasion, however, reflected on the effect that must result from the meeting of a man's full-swinging hand and an opposing mass of facial bones—the brush-off damage and minimum wincing of characters as portrayed in films notwithstanding.

For several years during his early days with Mother Nuclear, Walker had occasionally been badgered by a heavy-set site geologist who was a roustabout refugee from an oil well fire-capping company. Ben had been perfectly capable and willing to dish out his own tit-for-tat brand of verbal response to the bully's minor but annoying wrist-grabbing and hair-tousling tactics. That was plan A. He had also decided at that time that if things with the burrhead ever progressed beyond Ben's tolerance point, he would retaliate in a certain, precise fashion. On more than one occasion, with his irritation-threshold pressed, he had even hoped things would reach critical mass. This particular situation seemed very likely to test his historical Plan B.

Abruptly Walker's would-be assailant took a short, right-to-left chop, missing Ben's instinctively backthrust chest by a narrow margin. The bat's follow-through managed to connect with the left tail-light, rendering it useless. Foul tip. The sound and sight of exploding glass and plastic served as a catalyst for Walker's latent plan. He pointed to Amanda who had been standing just to one side of the car as Walker had been unloading their garment bags. He shouted, "Run!"

In the split second it took for his attacker to involuntarily glance in her direction and back to the object of his intentions, Ben made his move. He was scared, anxious and decisive.

Shifting his weight to his left foot he kicked hard with his right leg, the toe of his wing-tip catching the man full in his groin. Sacrifice hit. The batter fell to the asphalt, writhing and sobbing pitifully as he proceeded to return as closely as possible to his pre-birth position, seeking impossible relief. End of fight.

Ben quickly darted into their room and retrieved in one load everything he had just placed there, throwing it all in through the van's sliding side door. Amanda slammed down the back hatch and scrambled into the passenger side. The van lurched out of the parking space and accelerated around to the motel lobby, braking to a stop directly in front of the main entrance.

"Stay here," he said, "I'll be right back." At the counter he interrupted the desk clerk, "I'm sorry, attempted mugging. May I make a call from your lobby telephone, please?"

Now even more fully in possession of his wits, Ben placed his call then dropped the room key on the counter, saying to the bewildered, badge-wearing trainee as he turned to walk out, "Loved the room. Sorry we can't stay for the free breakfast."

Not until they were back on the primary highway and once again heading east, did Amanda speak, her voice cracking. "Ben, what is happening? Did you call the police?"

"The police? Hell, no; an ambulance!" He smiled. "I wonder how Buford Pusser, Jr. will handle things with the hospital admittance clerk. I can just see it. He'll be looking up from a stretcher, clutching his crushed balls and trying to dam the torrent from his eyes while at the same time attempting to produce his group health card, if Mirror Magic issues them to their offensive linemen."

She replied, still shaken but trying to grasp the situation, "Forget the narration, Ben. This is serious stuff. That was Sloan's man from the furniture factory, wasn't it?" And then added before Walker could reply, "Do you think he might have killed us?"

"I doubt it. Otherwise he would more likely have had a gun, or a knife at least. And he certainly wouldn't have announced himself. His orders were probably to scare me," Walker reasoned. "Are you okay now, 'Manda?"

"Yes, but I'll need special attention," she said as she leaned as close to Walker as her seat restraint would allow.

He leered at her so she could see his expression, raising and dropping his eyebrows twice while tapping ashes from an imaginary cigar with his right hand. "You said the magic word, Ms. Booth. You win five dollars and an evening with Wakeful Walker."

Amanda laughed, relaxing a little. "Ben, you chopped him down like a tree. Where did you learn that?"

"What's to learn? The School of Self Preservation. I'm a blue belt, you know," he joked, trying to keep it light. "Seriously, Amanda, I'm worried for you. I'm taking you off this patrol. I can't have you at risk like this." He added, "I'm quite fond of you, you know."

"Fond!" she squealed. "How'd you like to receive a 'blue belt,' Walker?" She drew back her small fist in a mock gesture, then popped her seat belt and threw her arms around his neck just as he pulled up in front of their evening's second choice of lodging. "Actually, I'm somewhat amused by you also," she said.

38

During the long drive back to Atlanta following the successful show, Ben had been contemplating while Amanda dozed most of the way. He said aloud, "Help me walk through something I've been puzzling over for weeks."

"Okay, let's walker." A snicker of a grin appeared on her face as Ben rolled his eyes at her.

"Now stay with me," he said. "We know that double M is selling blank mirrors to at least one large manufacturer in both the auto and furniture industries. And to who knows what other industries. And not just mirrors for mirrors' sake," he added.

"What do you mean?" asked Amanda.

"Well," he launched into substance, "suppose Mirror Magic is marketing to carefully selected national accounts which have built-in mirror displays for either private or public use and are strongly positioned through chain or captive outlets such as furniture stores and auto dealers, or in very high traffic locations such as public restrooms in fast-food restaurants and service stations? Wouldn't they be natural potential buyers of MM's uniquely-packaged hidden persuader hook?" He glanced at Amanda as his mind was racing with this line of thought.

So was hers. "Oh, my God!" she reacted. "The product appears to be simple blank mirror; but with an advertising and identity message invisible to the naked eye. Millions of them in place collectively become the ultimate subliminal broadcast medium." she said.

"Absolutely," Walker confirmed. "An invisible message carried by a product whose utility is so basic to man's inherent vanity that its usage is regular, frequent, and universal. In addition, it's effect not only approaches that of a mass medium but does so without regulation or labelling of any kind. And further, it's a product that could insidiously guarantee measurable results over a nominal period of time.

"And here's the sweet part of Sloan's hook; the advertiser doesn't know he's succeeding with the product until he tries doing without it. The business drops off so he goes back to what was working, as the MM rep is trained to suggest. But the sales rep is also ignorant of the true reason. He or she just thinks Magic's mirrors are wonderful.

"Now, here's where it all must lead, Amanda; double M may very well be planning to build other factories, and why stop short of international? Freight would be a competitive killer or would appear to be, and they wouldn't want to draw unnecessary attention to themselves in that arena. For all we know they may already be marketing under a dozen different private labels to avoid cries of antitrust."

"But they have no true competition," interjected Amanda.

"Correct. But they can't advertise an illegal advantage. They have to appear to be in a competitive posture," Walker clarified.

"But, Ben, where does the ad specialty aspect come in? How does our business relate to what you've just described?"

"If I'm not mistaken," said Walker, "the promotional product industry is small potatoes for Phil Sloan and Mirror Magic. But there's a hitch that has probably caused them serious concern."

Amanda held up one palm. "Whoa. Too fast; let me catch up. On our side of the equation, distributors attribute their success with MM partly to some marketing mystique—about which they have no motivation to be too curious. It takes form in their presentations as being simply a superior-made wall mirror that is a natural carrier for an advertising imprint. A wide range of models and sizes are available at different price points.

The appeal of the utility of the mirror itself ensures the visibility of the advertising message—essentially just like the thousands of other industry products. The MM product comes with its apparently superfluous, but nevertheless perceived value-added registration plate and lifetime warranty." She caught her breath, "Their biggest problem must be where to bank their profits."

"Very succinctly stated, Amanda." Walker tipped a make-believe hat. "But since marketing the same mirrors in an automotive, furniture or other outlet has nothing whatever to do with an imprinted advertising message, Sloan wouldn't have anything but price and delivery on which to peg his initial sales pitch. Again, they obviously couldn't disclose to their buyers, or even their reps, the true MM product advantage. If just one leak developed, the news media and then the public furor over invasion of personal privacy would hound them out of business overnight—if not into the courts. What do they do?"

It was late afternoon on a Friday and their half of the eight-lane perimeter traffic around Atlanta was heavy. Walker found the mainstream speed, more than ten miles above the metro limit, and he was able to concentrate as the scenario of events with MM continued to crystallize for him.

"Okay, here's where the art-science of puzzling requires a creative bent in working through Sloan's thought-warp," he said, as much to his rear-view mirror as to Amanda. "I doubt that vague and undocumented superior claims for a generic commodity such as commercial mirrors would cut much ice with purchasing agents whose performance reviews are based primarily on their success at effecting cost-savings for their employers." He was preparing a question. "With that in mind, Amanda, MM must have to resort to deep discounts to initially win an account. Now how do you suppose they later justify raising prices?"

"You implied the answer earlier, Ben," she said, "When you addressed the issue with respect to ad specialty distributors. After a sufficient period of time passes with their MM-programmed mirrors constantly pulsing the manufacturer's name, logo and slogan through millions and millions of shipped products to dealers, stores and other outlets, they simply claim credit for the unusual increases being experienced by customers. Then they could offer to withdraw the product, a reverse trial period for the sake of sales comparisons. And when customers come whimpering back, they double or triple the price. No one knows how to account for the difference, only that it exists. No downstream confidences are thus at risk, no potential leaks. And only a bare handful of people at Mother Magic knows for sure."

"Precisely," said Walker.

"Ben, the potential influence on people's minds is staggering. But I had no idea such a technology existed. Worse, if the message can't be seen by the naked eye and if, in fact, the technology resides exclusively with Mirror Magic, just what and how are we going to do anything about it?"

"That's a two-part question, and I don't do two-parters without a little incentive. I'm drowsy," said the driver. "I'm also in need of a back scratch," he added.

"It's only a few miles to the office and personally I'd rather relieve you at the wheel than at the itch," she retorted but then relented. "Don't fall asleep in the process and I'll do what I can. But if I see your eyelids do just one slow flutter, I'll tattoo you."

"Ooohh, promises!" he sighed. "All right, to business. First of all, devices do exist which can fix on a transmitter's wavelength, whatever the frequency, and then render the message in printed form. I don't think that's as important, however, as the fact that for all this deductive reasoning, Sloan by now probably realizes we have learned far more than he ever expected we would. As a result, Amanda, your life may be in jeopardy, in spite of my attempt to steer media and public attention to double M."

Walker then steeled himself for revealing the first part of an idea concerning Amanda which he knew would be vigorously contested. "The next thing I'm going to do is accept your public resignation from Baxter Products."

Instead of an expected sharp dig from her fingernails, she merely threw him a look that would have seared granite. "Resignation?" she said. "No matter your thinking, Ben Walker, you'll have to fire me to get me off the shelf. I'm far more interested in Baxter Products and in what really happened to Jon Baxter, as well as to seeing this thing through than in your supposed charms and any plan, however well-intentioned, to dust me off." She sat ramrod straight.

"Relax. I'll privately hire you as an independent consultant at the same rate you're now earning, with all the bennies thrown in. That'll do two things for us. One, with a public announcement of your departure, it'll take you out of the center of attention as far as MM is concerned. And, two, it will dampen the office scuttlebutt concerning our relationship. It's either that or I'll simply have to marry you," he added, looking straight ahead as if concentrating on the road.

Whoa! he thought. Did I say what I just heard? I mean, sure I've been thinking about it but I hadn't actually decided to go on record. Well, now I've done it. What'll she say? She can't turn me down, can she? She loves me! I mean I love her. Then you have to say it; it's part of the package. But that's how it happened with Susan, the first time around. Oh, well, too late now.

A pause. Amanda's initial ire was replaced with cunning. "You know, Mr. Walker, my mother once told me that some men have a difficult time with tradition, but that a smart girl should overlook some of that if things seem to balance. I'm going to accept your job reclassification and call your bluff on an offer of marriage, pitiful though it was. I'll accept no date for the latter, however, until this Mirror Magic thing is resolved."

She hadn't looked at Walker, but was expressing the same grin as he. Amanda had been satisfied with their relationship to this point, but she had given considerable thought lately to the notion that things must sooner or later lead in one of two directions. One option would let her be caught in the tender, but no-commitment trap in which so many of her girl friends had found themselves. The second had just presented itself in an unusual fashion.

39

Walker phoned Flyn Bascom that evening. "Flyn, would it be possible to get a week to 10 days of those high pay, low activity summer months that befall a professor with tenure and esteem? I need help, and only you can provide it. Baxter Products will cover your expenses and your going consulting rate. What'ya say, life-long buddy of mine?"

"Well, buddy, we can really only count our relationship from age 20 or so, not lifetime. The university esteem to which you refer depends entirely upon prolific publication, which means eyes on the screen and fingers on the keyboard—publish or perish, you know. And as for tenure, that only means that I can't lose my job for anything short of bedding the Dean's wife. Ouch! Janie just kicked me in the left shin. See the grief you visit upon me, buddy?"

"Nice flack job, Flyn. You must have a new writer. Now get this. It turns out it was Phil Sloan's trusted chauffeur and personal bodyguard I put into that North Carolina hospital. He's going to be laid up there a week or so with a quadruple hernia. That spells opportunity for us. Amanda knows which temporary service Mirror Magic uses and we think we can get you on as the goon's short-term replacement. There must be some solid evidence we can pick up through that cover, either at the MM office or at Sloan's home."

Walker could scarcely believe he was so matter-of-factly asking for Flyn's help on such a risky matter, but he didn't know who else to turn to in such a situation. He was even more surprised by the qualified acceptance.

"Ben-O, you amaze me. First you apologize to me for putting poor Kobsavich into some dirt job in Detroit and then you turn around and want to hire me as a footman, just because I'm black. Now where's your sense of shame?"

Before Walker could answer he continued, "Damned lucky for you it's summertime and the livin' is easy. Set me up and I'll catch the first plane out. Jeez. Run one little traverse across one stinkin' harbor with a man, and from then on he thinks he's a brother."

40

"Barton!" barked Phil Sloan from his office in the direction Flyn Bascom was sitting and waiting in the outer office, chauffeur's hat in hand. "Come in here, dammit!"

"At your service, Mr. Sloan," he said. Amanda was right, he thought, Phillip Sloan made Ichabod Crane look like Jackie Gleason. He was tall, thin, and hook-nosed, with deep-set eyes and unkempt, rat-brown hair.

Bascom had resolved to keep his talk to a minimum. He would be less likely to offer clues that might not be consistent with the stereotyped background of a man who drove a limousine for a living. He very much doubted Sloan would recognize his voice from the one brief phone call he had made to him about the interview request. He had already disguised his voice somewhat, at Walker's suggestion. Still, he didn't want to increase the risk of exposure any more than necessary.

"As I told you when I agreed to take you on for a couple of weeks, you don't strike me as a chauffeur-type. If the agency hadn't said you come well-qualified I'd have held out for someone with a little more hustle. What I want from you is presence. When I need you, be here. When I don't, be here anyway. Your job is to wait. Wait and drive. Is that clear?"

"Yes, sir, perfectly clear," he spoke slowly and carefully. "By the way, sir, your secretary said there was a little library somewhere in the building. It might have some city maps. I need to study some. I haven't been back in Atlanta long."

He hadn't worn any type of uniform since he had left the Naval Reserve almost ten years ago, but he found himself constantly wanting to adjust one item or another of his pawn shop ensemble. Once he even came close to saluting his erstwhile boss.

Sloan himself cared little about clothing. A part of his soul was reflected in his cheap, ill-fitting dress shirts. But it was his company and his call. No one riding on a Mirror Magic elevator with his majesty had ever accused the emperor of wearing poor clothes.

"I don't give a damn whether you sit in the office, the car or the john—just keep that beeper close enough to kiss. Now get out of here, I have work to do!" Sloan waved him away, scowling.

After three days on the job Bascom had gotten a feel for when, where and how often his services were needed. Sloan was very much a man of habit. Bascom was living in the still-hospitalized chauffeur's room next to the four-car garage on Sloan's sprawling, but spartan estate. A preliminary search of chauffeur Eddie Prater's room yielded only a self-help book on chauffeuring. Bascom found portions of it entertaining as well as informative. For example it read, "Assume the privilege when parking your limousine at the desirable front entrance location to whichever public or private building your employer wishes to make his entrance or take his leave. Once parked, open one or more curbside doors as if you are momentarily expecting the return of a celebrity, the owner of the building, or a cabinet-level member of the current White House administration."

The primer continued, "For insurance, make certain your uniform cap is properly in place and your most snobbish demeanor affixed. Stand by an open car door holding a clipboard on which you are seen to be checking off critical items. No one will question your privilege. Note: In the event your limousine is something as mundane as a mini-van, have it painted bright red."

Well, thought chauffeur-Bascom, tidbits he could perhaps use back on campus. He need only instruct a struggling graduate student in the rudiments.

After a more thorough examination of the compact premises, he found a security entrance card partially hidden at the base of an artificial philodendron. Neither the house nor the garage had restricted-entrance doors so he made short forays up and down the various MM office hallways in search of a door that might suggest anything curious.

Talk about sterile! How about antiseptic and neutered? The Mirror Magic building was not a hospital but a profits palace without imagination. The only magic in MM was the bottom line. A prospective customer or new employee might have expected mirrors to adorn the walls; there were none. After all, a profitable mirror was a mirror out the door.

On these reconnaissances Flyn always kept a map in hand, ready in an instant to ask about a metro area shortcut if his presence should suddenly be questioned. He came across as friendly, sincere and eager to learn. He was on one of his sorties on a below-ground floor when he noticed one of the entrances near a parking deck marked "Authorized Personnel Only." A security guard was posted within 20 feet of its code-entry door.

He could find no excuse to hang around for very long so he made a number of trips to the area through the remainder of the day. It was nearly five-thirty, close to the time Sloan would be beeping him for the trip home, when he observed more than a dozen people exiting at the same time. He recognized one black technician whom he had seen the day before in the company lunchroom. His name badge had read "Wilson, Glover." Very personal place, thought Bascom.

At that moment his beeper delivered its summons and as he turned to leave, a very striking female exited through the door and handed something to the guard. He said, "Thank you, Ms. Ver Meer."

Bascom paused, thinking she could only be Walker's wicked witch. He decided to risk Sloan's wrath by being several minutes late and walked up to the guard desk—letting the beeper continue to signal. "I'm Mr. Sloan's new driver, man. When he tells me to jump I got to ask him what color hoop he wants and does he want me to set it on fire first," he said, pointing to the source of the noise, "but I need some help."

The guard barely looked up. He had seen this new face several times already today and once was about to ask him his business. "What do you need?" he asked matter-of-factly.

"Was that Glover Wilson who just left? I met him yesterday and I want to ask him to have a beer with me after work. Do you know where he hangs out, man?" He was afraid he was overdoing it, but after a week of quiet observation he thought he had the black blue-collar *shtick* down fairly well.

The guard looked up, puzzled, then smiled faintly, "You mean *Bleeper* Wilson? Yeah. Find him same place every other workin' stiff around here makes for as soon as his shift ends. It's called The Church, just off Fulton Industrial, about a mile from here."

"They call him 'Bleeper'? Why's that, man?" Bascom asked.

"Well, story goes Old Glover used to swear so bad when he was only ten years old that one day his momma caught him and put such a guilt load on him about the Lord not likin' it and all, and then throwin' in a bathtub o' tears and hellfire promises, that he took an oath never to use the F-word again," the guard explained. Then he laughed, saying "But it don't keep him from bleepin' himself!"

41

Sloan did not drive. It set up feelings of lack of control which, ironically, he was able to reconcile through a hired driver. Bascom made a couple of personal stops for Sloan, then drove him to Hartsfield International for an overnight trip to New York. Sloan released him for the evening but not without performance feedback.

"If you don't value your job, Bascom, all you have to do is screw up again. Your job is to be ready to haul me around when I beep. I don't care who you're doing at the time but you had damn well better zip it up and have your ass sitting behind that wheel by the time I show up. I'll be back tomorrow afternoon."

Bascom's motivation for seeing Sloan nailed was beginning to approach the level of Walker's. He drove the limo to The Church, parking it as inconspicuously as possible among the many cars in the lounge's lot that sported Mirror Magic advertising front tags. He spotted Wilson sitting at a table with two other men. Two empties and one half-full beer bottle sat in front of each of them and his man was just waving off the waitress as she prematurely solicited them for another round. Bascom sat down at the bar and ordered the same brand of beer the stranger sitting next to him was drinking. He was still in his chauffeur's uniform, figuring that while it made him stand out it also identified him as local. In the middle of the heavily varnished, circular counter a thick, dirty-looking hemp rope hung from the clapper of a huge but badly tarnished bell. The bell was suspended 20 feet up and housed in a crudely built cupola. The Church's belfry.

Just then the other man at Glover's table got up, threw down a couple of dollar bills and laughed loudly, saying, "Gotta go home and tell the old lady I've been at church."

Bascom slowly turned on his barstool and stared in Wilson's direction until he finally caught his eye, then he walked over, beer in hand. "You're Bleeper Wilson aren't you? I'm Frank Barton, man. I'm new at MM—I've seen you around. Buy you a beer?" he asked.

Glover nodded but didn't offer the customary local soul-shake. Bascom sat down and raised two fingers for the waitress.

"Been drivin' for Sloan for almost two weeks, temporary. Hope to get on permanent in some other department when this gig is over. Any openings you know of?"

"Naw, man. You gotta go to personnel for that."

"What department you in?" Bascom asked.

"Damned if I know. I'm a screen printer by trade but the bleepin' union let management start messing with some of us about six months ago and now I'm on a special assembly operation. Shit, man, we have to kiss ass just to take a leak. We stick bleepin' numbered plates on the backs of bleepin' mirrors."

Glover ached to complain about his lot in life. Bascom had noticed that he was one of the few people in the bar who was not wearing either a wash-faded company polo-type shirt or a light-weight company jacket. Both models had a Mirror Magic logo imprinted on them. They were things Wilson resisted wearing since subconsciously he felt more comfortable taking jabs at MM when he wasn't wrapped in a company flag.

Bascom encouraged him.

"Matter-of-fact," his subject continued, if they don't get me off this job-downgrade shit soon, I'm gonna file me a griev-i-ance. It's a bleepin' contract violation."

"Don't blame you, Bubba. What do you do with those plates; screen 'em or stamp 'em or somthin'?" Bascom asked.

"Bleep, no, man, all we do is pull the numbered plates out of a box, match 'em up with the orders we got, then mount 'em in a recessed area of the mother-bleepin' mirror. Lousy job," said Glover as he hoisted his fourth bottle and drained it.

Bascom did the same, then said, "Now me, I kind of like working with my hands. Maybe there's an opening in engraving or something, like the department that puts the numbers on the plates." He wasn't certain how far he could push this line of inquiry but he was going to find out.

Wilson laughed. "You lookin' to move to New Jersey? That's all they need in Piss-cat-a-way," he emphasized the first syllable, impressed with the humor he found in so doing. Then he repeated it. "One Frank Barton of Piss-cat-a-way, New Jersey, bleepin' driver and engraver."

"Well, man, I just might at that. I'm from Jersey. I don't much like the heat down here and my girl's been after me to go back North. Who's the Man up there?"

His table companion suddenly looked hard at Bascom. He paused a moment, the quick beers causing a lag between the inclination and the decision processes. He slowly stood, placing both hands flat on the table's top, partly to steady himself but mostly to make a declaration. It had just come to him that he and the others in his small department had recently been cautioned, again, about talking to outsiders concerning any aspect of MM production. It had been presented in such a way that they understood competitors might learn something useful from what they might say and this in turn could affect orders and ultimately even cause layoffs. "I don't know you, Jack. Bleep off!"

Bascom had pushed too hard but the price had been right. At least Wilson hadn't taken a swing at him with a broken beer bottle.

Bascom was anxious to update Ben, but it was late. He would have time for that tomorrow morning before Sloan returned from New York. Lying in bed he wondered if Sloan was actually visiting on the Jersey side. According to his pocket atlas, Newark International could only be about 45 minutes from Piscataway.

42

"Well, Chesser," said Gam'man, "how do you defend Sloann now? I told you he would become reckless under pressure. His escalating influence over the years has not only altered the original game, in itself a violation of the guidelines, but because of his willful disregard for others' lives he may well have put our own situation at risk."

With the passage of many years, the increasingly lonely pair still made their harmless, regular pilgrimages to the Las Vegas gaming tables in order to test their abilities at influencing objects and circumstances. This was quite different, however, from the grand obsession to which their countryman found himself yoked.

"To tell you the truth, Gam'man," replied Chesser, momentarily looking up from his ever-present game of Canfield, "I am quite surprised. I no more endorse Sloann's activities than you, and frankly I believe his erratic behavior may grow even worse with the dogged persistence presented by this Benjamin Walker." They had been avidly following the infrequent but, to them, telling newspaper and television references to the business and personality conflicts between Mirror Magic and Baxter Products.

Neither Gam'man nor Chesser possessed distinguishing physical appearances that would permit them to be especially noticed in even a very small crowd, let alone the lemming hordes of the casinos. Their hair styles, their clothes, even their height and weight all seemed calculated to make them unremarkable. Only close and essentially unpermitted inspection of their hands would have revealed the basis for interesting questions.

To engage either of them in lengthy conversation, however, would have dramatically caused them to stand out. Fortunately for them, casino populations have great tendencies to adhere blindly to their courses. In fact, the pair's individual attitudes and opinions on nearly any subject would have betrayed them as anything but uninteresting personalities. It was for these reasons they kept themselves out of social circles of any type, including even the most casual acquaintanceships. Their screams for social interaction raged silently.

43

"Nice piece of work, Flyn," exclaimed Walker as the two sat, talking over a mid-morning pot of coffee and the cheese danish Bascom had picked up on his way over to Ben's comfortable condo. Walker had skipped his regular Saturday A.M. racquetball game with the Off-The-Wall Gang. He knew Bascom very much wanted another shot at Ellison and the partner of his choice, but Ben persuaded him a rematch while Flyn was posing at MM, even though it was cross town, might possibly result in someone from the enemy camp seeing them together.

"Great perks you throw in this package, Ben-O. You know you could stand enlightenment from state and federal government as to basic civilized benefits due employees and consultants," said Bascom dryly. He took enthusiasm from his own lead, "In fact, you, sir, are guilty of blatant exploitative practices and if I don't see some improvement in very short order I will personally initiate filing of a class action suit, and both the MMers and I will see your lily white ass hung out to dry, man!"

"I'm glad to see you're getting the hang of things," said Walker. "I was a little concerned about that."

"Okay," said Bascom, "but I still don't see how we're going to produce hard evidence for the subliminal plate scam, let alone something substantial to incriminate Sloan for the two murders. But you're right about one point; this blue collar doesn't fit very well. Fortunately, after I pick up the head Neanderthal at the airport today I have only two more wake-ups on my short-timer's calendar."

Walker summed up their position. "My inclination is to go to the police now with what we have. It should be enough for them to at least pick up Ver Meer and the chauffeur for questioning. With a little dramatic show-and-tell to suggest we know more than we do, one of them might even be willing to serve up Sloan in order to keep their own hides from being skinned. Flyn, maybe this life and death nightmare starring Phillip Sloan is about to came to light.

The phone rang. "Excuse me, Dr. Bascom," said Walker, showing a knowing smile as he picked up the telephone's hand-piece. "This will no doubt be the gorgeous blonde calling to see if Dick Tracy can come out and play." Amanda Booth, it was.

"Ben," she said excitedly. "I just heard something incredible on a network news brief. I don't know if it's good news or bad. Phil Sloan has been reported shot and killed in a hotel robbery attempt in Newark. They say he was shot twice through the head. You remember the arrogant female reporter who did your television interview several months ago—Lynn Michelson? Well, she was on tape just a few minutes ago and guess who she was interviewing? None other then our own wicked witch."

Stunned by the unlikeliness of the death of the object of his past months near-total focus, Walker's thoughts were on a roller-coaster. At first he felt cheated that he wasn't to be instrumental in removing Sloan from the picture. Then, in a brief moment of elation, he realized that the person directly behind the death of his mentor had been dealt justice. That gave way to the realization that Mirror Magic itself was in no way prevented from continuing its deception and fraud. Maybe even more homicides would occur in order to preserve the status quo. And who, other than the probable indirect murderess of Jon Baxter, was the logical person to take over the covert reins of MM's subliminal subversion of Business America?

"Amanda," he said, "how did they locate Tersa Ver Meer so fast, and what did she have to say?"

"My guess is that every major network probably has a lead on hundreds of high-profile public or private potential newsmakers in the country, including something on their most likely back-up," said Amanda. "Sloan would fit that category. At any rate, Ben, Ver Meer had no comment on Sloan's death. In her compassion, however, she did state that it would be business as usual at Mirror Magic."

Walker felt sick. He was already sitting or he would have sought a chair for relief of the nausea passing over him. Strange, he thought. It wasn't totally unlike his initial physical reaction to the news of Jon Baxter's death. With Jon's, of course, his heart ached. He had kept most of the hurt to himself, or had tried. Amanda helped him get part of it out in the open, and that had allowed some healing. The successive feelings concerning Sloan's death, first at having been cheated, then a false sense of triumph, and finally the logic that not a hell of a lot had changed, left him puzzling over his position.

From his own perspective, Bascom saw things at a near-end, and thus attempted rationalization. "Ben, you've been seeking relief from the emotions of losing your friend by taking direct action in any and every way possible. This job has turned you into a classic A-type personality. Let it go. With the demise of the force behind Baxter's death you're released from your self-appointed role of avenger. Let's get back to life with the living instead of preoccupation with the dead."

Bascom meant well but Walker now knew what he had to do. He had a great need to confront the object of his chase, either in court or face to face on the pavement. He had wanted to see Sloan suffer as harsh a sentence as the system would deliver. Lacking proper execution of either of those two acceptable alternatives, Walker's satisfaction would have to come from the collapse of Sloan's creation, or at least of those who would perpetuate Phillip Sloan's work. He must again focus on the puzzle, but in which new direction would he look?

Analysis. Jon Baxter was dead. Probably homicide. Now Sloan was dead as well, certainly his death was by design, but whose? No clue to that. But what had changed other than he had lost a beloved friend and mentor and a largely unknown but absolute enemy? The puzzle remained essentially unpieced. He had wept over his loss and taken Sloan's unexpected demise in stride, but he could not shake his obsession with Mirror Magic. In order to reinforce his commitment to solving the greatest puzzle of his life Walker resorted to one of his private rituals—summation-by-mirror.

He excused himself and strode purposefully to his bathroom. Walker stared into the mirror. He raised his left hand and forearm to a vertical position, the palm perpendicular to the glass. With his eyes focussed on his extended right forefinger, he slowly and deliberately brought it to within two inches of his left palm. He paused, then swiftly pressing them together he growled, "Lock on, Walker!"

This exercise was his way of taking a personal oath to pursue Mirror Magic and its executive executioners to the end of the road, wherever that might take him. It was no less an oath of honor for him than if he had drawn his own blood.

44

"How did the Ver Meer broad take it, Mario?" asked Anthony Bonnelli of his finance man and business and personal attorney, Mario Scipone. Bonnelli was revered in his New York crime borough organization—not for how he came to power, many others before him had entered the same way, but for his success in retaining it against those who would emulate his methods.

Scipone replied. "Just before I called one of the television networks as you suggested, to mention the broad's connection with Phil Sloan, I had a short telephone conversation with her. I told her our organization was responsible for the death of her boss and that first the police and then a TV reporter would be calling her about it. Talk about a piece of ice! She took it like I had called to change her hair appointment."

"And then what, Mario?" Bonnelli asked. Imagination was not his strong suit, single-mindedness was.

"I told her she had two options; one, if she had a problem working for us she would be next to go down; two, she could stay on and run the show for us at twice what she was making under Sloan. All she said was, 'Welcome to Ver Meer. Your place or mine?'"

"Okay, now meet with her and lay it all out," said Bonnelli. "I want to get things rolling fast now that we're committed to this thing. Elections are less than a year away, Mario. You know what to do."

He should. It was his plan. Mario Scipone had accidentally discovered several months ago, through union stewards on their payroll at Mirror Magic's New Jersey plant, about the strange secrecy surrounding the manufacture of apparently simple metal identification plates. He had put one of his people inside with instructions to find out what it was all about. Within a week he had learned that the simple plates were in fact wondrously thin, laser-programmed circuit boards mounted and sealed inside a thin metal shell. These plates were shipped from the northern New Jersey plant to Mirror Magic factories in Atlanta, Dallas, Chicago and Los Angeles.

Each of the five primary factories, according to Scipone's collective sources, received raw glass, screen-printed the advertising in backward format, then silvered the glass before finally attaching the New Jersey plant's specially prepared and consecutively-numbered warranty plates to the back of the finished mirrors. The carefully packaged mirrors were then shipped to MM's promotional product distributors for reshipment, or sometimes dropshipped directly to the distributors' advertising or promotional customers.

It was only when Scipone learned of Mirror Magic's expansion plans that he began to dig in earnest. That led to information that MM's latest mirror product would be made in many new sizes and shapes, and none would carry an advertising imprint. Scipone had understood that MM's business was manufacturing and marketing advertising-imprinted products through a specialized distribution network. What this latest development suggested to his analytic mind was a consumer market, not a commercial one. There was even rumor that MM had some sort of technological edge. All this reeked of new big-profit opportunities and he wanted more information.

Scipone had come a long way from his early days as a clerk in a poorly stocked convenience store fronting for neighborhood numbers sales. His handsome, All-American looks ensured he could pose as the captain in any college or professional football team photograph, but by an early age he had opted to fix plays rather than call them. Numbers running had not been challenging work, but as a teenager with both ambition and intelligence, young Mario soaked up every detail and nuance. The owner of the one-store operation paid off (in today's money) almost five thousand dollars for a four-digit winner on a one dollar ticket, and six hundred dollars for a correct three-digit pick. The odds were figured at ten thousand to one on four digits and one thousand to one on three digits. If Wall Street analyzed the numbers industry profits, their unanimous call would be to buy. The average customer in Scipone's poor neighborhood had spent about the same proportion of his or her meager wages as their counterparts do today, amounting now to four to five dollars per day. Many put down thirty to forty dollars with some outsiders risking as much as two hundred dollars on a daily basis.

It hadn't taken Scipone long to learn the numbers business knows no recession. In good times people look to improve their lot, in bad times, to catch up. Overhead is minimal. The police busted them two or three times a year, which cost their operation in fines what amounted to spare change plus whatever cash was found in the till. This was maybe ten percent of what was ingeniously hidden behind the false fronts of back room walls before the daily cash receipts delivery to the owner.

Similar independent small operations like Scipone's are in place today in many neighborhoods in most large, mid-sized and even many smaller cities in America. Each paying out as much as a million dollars a year in customer hits. Putting up with long hours, tedious work, boring conversation and the occasional shooting, robbery and bust are considered a manager's or owner's cost of doing business for five thousand to six thousand dollars a day in cash revenues. By declaring a generous store income, twenty percent of the actual take, an owner can cleverly pay some taxes and not have to live on a cash basis, in fear of displaying any of the trappings of the good life.

45

Scipone and Rocco Bonicotti, an ex-Big Ten defensive lineman well known in his collegiate days for a trigger-like response to simple game-book plays, had flown together from New York to Atlanta for a hospital visit. They were not care-givers. Scipone's pipeline network had it that one person might be able to provide them with a check on what they were about to be spoon-fed by Tersa Ver Meer. The source for telling of existing or potential difficulties just happened to be easily accessible, Sloan's long-time chauffeur and leg-man, Eddie Prater.

Apparently Prater had himself been mugged on an out-of-town trip, badly beaten and hospitalized on the spot. Just yesterday he had been transferred to an Atlanta hospital on the far west side. The irony of a designated wide-body being taken out by an amateur was not lost on Scipone. If the story was true, he would have some reason to question the savvy of the supposedly shrewd former head of MM, not to mention the hapless enforcer himself.

"We're from Mirror Magic, nurse, Mister Prater's employer. We'd like to see our friend, Eddie. We won't be long," Scipone said to the third-floor supervising nurse.

She stood behind a broad circular counter which offered quick access for the staff to all 12 of the patient rooms arranged in perimeter fashion around the station. They entered the room and immediately closed the door, just as Prater, roused from a light sleep by their entrance, looked up in surprise and instant suspicion at the two suited strangers.

The pair's leader raised his hand in a communicative fashion that signified quiet, stating in a low and very deliberate voice, "Please, Mr. Prater, my name is Mario Scipone. I only want to talk with you. If you cry out at any time, my assistant will crush your knee cap with his ball peen hammer. Rocco, show Eddie your hammer." Rocco quickly produced both the instrument and a sneer.

Scipone continued in the same conversational tone, "Of course if we were forced to operate, we know your screams of distress would bring a nurse to investigate, causing us some difficulty. Now, Rocco, show Eddie your muffler."

Rocco moved in close to Prater and jerked the pillow out from under his head, holding it only inches from his mouth and nose. The look of anticipation in the would-be assailant's eyes lacked only the command, "Snuff play, on two!" to execute whatever action his quarterback might desire.

Prater thought quickly. He could scream and possibly summon help in time to avoid serious damage. Given other circumstances, he would have done so and taken his chances, grabbing this asshole bodyguard—who would probably have been drafted by the NFL no later than the 78th round—by his greasy, stinking hair and slamming his nose hard onto the top of his own head. He knew that would easily break something. Then he could worry about the stand-up comic. Through most of his adult life he had maintained both the equipment and the will for such. But Eddie Prater's motivation was subpar these days, as was his physical condition.

First had come the recent humiliating and crippling injury by his uncharacteristic, but nevertheless total underestimation of the intended victim of a routine intimidation attempt. That was followed by Sloan's raving obscenities over the telephone about his incompetence. Now, here he was, laid up with complications. He was still drawing his salary, but for how long? Prater knew full well that if he hadn't known so much about Sloan and Mirror Magic he would already have been cut loose.

As it was, he stood to be silenced on mere whim by Tersa Ver Meer, his new boss. He had put up with that bastard Sloan for nearly ten years because of the money. For all his intelligence and self-confidence, Eddie Prater was lazy. He aced the things that interested him and flagged those that didn't. He would do almost anything for easy money, and nothing that required serious labor. Now, he thought to himself, he had better analyze the situation. The man said he wanted to talk. Was this, after all, opportunity come knocking?

"Okay, hotshot," Prater acquiesced, "so you're a helluva salesman. Pull back your accountant, here."

"That's a good patient, Eddie. Continue to cooperate and you may recover fully. If you should balk, Rocco will take it as a personal affront. Now, on the other hand, be extremely helpful to us and there's fifty thousand dollars in it for you to get out of the mirror business."

Scipone enjoyed leaning on people. It was immensely more gratifying to him than the cerebral part of the business, for which he was also well qualified. That's why he chose to go out into the field as often as he did when he could just as easily send an underling.

"Rocco, show Eddie the cash."

Scipone's instrument stepped closer to Prater's bed and pulled a large wad of bills from his coat pocket. They were held together by a heavy rubber band. He raised the bundle as if to hand it to the object of his play. Instead, he brought it down hard across the bedded victim's face, bringing only a trickle of blood from his nose, but a high level of irritation. Fortunately for Prater he knew how to temper his reactions.

Scipone resumed framing his proposition. "This is not multiple-choice, Eddie. You had better know one hell of a lot, or . . ." He sat down in the visitor's chair and crossed his knee, pointing to it. "Or, when we leave, the operation will have been successful but the patient will have a serious complaint."

Prater reasoned that if he had a chance to both avoid further damage to himself and to be paid in the process, he would have to sell himself as well as his information. He began his argument on the offensive. "Tell Jocko to lay the money on me right now, Scipone, and I'll send you away with enough information to get your nose so far up your boss's ass, it'll be brown for life."

With that remark Rocco was close to anticipatory orgasm, but he waited dutifully for the play he felt would surely come.

Mario Scipone had gotten to where he was in Bonnelli's wide-ranging organization largely due to his ability to correctly assess others. It was time for another such decision. He shook his head to restrain Rocco, and looked again at his subject.

"Time's wasting, Eddie-boy."

Prater went to work, saying aloud, "You know, I might benefit from this in other ways. I haven't been able to unload to anyone and it's a helluva bag to carry around. Okay. For starters, MM has special equipment that's used in the New Jersey factory to laser-program wafer-thin devices that are plated and then attached to their mirror orders."

"The world already knows Mirror Magic is in the advertising mirror business, Eddie. And I know about the lasered plates. What's special?" Scipone said, frowning.

Prater turned to Scipone's assistant and said in a patronizing tone, "Let me illustrate. Jocko, hand me one of my hundred dollar bills along with that pocket mirror lying on the sink. Good boy."

"*Rocco,* short-timer!" said the subject of Prater's deliberate miscues, as he grabbed both the mirror and one of the bill's still lying on the bed and stuffed them roughly inside the still-smiling patient's hospital gown. The slab-sided ex-lineman pressed heavily on the invalid's bandaged abdomen, causing a dramatic change in his victim's expression but not in attitude.

"Thanks so much," strained Prater, breathing with difficulty as he retrieved the bill, holding it straight up between his thumb and extended middle finger. Rocco had to be physically restrained this time. Scipone was forced to grin slightly at the controlled cockiness of their ill-positioned subject.

Prater continued his lecture. He folded the bill in half and then held it flat against the bottom of the small frameless pocket mirror. "Consider this bill to be one of the plates that are mounted on the backs of MM mirrors. What you want to know has everything to do with these plates. The unit is actually an ingenious device that, once programmed, continuously lasers its message to the mirror's surface in a wavelength just below human consciousness. In other words, Mirror Magic is big time into the subliminal advertising business—and I mean literally, 'being in the mind without our knowing it.' Mirror end-users are presented with subconscious advertising messages in addition to the more conventional influence of visual imprint."

Scipone was thinking. If the subliminal message couldn't be seen, yet the mirrors which carried it were being repetitively viewed, then the potential benefit to the advertiser was incalculably enormous. All this minus any censorship or regulation. He posed an objection, "I've never even heard of such a technological capability, but if I had, by logical extension the system would be high profile and therefore inherently jeopardized. I don't believe it."

"That doesn't mean it isn't true, Scipone," said Prater. "It's one hell of a secret. Sloan didn't share this information with his distributors, let alone with their clients—naturally. Otherwise the whole thing would go up in smoke. All anyone knows is that MM advertising mirrors get results. And whenever an advertiser tries to cut back and discontinue use of MM product, within a few months or a year at most, business drops significantly. As you would imagine, MM purveyors attribute the downturn to discontinuance of the mirrors and the promotional product medium itself." Prater was proud of himself for what he knew and how well he was able to communicate it.

"It's better than dealing drugs. It's not pervasive with the general population, but advertiser addiction nevertheless causes a lot of black ink to appear on the bottom line without the complication of every other cop trying to bust us. Mr. Advertiser ends up comin' right back home to Mama Magic."

"Eddie, you're full of shit!" said Scipone. "The only thing that keeps me from letting Rocco off his leash (Rocco was not offended by Scipone's insult, he only strained forward) is the fact that I can't explain the extraordinary secrecy at the Piscataway plant. You haven't even earned the one C-note you've already socked away. Give me something I can use. The meter isn't accepting your slugs."

Despite the disclaimer, Prater knew Scipone's interest was piqued. He played out more line. "I don't know how or where Sloan got his equipment. He just had it. He churned out the subliminally-processed mirrors for decades. It's taken a long time to build double M sales to where it is because he only had a few machines, no more than a dozen. Worse, he once told me, he couldn't buy or produce more. The inventor died or something and the technology for duplicating them is scrambled."

Eddie was really beginning to warm to his subject. Phil Sloan had held him in tight rein through a combination of a big check and a maniac's temperament. Assigning him essentially go-fer status while continuing to overlook Prater's potential contributions was a mistake, but it was typical of Sloan to underestimate everyone.

"Closing scene, Eddie" said Scipone, by now understanding exactly how he could exploit to the maximum the set-up that had dropped into the organization's lap. It was taking on beautiful focus. Still, he wanted whatever else might still be on the table. "You need a big finale, Eddie." Scipone leaned forward on his chair, having abandoned any effort to disguise his body language if not his verbal enthusiasm.

Prater waxed creative. "Try this on. Sloan recently moved into some other subliminal mirror arenas outside the industry. I personally thought was a big mistake," he shrugged.

"Oh, and why is that, Mr. MBA?" said Scipone.

"Simple," offered Prater, mindful that his tormentor had probably not yet made up his mind whether to ice him or pay him. "The visible imprint that is part and parcel of specialty advertising is the camouflage necessary for the MM scheme to operate successfully in the first place. Better to stay small and tight than big and loose."

A nurse came through the door with an announcement. "You gentlemen will have to leave now. The doctor is coming in on rounds."

"Give us another minute, nurse," said the somber-looking Scipone. "He's had some bad news about a friend's death."

"I'm sorry, but news or no news, when the doctor walks in, five'll be a crowd," said the nurse who exited, not noticing Prater's hand raised in mild protest.

"Okay, Eddie, anything else? I can't use a hell of a lot of this," Scipone said.

"Don't bullshit me, Scipone," whispered a weak but still-defiant Prater. The session had all but exhausted him. "Even I could push the lever on this one, if I just had the money and muscle like you guys. I'm not the only one who knows what I know, but none of it, or us, is much good without Sloan's bitch, Ver Meer. She knows how to make those programming machines sing. Sloan treated even her like a piece of crap, but I'd have sooner trusted him than her. What do you need from me, an engraved blueprint?"

Scipone studied his spent informant. "Eddie, lucky for you I like your style. I just don't trust your appetite. To curb it a little I'm giving you 24 hours to check yourself out of this hospital and out of the country. After that I'm putting an open contract on you. Anyone who brings me proof-of-purchase will pick up a quick

$10,000. If I were you I would never come up for air, much less share what you know with anyone else, if you don't want the value of your hide to double."

No sooner had they passed the medical duo heading for the room, than Rocco began asking for Prater's contract. Mario Scipone sighed and said, "We don't need to actually take him out, *Jocko*, we could have done that back there. For him to think so is enough."

46

"Flyn, I can't sleep," complained Walker after he had surprised Bascom with a phone call to Tallahassee at six in the morning.

"Ben, I have to be honest," said Bascom. "I really don't give a clam about your insomnia. Now, I like to hear from you, but do you have to call me with a progress report during the middle of a night's sleep?"

"You weren't asleep. You can't string six words together within 30 minutes of arising. Besides, you can't even remember the last time you weren't up before five-thirty A.M.. Look, I'm not calling on a whim," Walker's tone turned from light banter to dead sobriety. "I've spent half the night thinking through this whole Mirror Magic thing one more time, and I know what we have to do.

"Once again I need your help. Start your meter, if you will, Dr. Activist. I'll lay it on you as soon as you can get a flight up here. Give Janie my love and tell her you'll be back among the ivy and palms in a few days; rested, reflective, and more ready than ever before to begin another triumphal fall campaign."

Bascom hung up the phone and Janie said over the newspaper she had propped up on the breakfast table, "He con you again?"

"Yep. I think I've become his challenge. What if I told you this is the last time, my love?"

"Your nose is already long enough, Pinocchio," she grinned in resignation.

At Hartsfield the next morning, Bascom sat listening to Walker's re-focussed version of—was he saying *their*—mission? He interrupted, "Whoa, best friend. I admit I'm interested in this because you're involved, but this *I Led Three Lives* business is not contributing to either my career path or my health."

"Sure it is. You can build a best seller around this and you won't even have to research it.

"I've had some serious second thoughts, too, Flyn. I thought I was in this scramble because of Jon's murder. When Sloan cashed in I wondered why my obsession didn't abate. Sloan was surely the force behind the action. But my itch comes from having cracked mirrors on my mind. And now I think I know how we can scratch it."

There it was again, thought Bascom. He *is* using the W-word.

"Mirror Magic is going to receive another visit, Flyn. This time it'll be from both of us. They know you over there and you can get us through the front door."

"Ben, all this is either going to get us time in jail or serious injury—or both. Amanda warned me about your sudden late-in-life penchant for storming the gates. Begging the general's pardon but this particular troop questions the situation analysis."

"Look at it this way, Flyn, we need more information, but the enemy camp doesn't want to provide it. The military teaches that bad weather makes for good movement among the enemy's defenses because their troops tend to be hunkered down to protect themselves against the cold and the rain. This, then, is the logical opportunity for seekers-of-truth to be out in the field looking to learn, just like good geologists."

"Geologist," mused Flyn Bascom, 'one who would make a profession of studying the earth,' I remember now. That was in a former life, when I had my head into rocks instead of rocks in my head."

He was walking a fine line trying to decide whether his involvement was out of empirical interest in the subject or simply a matter of misguided friendship. Since he couldn't, he gave up and, rationalizing with a game if mixed metaphor, said, "Oh, well, damn the torpedoes, forward to our Mirrorloo!"

Security at double M had tightened since Bascom has been there on his earlier chauffeuring stint. They walked up to the lobby's reception desk which now held a bank of security monitors and one additional attendant. Flyn wore his old ID badge and asked to see Pauline Powers.

Walker had earlier phoned Mirror Magic from his office, inquiring if Tersa Ver Meer would be in today. Learning that she wouldn't and also that Sloan's former secretary was, surprisingly, working for Ver Meer, he made an appointment with Powers for late that afternoon. It had to do with a feigned malfunction with several fax machines in the building.

Looking uniformed in tie and short-sleeved white shirt under a logo-embroidered poplin jacket, they were cleared for admittance to her office. Bascom hung around in the hallway outside Powers' office so as not to be seen by her. Appearing to first check out her own fax machine, Walker then left to complete his maintenance effort elsewhere in the building. They hid themselves for more than two hours in a safe room located by Bascom, then carefully made their way through the deserted after-hours walkways, back to Ver Meer's office complex.

Bascom posted himself outside the door as lookout while Walker proceeded directly to the fax file basket near the same machine he had just inspected. Having previously had good fortune with such equipment in Jon Baxter's office Walker was anxious to test his new theory. People still weren't into full fax flow in a changing national communications system suddenly much more dependent upon electronic mail. A certain amount of trust was still reserved. Hard copy originals of fax memos were routinely kept, but rarely filed. Who knew where errant, electronically pulsed messages might end up in the dawning age of telephony? Something might have to be sent or received a second time.

Of special interest, only a dozen or so pages down from the basket's top-sheet, was a two-page report from a Mario Scipone in New Jersey to an Anthony Bonnelli. Walker read it shaking his head, not just because of its incredible content but also because it was left practically on display. He looked up as Bascom stuck his head though the doorway, urging him to finish. Walker had to share with him on the spot some of the information the fax contained.

"Flyn, Ver Meer's now a puppet for some new players. They appear to be more the definable, organized crime types than the corporate trash we've been dealing with all along."

"Uh, partner, it could get a little dicey around here if we don't move out within the next day or two," a nervous Bascom rejoined.

Unmoved, Walker continued his commentary. "This guy Scipone must be purely fascinated with the concept of instant teleprinted communications. Can you imagine how sloppy an overall operation he must run not to destroy or at least file any record of such a damning communication as this? Maybe it's overconfidence, I don't know."

Nearly finished with his rifling of the approximately 10-inch deep paper pile, he paused at the next-to-last archive. He read a little, then turned to Bascom, holding up his prize and making quiet, stabbing gestures at it with his forefinger. He hurriedly scanned the fax memo from Phil Sloan to an O. Gam'man in Las Vegas. "Whoa, Flyn, . . . this is more curious than enlightening. I'm going to make copies of both memos with the fax machine itself and put things back as they were, then we're out of here."

The machine made a minimum of noise, but it was after-hours noise. Walker's accomplice stepped back outside the office and turned, only to be staring face to face with the security guard, his revolver drawn and sweat profuse on his red, round face.

Walker heard a strange voice bellow. "Bascom! What the hell are you doing here?" It was said with a combination of authority and relief.

Flyn recognized the guard as the one he had questioned about Bleeper Wilson. His response was instant and relaxed, "Ms. Powers asked me to wait until the fax service guy finished up. He finally got the damned thing to stop sending New Jersey messages to New Mexico," he laughed. "He's just leaving. Oh, hey man, it looks like I may be driving some for one of the new bosses. Me, I'd rather be hauling around that tight-assed Ver Meer lady, but they didn't ask me. Thanks for helpin' out the other day, brother."

Bascom turned to Walker and spoke reproachfully to him as he came through the door, a stray but official looking notebook in his hand. "Come on, champ, they must be payin' you by the year. I got to go to the airport on Mirror Magic business."

Part Two

47

The next morning in Walker's office, Flyn Bascom let out a low, slow whistle as he re-read the two fax copies he had helped secure. "Your would-be intimidator and my predecessor apparently knew a whole lot more than would seem to be justified by his position. He certainly coughed up a lot of information to Scipone, for whatever the reason. I wonder why old tight-lips would have confided so much in Prater in the first place?"

"Who knows?" shrugged Walker. "Maybe Prater was just nosy. Point is, we now know absolutely that: a) Ver Meer engineered the 'accident' that ended Jon Baxter's life, b) Phil Sloan master minded Mirror Magic's expanding efforts to subliminally, and illegally, influence viewers of its mirrored products, and finally, c) a faction of organized crime has taken effective, if not corporate, control of the tightly restricted subliminal message processing at MM. With death threats to Terrible Tersa, their interests in Mirror Magic are obviously major."

Walker continued. "But just what can be made of this mysterious second and older memo faxed to a name-smudged Las Vegas casino? It's dated several days before Sloan was killed—I surmise by the Scipone and Bonnelli crowd. As loose as this bunch is I doubt they even know about Sloan's memo to this Gam'man. It's a cryptic read, 'Unique opportunity. Expect your help with equipment. You and Chesser must be suffering in the extreme by depriving yourselves of basic needs. Call me or I'll have to send someone.'"

Bascom picked up his overnight case and started out the door. "Could be anything, Flyn. Sounds to me like an excuse for a Walker-

and-Booth junket to sin city. Now, if I may be excused, I have to see to my ABC's. I know you think preparing a course lesson plan is akin to one of your industry distributor's picking up the phone to take a calendar re-order, but it ain't Ben. And don't call me, I'll call you."

48

"Ben, sweetheart, first you spend yet another evening with Flyn doing industrial espionage. Then immediately upon your return you whisk away to Las Vegas the only remaining member of this twosome interested in the day-to-day welfare of Baxter Products," said Amanda.

Walker started to counter but her barrage had just begun. "But as if that weren't enough, you don't even have hotel reservations for us. So here we are, checking out half-a-dozen hotels before you settle for the one with the best free lunch in town. And now you drag me downstairs at Circus-Circus to watch some clown run through a juggling routine. Don't we have work to do?"

Walker looked at her with one corner of his mouth made into a deep dimple, reflecting his chagrin. "I told you we had to find which hotel, if any, this guy Gam'man calls his gambling headquarters. We got lucky and found it. Now I want to catch a glimpse of him. I put a couple of top-line Baxter Products samples on the bellman and he described our subject for me and tipped me off that our boy frequents this act. It seems he fancies these object-manipulation bits. You know something? This is great stuff! Ellison should be here."

The performer's tipsy-appearing male assistant was introducing items into the juggler's start-up routine, one at a time on the juggler's cues. First came an apple, joined in turn by an orange. Then in place of the lemon tease the assistant first held up, in flew a long-bladed knife. Appearing unsettled over this, but without a drop, the fretting juggler again called for the lemon.

In came a second knife, apparently causing the performer to lose his composure, but not the four juggled objects. After some icy looks in the direction of his assistant and comments about cheap help, he broadly mouthed a request for a ball, while appearing to struggle with the four items being juggled two-per-hand. The confused assistant puzzled over a variety of balls lying on the stage table; the audience howled as he selected a bowling ball. The juggler gasped as it came to him in a low, two-handed, but perfectly-timed throw which he caught in a staggering and exaggerated recovery, all the while cursing his assistant.

He made several complete passes with all five objects, then dropped the bowling ball. He placed one foot atop it while throwing the two pieces of fruit high into the air, followed by the two knives at a lower height. Seconds later the two knives fell to the wooden stage floor, points down and quivering, one on either side of the performer. He then caught the fruit, one piece in each hand, sweeping his arms back in a triumphant flourish.

The recorded music came up and the performer took a grand bow on the final note. The audience, children and adults alike, applauded furiously, exchanging amazed glances with their neighbors. Amanda said upon the act's conclusion, not nearly as impressed as Walker, "Ben, what are the chances of us actually spotting your . . . " Walker interrupted her.

"There he is, the one who just stood up in the front row, applauding. The one who looks like either Larry of The Three Stooges, or Telly Savalas in a cheap toupee. Stay here, Amanda," said Walker. "I'll be right back. I just want to get a closer look." He eased down next to the object of his search and satisfied himself, even risking a glance at his face while managing not to catch his eye.

Walker knew he needed to make a clear ID, but hadn't the foggiest notion what he would do with the knowledge.

49

Ben and Amanda had located their man, gotten a room at the inn, and even managed to be booked on the same floor as Gam'man. They didn't yet have a game plan and they hadn't eaten, so after they had refreshed themselves in their room they went down to one of the show lounges for dinner and planning. No sooner had they walked within earshot of the live big band sound pouring through the huge open doors of the lounge than Walker began grinning and snapping his fingers to the one type of music he found so satisfyingly infectious. They were barely through the doorway when Ben whirled Amanda out onto the well-trafficked dance floor, covering it with fast-paced steps and tight-spins with his grinning, head-shaking partner.

While Amanda didn't share all his passions, she nevertheless found Ben's out-of-era music interesting enough to want to know what had fostered it. "What's the name of that vaguely familiar tune, Mr. Astaire?" she asked, out of breath and back at the floorside table that had cost Ben a $20 tip.

"Why, thank you, Ginger," he smiled. "It's really no step for a dancer. But in answer to your question, that tune may well be the world's most famous theme song: Benny Goodman's 'Let's Dance.'"

Her question set Walker off on his big band tangent. "Goodman had a three-hour radio show in 1935 that ran for nearly six months and was the longest sponsored musical program that had ever been broadcast to that time. He was one of the gods of swing," he said with semi-reverence.

"Interesting" she said, "I enjoy some of the big band sounds that seem to be coming back in vogue now, too, but I prefer the more contemporary appeal of a Harry Connick, Jr. You'd call his music swing, too, wouldn't you?"

"Well, yes, when he bothers to play it." Walker was a purist with respect to his music. Swing and its artists were sweet history for him and that history began in 1935 and ended in 1946, although experts recognized its roots as having come from the native American music—jazz—as early as the 1890s, in New Orleans.

"But," he continued with his narrative, "the epitome of these artists, to me, was the swinging-rhythm arch-rivalry between Benny Goodman and Artie Shaw. Well, throw in a little Woody Herman and Harry James, but that's about it. I dote on it."

Amanda was still curious and very much wanted to draw him out. She wanted to learn more about what made her man run. She had decided she was going to allow Ben to chase her until she was ready to be caught. "How did you come by this motivation?" she asked. "It's just not from our era."

"I'm not certain. It sort of developed over the years. My father loved the big band music. He wasn't a professional musician but when he was only 18 years old he travelled while selling for an Iowa agricultural feed company and on several occasions he got fill-in jobs playing trumpet for big bands like Lawrence Welk." His eyes moistened as he thought of his father and the early mentor role he had filled for him.

"Your father must have been a great influence on you. I'm sorry I never got to meet him, Ben," Amanda said softly. Tell me more about him." Opportunities to get to basic understandings about someone special are usually fleeting and often develop spontaneously. Amanda didn't want to overlook this one.

Walker smiled. "He was my first hero, a charismatic competitor at whatever he undertook—from his music, to selling, to the telling of a story. Let me illustrate his ability to seize that rare moment that most of us don't realize is even galloping upon us until the event is long gone. The story is a two-parter. Part one sets it up.

Dad was at the Marine Recruit Depot in San Diego, California, in the spring of 1944. He had badgered my Mother into finally signing the papers legally necessary for him to enlist at age 28 with three children at home and four brothers already in military service.

I wouldn't be born for another seven years yet. Dad had been breaking horses for a civilian mounted patrol in Des Moines and Mom was an inspector for the same ordinance plant where Dad was working, making heavy caliber ammunition." Walker was a fair story teller himself and he knew how to weave in a few background details to make it more interesting to the listener.

"My mother thought his obsession to enlist in the military was stupid. She would have to manage with very little money and three little children plus her own mother to provide for. She agreed only on the condition that he not join the Marines. Well, of the 35 Navy enlistees in Dad's group he was the first of seven that a Marine Captain 'volunteered' for assignment to the Marine Corps. I remember Dad telling me that when he objected by telling the recruiting captain of his age and the number of his children, the Marine officer replied with, 'Perfect, I like a man with maturity and responsibilities.'" Walker laughed.

"That doesn't seem fair," said Amanda.

"It wasn't, but it's the hand he was dealt. He made the most of it. The second part of the story makes the point about my father seizing the moment," he said.

"Ten days before Dad was due to ship out to Camp Pendleton, California, for advanced infantry training, to which he was looking forward—as he used to say, like a hog about to be castrated—he ran into a former high school band director who recognized Dad and told him about a base band being formed. The director added that the band wouldn't be leaving for Camp Pendleton for a while." Ben shook his head, smiling.

"Dad phoned Mom immediately and told her not to sell his trumpet, as they had earlier decided to do, but to send it to him right away. He had one week to practice before the audition for trumpet players, but he hadn't played the horn since his first and only year in college, 11 years prior. He had been known to have an 'iron lip,' but he wasn't very good at reading music. Anyway, the trumpet arrived and he was moved into the band barracks and started to practice six to eight hours a day. He wanted that deferment desperately, however brief it might be."

"Would that have kept him stateside?" asked Amanda.

"All Dad knew was that it would have slowed down his being shipped out. He ultimately fought in the South Pacific on both Guam and Iwo Jima. But back to the story.

There were 22 guys auditioning for two remaining spots in the trumpet section. Dad had won first place in a state high school trumpet competition for his play of 'Flight of the Bumblebee.' If you're not familiar with that tune, Amanda, it's a demanding arrangement full of rills and glissandos. But Dad had played it a thousand times and he knew it inside out, so that's what he practiced in order to get back his 'lip.'

"Then came the day for auditions. He went early and sidled up to the cracked door of the auditorium room to observe what was going on. He soon realized something very interesting. The director would flip through the sheet music and ask each individual trumpet player, as he came in, if he knew those songs. If the Marine said 'yes' he would keep going until the player said 'no,' then the director would ask him to play that tune. Poor bastards."

"What happened on your Dad's turn?" Amanda prodded needlessly.

Ben laughed again. "When Dad's name was called he went in and the director began the same routine. But as he flipped through the sheet music asking Dad if he knew this, that and the other, Dad would reply enthusiastically, 'Yeah I know that, yes, yes, yes, I know that,' until he came to 'Flight of the Bumblebee.' Then he said, 'No, I don't.' The director said, 'Play that.'" Ben broke up at his own story, then continued.

"Dad was a showman. He said, 'Flight of the Bumblebee?' The director was emphatic. Dad put the music on the rack and looked it over carefully as he knitted a little frown onto his face. Then he cleared his throat and his trumpet and purely ripped into it. As Dad told it, during the other auditions the director would gaze out the window while each guy blew out his guts with unfamiliar tunes. He did the same before Dad started to play. But after the first few bars he had to look directly at Dad because he was playing the hell out of a very difficult piece. When he finished, the director said, 'You never played that before, huh, Marine?' Dad just grinned and the auditioner said, 'Report to the band, Private.'

"What a great story, Ben!" said Amanda, beaming at the fairytale ending.

"And to top it off," he said, "the next day the band was out on the parade field playing 'Colors' and a Chief Warrant Officer who was the assistant band leader stood by each player, listening to him. After he listened to Dad he said, 'Walker, you don't play well but you damned sure play loud, and that's what I like.'

"Now I understand how it is that your taste in music carried over a generation," said Amanda. "Osmosis."

"Thanks for asking, Love. But enough of that. Let's order dinner. We have devious plans to lay and a short time in which to do it." He wobbled his eyebrows and Amanda laughed. Tonight she had indeed learned something; her man was a cross between Harry James and Groucho Marx.

50

The next evening after they hadn't been able to find Gam'man at either of the two early juggling performances, Ben and Amanda congratulated themselves when they spotted him at one of the gaming tables—apparently alone. According to plan, Amanda took up a place next to him, smiling and hesitantly mentioning aloud that she was a novice at Baccarat, but maybe she could catch on before she lost too much of her boyfriend's money. Gam'man didn't seem particularly interested, however, only commenting politely that she might be better off at the craps table. "Better odds, my dear," he offered his minimal advice.

He was a subtly odd-looking individual. Not at first glance, but if one studied him it seemed that some of his features were just ever so slightly different. Difficult to pin down except for one somewhat disconcerting characteristic: his fingers seemed to have a third joint. They didn't really appear any longer overall, but when they grasped a beverage glass they seemed to clasp the vessel rather than grip it. Well, Amanda had once seen someone at college with a similar digital aberration so it wasn't absolutely unusual.

Seeing that Amanda was well-positioned to cover Walker during his clandestine check of Gam'man's room, he used a house phone to call housekeeping, asking for a larger-wattage light bulb to be brought to room 1250.

"I'm on my way up now from the main floor," Walker spoke as if he could hardly contain himself. "I've just hit the jackpot of my life and I want to count it in a good private light, ma'am. You tell whoever brings up my bulb that I'll tip her a hundred dollars. Yes, siree, a hundred bucks."

He knew there would be no delegation of responsibility. Up to now he had been getting by nicely with a few five-dollar bills and generous distribution of some hand-picked samples of BP products. The price for special services had just gone up.

He waited until the maid was just coming out of Gam'man's room, a frown on her face at apparently missing out on her promised bonus. She had been stiffed many times, however, and she knew her life had many more yet to come. From around the corner, Walker suddenly appeared and placed his hand on the still-opened door, a smile on his face and his tie askew, with a wad of bills held in his hand. "Now, how much did I promise you for the light bulb, little lady?" he said, slurring his speech.

The maid looked worried. She also sized up the look and smell of the apparently lucky gambler. He didn't appear to be one of the high-rollers who were regularly 'comped' their rooms, but more like a typical conventioneer who had hit it tonight and would surely lose it all tomorrow—with interest.

She valued her job and was about to ask to see his room card when Walker pulled out two one-hundred dollar bills. She took them quickly, thanking him and moving out of the way, blinking her eyes twice as if to square with practicality her rare compromise with integrity and hotel policy.

51

Walker hoped for anything which would take some of the mystery out of the Sloan-Scipone-Gam'man puzzle. He knew full well that he was at risk, both with the bad guys and with the law, but he reconciled his actions with the gravity of the need. He had no idea what he was looking for but he would surely recognize it when he saw it. It had been proven on several occasions that this group, as a whole, tended to be lax with records and security.

Now that he was inside the room and looking around, what was this? Apparently two people were occupying the suite. It featured a single over-sized and well-appointed living room with a bedroom and bath at either end of the room, but with only one door to the hallway. Both occupants were apparently staying for more than a few days since clothes were hung neatly and no suitcases were sitting around.

Having no idea of how little time he might have, Walker immediately began searching for anything that might address either the individuals or their business. On the desk in one bedroom he noticed what appeared at first to be an odd-looking reading lamp. The device had a large, circular, fluorescent-type tube. In its center was a thin marble obelisk with a platform at the top supporting a rectangular, open frame. Curiosity obliged him to press one of several switches located at the base of the device. Doing so caused the tube to lighten to a brilliant blue. A single line of copy suddenly appeared within the reference frame, which read simply, "Gamesman Guidelines."

Walker could understand the bluish cast to the light compared to the white of fluorescent light or the reddish-orange glow of a neon lamp; it was probably due to a few drops of mercury having been added to the inert neon gas. What intrigued him, aside from the ambiguous words themselves was the automatic alignment of the strangely ornate type. It remained perpendicular to the line of sight of the operator, even though he circled the object to test the effect. He could think of no particular user benefit to such an otherwise marvelous hologrammatic feature, but he filed it away in his mind. Unable to coax any further display from the machine he abandoned that attraction for other, more potentially concrete clues.

In a drawer next to the bed in the same room was a leather-bound diary with a gold foil-stamped 'O. Gam'man.' Trying to make an association with the title he had just seen, he puzzled, Gam'man. Gam-man. Game-man, gamesman! Contraction for gamesman? But games? What kind of game? And how would that be relevant to anything?

Walker had read only two pages when he knew he would have to steal the diary. Borrow it. He was not immune from the need to rationalize even marginally unethical decisions. Just then he heard the unmistakable 'click' of a room entrance card releasing the living room door lock. He had a 50-50 chance of avoiding instant detection and confrontation. His mind flashed the possibilities. He liked one. The diary certainly belonged to Gam'man and since Amanda was likely to be occupying his attention, the entrant was probably the inhabitant of the other bedroom. The visitor thus would have no reason to come into Gam'man's private room from the common room. But how to exit? The real problem came down to which of two events would come first; Gam'man's eventual retirement from the tables or the visitor's retirement for his night's sleep. Unless of course the roommate was a female and she chose to offer up a little nightcap for Gam'man when he rolled in.

Chesser was tired, not from any activity of his own, but from watching the annoying seesawing of Gam'man's evening fortunes. Gam'man's gaming activities were quite unlike those of Chesser, who would cease gambling altogether in the second half of any four-hour session whenever he had lost approximately one-half of his initial stake. Almost invariably Chesser doubled his stake within the first few minutes of gambling, but this system ensured him a minimum 33⅓ percent return on his investment and caused no undue suspicion on the part of the various casinos in Vegas. He rotated among them during their regular week-long visits.

Chesser still revelled in the excitement of the risk, minimal as it was compared to Gam'man's. Chesser's associate was not really concerned with return-on-investment, only with participation. Accumulation of proceeds, beyond those required for their modest needs away from the casinos, did not appeal to Gam'man. Being at the tables did. In fact, to avoid the disastrous consequences of being banned from the tables as a 'counter' or other equally undesirable gaming customer, he deliberately lost considerable sums from time to time. This entitled them to a complimentary suite any time they cared to clock in on the floor. The real source of their income fell to the reliable result of Chesser's Rules-of-Ration.

Now Chesser had decided to view again the casino's closed circuit video presentation of how-to-play. He knew it almost verbatim, but he enjoyed watching the croupiers' deft moves as they controlled the game. But first he would change into his night clothes before returning to the living room and a warm beverage. He hit the TV's remote 'on' button and got up.

Walker could hear both moves but had hidden himself in the walk-in closet and could see nothing. He broke out in a sweat until he heard a muffled sound that suggested it had come from the opposite bedroom. The uninvited visitor quickly exited the suite and proceeded hastily to his own room.

Walker just as quickly packed both his and Amanda's things and called for his bellman by name, checking out via computerized room monitor. He then found Amanda still gamely at her assignment. She caught his high-sign and excused herself politely, saying "Oh, I think I see my boyfriend, Mr. Gam'man. Won't he be surprised that I quadrupled his money. Thank you so much for your help. I hope we meet again."

52

Mario Scipone was troubled. He usually was given the nature of his business and that of the man for whom he worked. It was true Tony Bonnelli had slowed with age and Scipone ran things on a day-to-day basis, but the old man liked to serve up little reminders every now and then as to who still sat at the head of the table. This latest upset was mellow compared to some. Scipone had been pressing for a new direction altogether and recently it appeared that Boss Bonnelli might finally be ready to relinquish his watch.

It was Scipone, the underboss, who had turned up the subliminal mirror scam of Sloan's, and it was Scipone who had made much of its potential for the organization. His initial exuberance over the prospects stemmed almost as much from the mere discovery of the incredible—and wonderfully undercover—operation by Mirror Magic as it did from the opportunity to take what Scipone saw as the biggest single step forward in the history of the Bonnelli family.

"Tony," he said, "with our newly-found potential ability to influence the outcome of elections we could move into new territories as well as new businesses. We can offer the other bosses new revenues while we still take a healthy cut. In five years we can control all of New York and then look to the rest of the country. They'll line up behind us like we were doin' the 'Bunny Hop.'"

Bonnelli didn't see it that way. "Mario, bigger don't mean better. Bigger soaks up cash and causes jealousies you can't control. If I had the energy today to stay on top of things I would say to you, 'No, stick to what we know.' This Mirror Magic thing is a rich vein in a small mine. It's true we could be carrying out gold for a while but we'd wind up advertising 'success.' And that ain't good in our business."

He slumped heavily into his overstuffed desk chair and swiveled to face Scipone with a deep sigh. "But . . . ," he said, "the love for the struggle has gone from me. These days I worry more about a good healthy crap than I do about money, power or women. You'll be sitting in this chair before long. Maybe you're right and the times have passed me by. Do what you think is best. But one thing is sacred; do not cause me embarrassment. For that sin, should you live, even the capos and soldiers would desert you."

53

Once Phillip Sloan had been eliminated from the Mirror Magic picture, Scipone's next step was to remove double M's corporate attorney. It wasn't difficult since the law firm's principal was quietly eager to be out of the MM loop due to the many marginally legal requests they had been asked to deliver over the years. The underboss effected a controlling-interest stock purchase of Mirror Magic in the name of one of the Bonnelli family's holding companies.

Tersa Ver Meer, Scipone's newly installed Mirror Magic president, sat cross-legged opposite him while he occupied her desk chair in the Atlanta office. He was animated, painting the scenarios of his new business plan which she was more than competent to administrate. In fact, once he had explained the election-influence concept, she was way ahead of him and quickly became bored with his redundancy. Typically, in such tedious situations with virile males she would first tune them out, and then, with ever so slight shifts in her posture and facial expressions, begin toying with that most convenient focus of her contempt for males in general—the man himself.

She could no more resist her ingrained nature for male seduction than her much younger and estranged, but happily married sister could avoid looking like the Sunday morning choir singer that she was. Tersa Ver Meer enjoyed—if that was the word for someone who had long ago put her emotions on automatic pilot—her ability to cause men to react predictably to their ill-concealed lust for her.

Her deeply tanned and bared legs were accented by her four-inch high, red-heeled shoes. One of these 'triggers' she began slowly but rhythmically pumping while Scipone talked. His attempts to keep his eyes fastened on hers would have been more comical than stimulating to anyone but a voyeur. He had already taken her once since they first met, but that had only fueled his lust rather than satiated it.

She had underestimated the capricious nature of Mario Scipone, however. He suddenly lunged from where he was sitting behind her desk and grabbed her cheeks and chin in one hand, pressing them painfully between his thumb and fingers. He spoke to her from what passed as his soul. "Whore, if you don't un-train yourself to appeal to my maleness when we are at work, I will personally disfigure you in such a way that would cause even the sorriest pimp in Manhattan to reject you."

He released her but continued his harangue. "The fact is that if you didn't have certain unique knowledge of the subliminal-processing operation you would be of no use to us whatever. But for that, you are as expendable as yesterday's newspaper."

Ver Meer was not intimidated. She had been to the edge many times before. She was first of all a survivor, and it was for that reason that her response was an apparent capitulation. "What's your pleasure, boss?" Had she not uncrossed her legs and pulled slightly at her dress at the same time she smiled, she had no doubt that Scipone would have hit her squarely in the mouth, thereby, ironically, continuing to heighten his growing anticipation. It was she, after all, who was in control.

For the moment Scipone brought himself back to the business at hand. "I'm returning Mirror Magic's subliminally-programmed products exclusively to this specialized advertising business. Offering our product benefits to larger, but non-advertising based industries only increases our risk for exposure." He would give credit to Bonnelli for that concession so that he might go forward with his own much more intriguing political agenda.

"Terminate all activities and contracts in that respect, Tersa, my lovely. Simultaneous with that action we will begin to offer overt financial support to those metro New York and Jersey borough and city candidates who have only," he emphasized the next word, "marginal chances for winning election. "That will be an unexpected but greatly appreciated monetary blessing for them.

"That, combined with a new distribution to the electorate of massive numbers of subliminally-processed pocket mirrors, plus the charitable donation of thousands of city-wide public restroom wall mirrors, will guarantee our success at the polls."

Ver Meer gave voice to the obvious objection. "Since MM is headquartered here in Atlanta, what would be the supposed motivation on the part of a suddenly benevolent Mirror Magic for such a magnanimous public works program in New York City? Only one plant is even located in the general area, and that's in Jersey."

She was correct in her quickly-formed suspicion that Mario Scipone relished his call-the-shots role in the 'new' Bonnelli family.

He responded, his ego as a planner being stronger than his normal male chauvinism. At least for the moment. "Mirror Magic will simply be the new kid on the block who needs to establish credibility within the community. We'll move the headquarters to Long Island, employment problems or no. Or wherever in the area you can make the best deal. The Jersey operation stays where it is, I don't want to upset that situation.

"And leave the new North Carolina deal alone as well because we'll certainly need the additional capacity. I want it all up and running within six months. That will give us at least another six months before the campaigns heat up. Baby, we're gonna run New York like its never been run before."

"We, Mario?" she said in her usual caustic tone. "Like maybe you're cutting me in for more than a car lease and a week-to-week salary when you just finished bragging that once you get the hang of Sloan's cute little machines I'll be dead weight?"

"Okay, I was hot at the time. Fact is," he admitted, "we need your experience as well as your expertise to keep up both appearances and profits in this promotional products business. It's our perfect cover. Once we move into Boston, Philly, Miami—yeah—and maybe Chicago and L.A., too, we'll even offer expensive but guaranteed protection for drug operations."

His eyes blazed and his voice cracked as he caught a glimpse in neon of his grandiose schemes. "Hell, with our people in office we'll have everyone standing in line with sacks of cash, waiting to purchase 'Scipone Insurance.'"

He had worked himself to a fever pitch, caught up in the enormity of one man's falsely based, but nevertheless accelerating warp of infallibility. He needed a release from such heady stuff and his attention was easily diverted. His mind was quickly riveted by the incredible taunt Tersa Ver Meer continued to present with a minimum of effort.

Scipone stared at the bright red-tipped and ripened legs, again crossed and slowly pumping to a personal rhythm that communicated a universal message. Scipone's groin made a command decision which dramatically shifted the emphasis of the moment. It only remained for him to choose a location; the floor or the couch. Tersa Ver Meer could have cared less. For her the moment had already peaked, with Scipone's base instinct having been brought to heel.

54

The business of Baxter Products was decidedly bearish in a bullish economy. Sales volume was off, the order count down, projects were delayed. Things were being run by a rudderless committee. Walker fully realized all this only because Amanda had pointed it out. Everything but MM had been pushed to the back of his mind. He hadn't even been making it to his standing racquetball game. He felt that he must not be distracted by anything in dealing with the deepening Mirror Magic threat posed by Ver Meer, Scipone, and now, possibly, by Gam'man and Chesser as well. He had taken himself out of everything else. Forced to face the situation he now made a decision to reverse himself on an earlier one.

"Amanda, you know our corporate objectives and marketing plan as well as anyone, and you have a better feel for what's actually happening in the marketplace. Since I can't clone myself in order to follow two critical paths at the same time, tomorrow morning I'm going to announce your appointment as acting executive vice president. Congratulations, once again you're an employee."

Amanda Booth wasn't expecting this turn of events. She was flattered and excited by the responsibility, which she knew she could handle. Or at least she could once her stamp of resolution became as crystal clear to the others as it was for her. She would much rather have stayed a part of the MM chase, but she knew instinctively that this was a correct decision by Ben.

Downplaying her true reaction, Amanda said dryly, "Before you leave town again, Mr. Walker, please so advise payroll of the change. I don't want to have to be invoicing the company like a common consultant for my grossly inflated new salary."

"Whoa, Amanda. That's exactly why the title includes the word 'acting.'" said Walker. "This development isn't in the budget. In fact, I was hoping you'd go along with the same pay rate as before since I'd have to get the full board's approval for such a move. Right now Muriel Baxter is out of the country."

"Ben Walker, you cheapskate! I know damned well you're putting me on. You wouldn't need board approval at this place if you wanted to open up a satellite factory on the moon. If my first check doesn't reflect a healthy increase in what you've been paying me I'm going to kick off a new national promotion and it will cost you dearly—dear." She caught her breath and continued, "I'll offer unlimited free speculative samples on the entire line—to some 9,000 distributors. You'll wish you had tripled my salary."

"Now you're talking like the marketing genius I know you for, Amanda. Great idea! You'll probably double our sales and profits before the year's out. Be certain to put my name on the offer."

He knew he could find a compromise somewhere out on his limb. Actually it was becoming more of a rope-walking trick—working with a lover in a corporate environment. The fact that it was poor judgement to begin with may yet prove to be the least of his problems, he thought.

The exchange with Amanda, however, had caused him to relax somewhat from the tension that had been occupying and building in his mind based on what he knew awaited him in the days ahead. Right now he needed a second strong ally, and then a plan. He knew where to find the former but he had no clue as to the latter.

55

Walker caught a late Saturday morning flight to Tallahassee. Flyn and Janie Bascom picked him up at the airport. Janie was at the wheel and surprised them both when her husband inquired of the luncheon menu.

"I don't know," she grinned. "You'll have to ask the waiter at the lodge. This cook is taking the afternoon off with two handsome men."

The 'lodge' was a 1930s-built spa hotel situated about 15 miles south of Tallahassee in a rural area of Florida's eastern panhandle where the term 'sparsely populated' meant most communities counted their population in the hundreds, if not the tens. The Springs sat hard by a 185-foot deep, cold, clear-water spring. It was locally famous, not much commercialized and recently taken over by the state. Its role as background for a few Tarzan and later, James Bond, movies yielded to slightly greater tourist interest in Old Joe, a famed 200-year-old alligator now deceased and stuffed. He sat surveying his territory from a perch in the Old South, high-ceilinged hotel lobby. Walker had visited many times as a student and was pleased to re-visit.

The more temperate Panhandle had been *the* Florida area for snowbirds from Europe, as well as North America, prior to the advent of refrigeration and air conditioning. The southern half of the state, before that civilizing technology, offered only a hot, damp, bug-and-jungle environment for resident or visitor.

The threesome stepped out onto a Hemingway-imagined, screened veranda where the building's curved red-brick tile roof was brushed by air-nourished spanish moss hanging from host hardwoods. Janie had made reservations for them. After a delicious and not-so-light lunch, she insisted on taking Ben for a short tour of the grounds, complete with a one-story ride in the operate-it-yourself vintage elevator with a steel, accordion-like, inner 'safety' door.

Rejuvenated, they then drove to the Bascom house. All this was calculated by Janie Bascom to allow perspective to set in before discussion of the Mirror Magic problem Ben kept heaping upon Flyn and—by implication—herself.

No sooner had they walked through the front arch of the Bascom's spanish-style home than Walker posed a question, "Flyn, what do you think will be man's greatest challenge in the decade following the '90s?"

"Whoa, Ben. Mind if I have a seat before I tackle trivia?" responded Bascom.

The two men sat heavily, the luncheon dessert making its contribution. "Okay, here it is, since you ask. I opt for problems caused by increasingly frequent and sustained power failures. In fact, they may periodically paralyze the more heavily industrialized societies of the world.

"Seizing on that fact, Mr. Walker, the front page events will be claimed by terrorist-like 'have-not' groups. They will correctly perceive that traffic light chaos is the ultimate weapon by which they can command the instant attention of the 'haves.' There's no risk of retribution that would endanger themselves or their own families. All demands will be met." He smiled faintly, his eyes widened as he extended two open palms.

Walker laughed. "Sorry I asked, professor. I was hoping for a simple 'I don't know, what-did-you-have-in-mind?' response."

He sighed and prefaced his own answer by bringing both of them up to date with everything that had happened to himself and Amanda during the Las Vegas trip. He ignored their head-shaking.

"Now," he concluded, "how does one fight—let alone succeed—against patently illegal but so far unprovable manufacturing and marketing competition, including murder, (he omitted the qualifier 'of a close friend') which we believe to be rooted in organized crime's interests? And as if that weren't enough, the two most unlikely characters imaginable have apparently invited themselves to dinner."

Bascom and his wife looked at each other and then at Walker before Janie deadpanned, "Give us a feel for what these 'guests' dining tastes run to."

Skeptics, he thought. Attack this intellectually, not emotionally, Walker. He paused for breath and for some degree of order as to how he might frame his random thoughts. If he were going to get serious support from his only true outside resource he had better be convincing to both of them. The pair came as a package.

"I've already told you something of this Gam'man character," Walker continued. "But let me be more specific. First of all, Amanda observed him very carefully, having spent more than an hour with him at a gaming table. He is quite unassuming.

"Of a more concrete nature, I have in my possession his personal diary. It is difficult to understand, but I've gained some startling revelations." Here it comes, he thought. "It's the diary of an alien life-form! Seriously! I've no idea why it is written in English unless it's because they've been among us for a very long time.

"This is the first time in my life I have ever used the words 'alien life-form' in a thoughtful conversation," he said. "I've always bought into UFO's just because of the volume and the sheer persistence of minor evidence over so many decades, but as for encounters of the third kind . . . "

Walker looked at Janie, then back at Flyn. He said, "That was the reason for my earlier philosophical question. Once reports attributable to credible witnesses are made public, official or otherwise, I think I can safely say that these aliens' story will be considered the high-water human interface of the millennium. How do you two think such a bombshell will impact people around the world? And what do you make of it personally?"

Since his and Amanda's return from Las Vegas Walker had not wanted to focus on anything but the subliminal-plot intricacies, but he could no longer simply ignore the incredible ramifications of the apparent extraterrestrials. He was bursting to explore its meaning with the Bascoms.

Janie took the lead. "Well, if you are indeed correct in this, Ben, before it's through it will probably be referred to as the first officially authenticated ET contact in the history of man, thus the end of the cultural isolation of the human race. We will therefore no longer be 'it,' as most people prefer to think of man and intelligent beings."

Personally, she had always expected that such initial contact—inevitable, in her consideration—would be peaceful versus hostile, but she had never given a thought to the introduction being competitive, which is what the circumstances were suggesting.

"First thing you know they'll be buying out the Japanese," she added. Humor masked her fear. Having given perhaps too quick credence to Walker's claim of the existence of aliens on earth, Janie now found herself rejecting it from a philosophical perspective.

Flyn picked up the thread. "Well, I don't believe this contact with your Gam'man represents anything other than what it has been. Theirs must certainly be a private effort if these two are indeed extraterrestrials. If they were part of a representative governing body—or even if they were merely riding 'point' for some collaborative thrust—then contact would not have been coincidental as this has been."

He, too, had considered the subject of intelligent alien contact on more than one occasion, although he and Janie had never had an open discussion of the matter—probably because it would have seemed too frivolous.

Bascom introduced a different line of thinking. "I believe we can safely assume that this is not the leading edge of an invasion of any kind. We probably have more to be concerned about with Japanomics and volatility in the Middle East and Europe then we do from the Gilligan's Islandesque appearance of these two supposed extraterrestrials. This is not to down play the very real threat posed by Mirror Magic, Ben."

Walker wanted Bascom's rationale for that statement. He obliged. "What we see is probably what we get. Consider that even for a civilization far advanced from our own it would be enormously expensive, and technically, extremely difficult to justify anything like mass interstellar travel. Remember, we're not talking a mere quarter-of-a-million mile jaunt to Earth's only moon, or even a six-year sabbatical to Jupiter in our own solar system. What we're talking about in our technologic time reference is a hundred human lifetimes, one-way, just to bring a few folks around for a 'how-y'all-doin' visit."

"So, then, just what would they be doing in our neighborhood?" Walker asked.

Bascom proceeded to hazard a guess. "Well, if you buy my previous reasoning, then it follows that only the most extreme crisis could justify mass movement of a civilization. Since neither Gam'man nor his associate have appeared to anyone either out-of-breath or with the ultimate block-busting announcement, we can safely assume we aren't about to be colonized. Further, since these folks don't seem to be taking over governments or cities, or even abducting citizens, then these very few visitors may be here merely by accident."

"Accident?" Walker shook his head. "You mean they blew a transmission?"

"Well, if they were actually vacationing I don't think they would be spending their time playing Blackjack," Bascom made his point. "Individual interstellar travel would be far less prohibitive, given that the technology for its accomplishment existed. But that's about as far as I can take it, Ben, and I may be way off base at that."

Janie wasn't satisfied. "So, where does that leave us?" she challenged. "And why do you, Ben, feel so compelled—and me so apprehensive—about your use of the dreaded 'we' pronoun linking Flyn with this never-ending Mirror Magic adventure-turning-nightmare?"

"Janie," comforted her husband, "you know we're all hooked on this." He took her loosely in her arms and looked at her compassionately. "I know your concern is protective but Ben-O here represents the original minority, sweetheart. He's a certifiable do-gooder with honest but hallucinatory tendencies and, unfortunately for us, a best friend.

"Look," he added, sensing her need for positive reinforcement, "when this is all over we'll take some time off together and travel. Professor's honor." He bussed her lips and released her gently.

With that issue somewhat laid to rest, Walker launched into his now fast-forming scenario. "This has gotten far too big for us. We need serious help. Plan A is to take the whole schmear to a federal agency—the National Security Council, I would say. We can present what evidence we have of the extraterrestrials and their obvious trespass in everything American—from falsifying birth certificates, to counterfeiting social security and draft registration, to bogus driver's licenses. Not to mention their possible involvement with Sloan in unfair business practices.

"We add to this collaboration with organized crime and that's it. Zap! The NSC will either corral 'em for trial or assassinate 'em and then cover it up. In either event, Mirror Magic will be out of the subliminal advertising business, Jon Baxter's death will have been properly avenged, and you and I can get on with our own lives and interests."

Ben liked the tidiness of the idea far better than the odds for success. He really felt this was a legitimate matter of national concern. He also felt the need to be solicitous of the pairs' input even if he had come to town for the Bascom's rubber stamp of approval for whatever course of action he decided upon.

"What do you think, Dr. Bascom?"

"I prefer Plan B, whatever it is," he said dryly. "Ben, don't take this unkindly but we're going to need to see some hard evidence before the Flying Bascoms are willing to take on a new catcher for this no-net act.

"And I don't think others are going to buy in. We're talking about the Feds. "You won't need me for this sortie anyway. Go ahead and get it out of your system. When you're through butting your head against granite come back home to regroup."

"Thanks for the support, sport, but I think you're wrong," Walker persisted.

56

Two weeks later Walker was back in Tallahassee relating to Flyn Bascom the classical failure of an unconnected novice trying to find a receptive ear within the bureaucratic (i. e., lip service-sympathetic) tangle in Washington D.C.

"The best I could do," he explained, "was an appointment with three different assistants-to-the-assistant of departments which had no apparent relationship whatever to the NSC. They all clucked and said how much they appreciated my coming forward with such information, but that my commercial competition problems were a part of America's strength—free enterprise, you know—even if that meant as one quintessential bureaucrat put it 'lasers from outer space.'

"The absolute best I can hope for, Flyn, is that they put my report in a jacket with my name on it labelled, 'Communist/Paranoid/Dopehead/Bears Watching.' Trouble is, that means it'll be two years before they get around to putting a tap on my phone. By then the barn door will have been open for so long all the antennae-folk will have deeper burrows and newer scams."

Bascom was unsympathetic, "Okay, you had to do your conscience-thing, Ben. Now just say the magic word and you win $10. It's a common word, something you find around think-tanks."

"Plan B," said Walker. "And I worked it out on the flight back. Let me lay it out for you. The civilian/scientific committee that was formed to develop project objectives for the flight to Jupiter and beyond, which was launched in October of 1989, meets regularly and is scheduled to convene again in Washington in less than a month."

"That's interesting," said Bascom." As a matter of fact, Janie's best friend is the part-time liaison for the academic coordination of this committee. It also has a standing member here at the university."

"That's right," Janie chimed in. "But not much has been happening in the early months. Frankly, I haven't kept tabs on things of late. I've been too busy acting a cameo role in 'Murder, They Wrote.'"

"She could be very useful—your friend," said Walker. "And we have one other wild card as well. My trip to D.C. did put one little check in the pro column. The new House committee chairman is none other than Buddy Jamison, the former Florida state representative whose advertising campaign I managed during my senior year. You remember him, Flyn."

"Of course. The highlight political event of the decade," he said semi-facetiously.

"Well he's a ranking member of the U.S. House of Representatives. I don't know why I didn't contact him first. I guess because we had lost contact with one another over the years. Anyway, I ran into him in Washington at a low-level reception I was trying to crash on my last-ditch day in the city. He was on his way out but he recognized me and cleared me to get in. He seemed to be delighted to see me again but didn't have time to talk.

"We met for lunch the next day and I cashed in an I.O.U. on the spot. He told me about his new chair with the Jupiter Committee and the upcoming meeting. I figured any hearing was a good hearing for our purpose so I told him my story. I was worried about how he would react, but with some convincing he agreed to put both you and me on the agenda."

"What's your thinking on this, Ben?" asked Bascom.

"We need this forum. We can use it to get some publicity and create legitimate media interest in pursuing an otherwise too bizarre story. The national news media know that highly visible, government-affiliated committees, reputable scientists and leaders shun tabloid coverage. Once we loose hungry newshounds in the direction of Mario Scipone and Tersa Ver Meer there's no telling exactly what might happen, but they may very well flush a fox."

The next day, after Walker had returned to Atlanta, Janie Bascom entered the double-desk home office and den where Flyn was working. A look of anxiety was on her face. "I'm afraid for the kid's safety if the exact subject of your appearance before the Jupiter Committee should leak out before the actual hearing. I pressed my committee liaison friend to make certain that both the meeting and the general agenda gets a lot of academic-community press attention. And that's what's troubling me.

"The national wire services will probably pick up the story and a fair public splash should result. But if Mirror Magic should get wind of Ben's plan to set them up as point party for the ET's . . ." She trailed off.

Flyn Bascom could offer little in the way of reassurances. In fact none of them had the remotest idea as to the astonishing nature of the world (public and private) reaction about to be generated as a result of The Walker Testimony.

57

"Am I to understand then, Mr. Walker, that you, supported by Dr. Bascom here, claim to have actually met with an extraterrestrial? In fact, have spoken with one? And that there are many others across the country who have also, although unknown to them at the time?"

This was Chairman Jamison, playing the typically skeptical government-funded committee leader role to the hilt. He had gone over the scenario of the pair's planned revelation and was still trying to devise a credible reason not to have shared it in advance with his colleagues. Jamison could barely believe he was actually entertaining such a witnessing before his committee as it was.

Three different elements had allowed it to happen. One, Jamison trusted Walker and his judgement. Two, he knew the story was going to come out, (he certainly knew Ben Walker well enough for that). And three, he wasn't about to throw an opportunity for such rare potential publicity to anyone else's group. Certainly not NASA or the opposing party's cabinet.

"To simplify my answer, Mr. Chairman," said Walker, seated side-by-side with Flyn Bascom as he spoke in the direction of Jamison and the maze of network microphones and cameras present, "you are absolutely correct. As to why Dr. Bascom and I are breaking this story here and now, it is imperative that some group do so. Why not such a prominent (well it would be from now on) and relevant body as the Jupiter Committee? What better-qualified group to undertake official overtures with these extraterrestrials?"

Walker had them exactly where Jamison wanted them. Every single person in the room was tuned to Ben Walker's every word, syllable and inflection. It was no time for anything but the presence of authority, clarity and—he was thinking about the most important element of all—brevity.

Walker continued, "I need not remind viewers and especially scientists, other academics, and certainly the politicians and the military—worldwide—of the unimaginable body of knowledge to be gleaned from such an intelligence. How long have our guests been here without an official of any kind stepping forward to welcome Earth's first truly authenticated representatives to visit from outer space? If they are from an environment that has no understanding of how to initiate cultural overtures without encouragement by an official welcoming body, what would they do but go underground?" Okay, that was a reach but it provided a cue for Jamison to direct the assemblage.

"As the committee is well aware," said Jamison. "Three years ago this very body supported passage of the Alien Protection Law, after more than two months of house and senate debate about the wisdom of anticipating the rights of official visitors from another planet. This law clearly protects the rights of peaceful and properly verified aliens. The act neither provides them with any sort of diplomatic immunity nor investigation of them—or their agents. You have the floor again, Mr. Walker."

The witness continued. "Mr. Chairman, Dr. Bascom and I have put everything in a summary report, including the last known Las Vegas hotel address of Msrs. Gam'man and Chesser." Walker glanced at Flyn, concluding with, "If you cannot locate them there I suggest you contact their Earth contacts at Mirror Magic Corporation, a Mister Mario A. Scipone and a Ms. Tersa J. Ver Meer. Thank you, ladies and gentlemen."

58

There was no public panic at the headline news, as so many government authorities had feared would be the case and as dozens of them had so smugly said in subsequent phone calls to the offices of all three—Jamison, Walker and Bascom. When pressed by Jamison, however, the callers conceded that had the government released such information it very likely would have given rise on the part of the public to serious military concerns.

Contributing to the relative calm was surprisingly responsible journalistic leadership (tabloids aside). For some reason the bombshell news did not even warrant the lead story in Walker's hometown papers, *The Atlanta Journal/Constitution*, during the first few days following the Jupiter Committee's unplanned disclosures. Within a week, however, the story began to seize the public's fancy. It became the topic for the talk shows and was the conversational lead-in for most people at both work and play, all across the country.

Walker and Bascom jointly accepted a very few of the dozens of invitations to comment on the subject, but interest in their appearance began to wane when it was seen that they stuck to not much more than what had earlier been released. They preferred, instead, to redirect attention to Mirror Magic, Scipone and Ver Meer, along with emphasizing the connection between the ET's and the now deceased MM chairman, Phillip Sloan. The only 'new' news was finally and apparently reluctantly offered by Walker, who casually mentioned that both Sloan and Mirror Magic had been the subject of his television interview with Lynn Michelson earlier that year. That caused a wild scramble for the tape and once it was located, the dragons were truly loosed.

The credence lent events by the Jupiter Committee and its members, combined with the re-release of the Michelson/Walker interview, began to take on the appearance of official confirmation of the presence of extraterrestrials on Earth. It began to wave across the peopled face of the globe like the grandfather of all tsunami. The famous Halloween broadcast by Orson Welles seemed like a child's trick-or-treat prank by comparison, and many viewed it in just that light.

But then a startling series of developments began to take place. Perhaps things were influenced by other historical events as well, and contributed to people getting caught up with the overall moment.

Some attributed the chain of events' beginning to Mikhail Gorbachev's stunning, but iceberg-tipped announcement of glasnost. This directly influenced subsequent Eastern European democratic revolutions and their attendant chaos. Following on its heels, the middle-Eastern oil and scud madness did nothing to defray international paranoia about both economic and political world re-ordering.

A totally unanticipated result of the 'Jupiter Announcement,' as the press dubbed the event, was the human one—a unifying effect on a near-planetary level. As one public television news-hour anchor put it in summing up one evening's program, "Perhaps for the first time in history events have been set in place that will ultimately make for a true world community."

Because of the possible existence of the ET's, there seemed to be an unlikely bond developing between Soviets and Americans. The almost impossible to imagine peace meetings between fundamentalist Arabs and Israelis became more substantial. If those unlikely alliances were somehow predictable, even given their circumstantial or traditional distrust, the truly amazing call to forget-and-forgive was predicted by no one; centuries of inherent enmity between the Japanese, Chinese, Koreans and other kindred Asian cultures, was washed away by the common bond suddenly uniting regional Earth cultures in the face of an other-being reality.

Back in Baxter Products' offices in Atlanta, Amanda Booth was reading to Walker from the J and C's Sunday opinion-editorial page. "Ben, this is incredible. Still without hard evidence, but probably due to both the lack of the U.S. government's denial and the latent wish of many for the realization of intelligent alien life, people are not only buying in but are ascribing moral as well as religious values to the revelation.

"Listen to this, 'Not only has the demonstrated existence of other-world beings brought common goals to light for most of the heavily industrialized nations of the world, but third-world countries have scaled back decades old civil conflicts and political demands upon their neighbors. Even those governments which tend to re-focus their own economic, social and political ills and ambitions onto holier-than-thou attention-diverting terroristic activities have begun at least mouthing planet Earth slogans.' Ben, what is happening?" asked Amanda.

"Certainly far more than we bargained for," he said. "Unfortunately, it isn't all positive, Amanda. Did you read the *Newsweek* story about one small African nation's beleaguered leader trying to save his political ass by announcing to the starving masses—if any were listening—that their salvation was at hand by virtue of the ET's, and that he would take their desperate plight directly to the visitors? Clever. That'll buy him maybe a few months, so long as he doesn't actually make contact with any of our friends and then have to report a summary refusal. That messenger bearing bad news *would* be shot." Walker laughed too loudly trying to distract himself. Then as quickly, he turned somber.

"Amanda, much more importantly for the moment—for me, at least—is how the mirrors-and-mob bunch is doing. Their temperatures must be getting a tad high. But what I would really like to know is how all this publicity is being taken by Gam'man and his sidekick. We really have no idea as to how they fit in with all this, and I'm beginning to feel a little guilty about our having assumed their implication with Sloan and Mirror Magic."

She replied simply, "Why don't we ask Gam'man? Maybe he would see us. I have his phone number; he gave it to me at the gaming table. He said he didn't normally enjoy the company of strangers, but that he had on this occasion and he was pleased to have made my acquaintance. Don't you remember my mentioning it as we were leaving the casino hotel?"

"I do now that you remind me." He didn't at all, but neither did he care to admit not being aware of something he should so obviously have retained. Her idea was a solid tactic: mount a frontal attack. That the feds hadn't yet taken the two visitors into custody—in spite of the Alien Protection Act—was difficult to believe, but they had better act on the opportunity quickly. Laws could always be amended.

59

The flight to Phoenix was right on time and the limousine had Ben and Amanda across town in less than an hour to the resort hotel where they were to meet Gam'man for lunch. The press had been relentless in their attempts to contact the alleged extraterrestrials. The harried pair had made good their secret exit from Las Vegas. They returned to their welcome mountainside home in the shadows of Camelback Mountain, but in a condition of near-panic.

While en route to their incredible rendezvous, Amanda had asked Ben a question which had been on her mind since the earlier phone call to Gam'man. "How on earth are you possibly going to make good on your promise to extricate them from this impossible situation?"

"It was a commitment made partly under duress. You know they would agree to see us under no other conditions," Walker reminded her. "But more than that, I have been studying Gam'man's diary more closely and I should have appreciated one thing in particular when I first picked it up. I've been paranoid for more than a year now over anything or anyone with the least possible connection to Jon Baxter's death and the Mirror Magic operation, but the plain fact is neither of these individuals are directly tied to Sloan's scheme."

"Do you think they'll trust us?" Amanda asked.

"Now it's a curious situation," Walker replied, then elaborated. "Gam'man obviously considers you a friend, although he had precious little on which to base it. For obvious reasons the pair must have few friends—perhaps none with whom they can truly share anything. Maybe Gam'man appreciates not only my offer to return his diary, but puts even more weight on my offer to apprise them of what is going on. And it was no small matter that I was able to convey my thoughts about what they must do if they are to survive eventual arrest, intense interrogation, or worst of all, possible global deification."

A casually-dressed man approached them as they were sitting in the resort hotel's magnificently backdropped open-air restaurant. The soft April sunshine and the cactus colors had quickly refreshed them. "The Walker and Booth party?" the stranger inquired. They both nodded, not knowing what to expect. "My name is Chesser," he said. "Isn't this a fine mess Ollie has gotten us into?"

Ben and Amanda exchanged perplexed glances. Would this evermore curious adventure turn out to be nothing but that? He pointed to another table across the patio and then led them to where their host was seated.

"Ms. Booth, it is a pleasure to see you again," said Gam'man, standing to greet them. "And to meet you, Mr. Walker. Please, have a seat. We can have lunch and then drive to our home near here. You've met my associate. You'll have to excuse his penchant for offering vaudeville-comedy cliches for simple greetings. If you'll pardon my directness, Mr. Walker, do you have my journal with you?"

"Certainly, Mr. Gam'man, I . . ." He was cut short.

"Please. No, 'Mister,' if you will. Just Gam'man. It's a title in itself."

"Yes, of course," said Walker. "And I apologize for having stolen your personal journal in the first place, but you two have a bit of explaining to do, if you wouldn't mind." Ben handed the diary to him. "If I am to help you at all, I must have the facts. At that, I'm not certain there is a way out of this that will suit you. But first allow us to treat you to lunch. After all," he laughed, "this meeting alone has a book in it." Then, more seriously he added, "I'm certain you can appreciate the historical significance of this visit, at least from our perspective."

"Of course," said Gam'man. "We have been dreading it all our lives on Earth. There is no telling where it will end. By all means, ask your questions. We will soon enough, I fear, get down to the real business at hand."

Well, thought Ben, there are no precedents for this conversation so I might as well take it head on. "Quite right, he said. "No one on Earth has yet visited another planet, much less 'done lunch' with a representative of one." He and Amanda exchanged amused glances. "We have, of course, detected apparently unintelligible radio waves from elsewhere in the universe and there is much circumstantial evidence for life within our galaxy if not the solar system. Still, to actually confront not only living proof that there is obviously parallel life, if not identical . . ." He trailed off, then asked, "Are there differences, gentlemen?"

Chesser, the interlocutor, spoke up first to the other's frowned disapproval. "In what respect do you refer, Mr. Walker? Physically? Chemically? Biologically? Actually, very little."

Amanda spoke up. "In exactly which 'little' ways do we differ, Chesser?" She instantly regretted her question, feeling she must sound like a daytime television talk show host asking deliberately presumptuous questions.

Chesser continued, ignoring Gam'man's second audible sigh over the past five minutes. "Frankly, I don't know how to address such a complex question, Ms. Booth. But we're not offended by your asking, you understand.

"For Gam'man and I these differences have never been a problem. I have read many of your philosophers, however, and one in particular expresses why differences between beings are relatively unimportant in the big picture. If I can correctly recall your longshoreman-philosopher Eric Hoffer's quotation, 'How many and deep are the divisions between human beings! Not only are there divisions between races, nations, classes, and religions, but also an almost total incomprehension between the sexes, the old and the young, the sick and the healthy.' Now, his last sentence on the subject summarizes my point, 'There would be no society if living together depended upon understanding each other.'"

The First Lunch, as the media would whimsically record this meeting, subsequently fell to platitudes about the food, the recent weather in Georgia and Arizona, and the country's general economy. Both twosomes suddenly realized that—in a manner of speaking—they were 'officially' representing the most alien of sides in the history of Earth, and were not properly prepared to beneficially engage the other, at least in that context. When they got down to specific business it would be different, at least for Walker-Booth.

At the extraterrestrials' modest but beautifully situated home on a flank of Camelback, the four of them sat face-to-face with few of the apparent communication or physical differences typically foreseen by Asimov, Roddenberry or Sagan. Walker was certainly aware of this meeting-of-the-millennium but he didn't want to lose the advantage.

Mindful of his purposes, he chose to employ intimidation. He intoned gravely, "Gam'man, it is only a matter of time before the U.S. federal government will place you and Chesser under arrest on one pretext or another. Probably because of the illegal activities in which you are apparently engaged with Mirror Magic and organized crime. Please tell us your story so that we may be of some help."

Gam'man cleared his throat and redirected. "Could we provide you with a conventional beverage or some sort of hors d'oeuvre, my friends? Our own palates' preference in that respect runs to warm, non-sugar beverages and heavily salted peanuts but we have other selections."

Both politely passed. Chesser offered them a choice of cigars from a beautifully-carved marble box, taking one for himself when they demurred.

Gam'man frowned and attempted a rebuke. "You don't smoke, Chesser. Why do you play such games?"

"No, of course I don't, but I do relish observing the panic that the threat of such an action tends to create these days." He was indeed delighted just to evoke a minor discourse on the subject—any subject—although he was disappointed in the relatively mild reaction of their guests.

All were by now comfortably seated, a world globe resting on an end table next to Gam'man. He began. "In your year of 1894, Chesser, Sloann—known to you as Philip Sloan—and I were placed in confinement on a colonized moon of our planet, Jun'or. It lies in a solar system within the Milky Way galaxy, but your astronomers have probably not even assigned it a number. After all, there are some 400 billion suns in this galaxy alone. Anyway, we had been sentenced to a life civil detention term.

Amanda gasped, "For what heinous crime? Murder?"

Embarrassed, Gam'man winced. "For lack of an equivalent term in your language, it was for what you might call overzealous entrepreneurship."

Chesser interrupted, a look of pride on his face. "There is a term; it's called counterfeiting. We duplicated a complex machine used to manufacture monetary units of each of the leading nation-states on our world. That was the beginning of all of this, I'm afraid," he sighed.

Gam'man continued. "The details of planning and the opportunity for our escape took us more than five of your Earth-years and then another 40 years to reach your planet, traveling at velocities far exceeding anything your technologies have even conceived.

Chesser chimed in once more. "Your planet's current pursuit of all of its various fossil and even nuclear fuel drives lie in entirely impossible directions for anything that will ever permit commercial manned travel beyond your own Earth-moon plane." It wasn't meant as either lecture or instruction, but merely as interesting conversation.

Walker empathized, "Well, I can imagine how poorly such a criminal violation as yours would be received in our own various Earth societies, but still the punishment does seem a bit harsh for a non-violent crime."

"We were labelled by the Jun'orian planetary government as the three most dangerous criminals on our world," said their host. "In truth we weren't, but just as punishment everywhere is preferred more for deterrence than rehabilitative purposes, we received the maximum penalty allowed by our laws. Since we had been so ingenious as to contrive a plan judged so antisocial as to land ourselves in exile-prison in the first place, we reasoned we could also come up with a better alternative to life than that which was facing us."

"But Gam'man," said Amanda, "how did you ever stumble across Earth of all places?"

"A very good question," Walker hitchhiked. "While laymen like us have little familiarity with the estimated numbers of planets potentially inhabited by intelligent life within our own galaxy, let alone the billions of other galaxies—and even granting that your race or culture possesses interstellar travel technology—what are the odds of your being led to this particular planet?"

"It really isn't that amazing," replied Gam'man. "It was no coincidence at all. We had access to excellent prison library resources that drew on the total body of Jun'orian-amassed cosmic knowledge. Public reports existed that revealed long-time surveillance of your planet. In fact, Earth is one of only two other planets known to our civilization to harbor intelligent life. Jun'or continues to surveil your planet even now, utilizing craft that your technology has no way of neutralizing, even on the not so rare occasions when they have been sighted. It is Jun'or's federated philosophy and policy not to physically or communicatively compromise their presence to an alien race. Obviously, since Chesser and I, not to mention Sloann, were outcast, we went our own way. We do not know how to judge our risk should Jun'orian surveillance crews discover our existence."

"I better understand the reasoning behind such a policy of isolationism than I do the capability for it, Gam'man," Walker said.

"I can't comment on the latter, but the former was borne of experience, Mr. Walker. More than 500 Earth-years ago, when the other of the two habitable planets known to us first revealed themselves to our own much less advanced civilization, the results were nearly catastrophic. While individuals within the general population held varying degrees of belief concerning rumors of unofficially confirmed contacts with alien life on Jun'or, when the fact was ultimately and responsibly revealed by government, it created tremendous religious havoc and upheavals. These included a generation with incalculable feelings of individual loss of self-worth, and even a diminished sense of race-significance. This was followed by increasingly hostile and violent attitudes planet-wide, resulting in civil disturbances and devastating economic repercussions that stretched over three of our generations. We have tried not to make the mistake of others."

Ben and Amanda were having trouble assimilating the input. Each item created its own set of questions, but this wasn't a time for two-way sharing and discussion as it was for confession on the part of their hosts.

Those hosts were obviously having problems of their own, being uneasy at the unknown effect of the revelations they were making. While Gam'man tended to trust these two beings and recognized the fact that they were not the authorities they might have to face before long, he nevertheless had to deal with truly universal 'fight or flight' tendencies.

Amanda broke the silence. "These, then, were the reasons which compelled the three of you to somehow escape—to Earth—and then select a city in which to meld with the local population, rather than announce your presence?"

"Precisely," nodded Gam'man. "By monitoring random electronic transmissions we judged one of the second-tiered U.S. communities would be the least objectionable for our needs of anonymity and freedom. We at first considered Atlanta. Actually, Sloann felt most strongly about that particular location. He is the only one who really did research on the matter. Chesser and I were finally more inclined toward someplace more remote yet stable and state-of-the-art, maybe in Canada or Australia. Ultimately, we two chose this locale and Sloann went his own way. It took us better than seven years to acclimate and assimilate ourselves to your Earth-American culture and physical and colloquial environment. Only then did Sloann position himself within your industry."

"But that picture is contrary to the Mirror Magic scenario which has led Amanda and me to where we are at the moment," challenged Walker. "Why did you put yourselves at odds with our particular industry?"

"But we didn't," interjected Chesser. "Only Sloann did. He was the maverick. We were equals in the original counterfeiting enterprise and even so during our confinement. But when we landed on Earth we were no longer able to influence him. He alone became responsible for his actions."

"How did that develop?" asked a frustrated Ben Walker.

Chesser continued. "Sloann quickly identified and removed the only pieces of adaptable advanced technological equipment on board the interstellar-circuit maintenance vessel we had commandeered for our escape. Specifically, the equipment I mention amounted to a small number of subliminal treatment units used in a prisoner attitude-modification program. This equipment was listed on the craft's manifest as having been recently returned from routine re-crystallization—the Jun'orian warranty equivalent of 50 years or five-million miles," he chuckled.

Gam'man glanced at Chesser with dismay but picked up the thread of clarification. "Both Chesser and I had been successfully subjected to the program and had in fact become model outpost residents. We were fairly well adjusted to our environment, if not our future. Sloann, however, absolutely rejected adaptation, and his natural zeal for influencing others—just for the sake of keeping score—was only magnified."

Walker was about to ask how their individual attitudes had carried over in their new home. He was becoming caught up in the story. These beings' personal accounting was focussed on the detail rather than the stupendous fact itself. They were merely survivors and happy to be such.

Gam'man sensed the need to continue his recitation of historical, personal events. "While we were confined we thought nothing of Sloann's heightened obsessions, since they really made no difference. Perhaps we should have been more concerned for his own well-being," Gam'man mused aloud.

"At any rate, we made good our escape. Following that we thought his initial attempts to make a minor impact in one of your smaller industries would be harmless enough. Certainly no more harmful than the influence conceded by whole populations to the major companies in American society solely because of their economic ability to purchase access to the commercial sights and sounds communicated to the masses.

"The fact is, we took only a passive interest. Chesser and I had our own modest agenda. If we had been pressed to evaluate Sloann's activities we would have said he merely wanted to compete aggressively for accumulation of your monetary units. We were wrong."

The conversational process with these extraterrestrials, thought Walker, is not much different than with most any other group save for one minor thing; their relative lack of gestures while talking. This was an express part of normal human conversations by both young and old.

Another thought elbowed its way forward. "Gam'man, how old are you and Chesser?"

"Age? I don't know whether to feel complimented or insulted. How old do we look, Mr. Walker?"

"I don't know; it's difficult to judge. Perhaps 40," Ben responded, knocking 10 years off his best guess in spite of what they had already told them.

"Ah, then," replied Gam'man. "I am certainly not insulted, Mr. Walker. After all, as you say on Earth, 'Age is negotiable.' In our case, however, it is also relative.

To explain, Jun'or travels around its single sun in 176 days, roughly half that of your Earth-year, but our average life expectancy is nearly 250 Jun'orian years. That translates to 121 of your years. Though we don't look more aged than your typical early-retiree, Chesser is past 100 and I am nearly 110 of your years! Your planet has been good to us.

We have no way of judging, however, how nearly 50 of your Earth years have affected our biological ages. And, we suspect we have not been totally immune to Earth bacteria, in spite of our surprisingly good health for nearly all the years we have been here. So we show our age, Mr. Walker?"

Walker turned to Amanda and winked, "No, that's no step for a pair of dancers."

Turning to Gam'man, Walker now sensed more than ever that there shouldn't necessarily be unreconcilable differences between two given cultures. At least not where individual performance and recognition played such an important role. He even wondered in a semi-distracted moment if promotional products were used on Jun'or.

Again, apparently intuitively, Gam'man deftly picked up the thread Walker was idly weaving. "We have learned of two more subtle, but still distinct differences in our cultures, Mr. Walker. For one, Jun'orians tend to react predictably to outside group threats with individual attitudes of divisiveness and rancor, whereas Earthlings tend to band together in response to either perceived or real other-group threats.

"Perhaps this is only when the threat is to one very broadly-allied group. We do notice that this banding together tends to be over physical or material matters as much as conceptual ones. Good examples of this are illustrated by your many world-wide wars. The bigger the apparent threat and the broader the group threatened, the greater the rally, while the more factionalized the problem the greater the apathy.

"Well . . ." Gam'man caught his breath, embarrassed at both the length and the context of his comments. "I seem to have taken on my associate's tendency for philosophizing."

"And what is the second difference you mentioned, Gam'man?" asked Ben, his interest in this pair could not be concealed.

"As I have indicated, Mr. Walker, our original heightened desire for undue influence over others—for game's sake, truly not for material gain—did lead us to excesses, then to prison confinement. Our tendencies were artificially suppressed, and ultimately we managed escape to subsequent freedom here on Earth.

"Now Chesser and I want merely to fully appreciate what we have and what we may expect to have. It's called 'happiness.' We have had a difficult time coming to terms with this notion since Jun'orian culture places far greater value on box scores than on peace of mind. We have long wondered if such a simple concept of life is as inherently difficult to comprehend for Earth people as it has been for us."

The scientist in Walker had expected input from these aliens to be on a more mechanical plane, something that would have arithmetically awed him, rather than responses that labelled them Everymen.

It was time to close out the discussion for the time being, thought Walker.

"Gentlemen and Amanda, we still have to deal with the very real problem of double M's continuing and damaging application of Sloan's process. Mario Scipone and Tersa Ver Meer have likely been distressed by events, but hardly shut down. We need the collaboration of my friend and sometime partner in this expanding Rubik's Cube. Would you mind flying back to Atlanta with us to meet with Dr. Bascom and to explore further the possibilities for your survival?"

"Very succinctly put, Mr. Walker," said Gam'man. "We are at your disposal."

60

The two Earthmen and the two Jun'orians sat facing each other across the solid walnut table in Jon Baxter's former office, now the Board of Directors' room. It was the first formal meeting—if not official—between representatives of Earth and another planetary body. Earth's representatives glanced at each other with looks that read, "Can you believe this?"

Gam'man and Chesser looked even more ill at ease. Flyn Bascom began the dialogue by rephrasing the question Gam'man had earlier posed for Ben; what did he and Chesser hope to yet accomplish during their remaining lifetime, which would be spent on Earth?

"Thank you for that direct line of inquiry, Dr. Bascom. Please let me illustrate something in the course of my response," said Gam'man. For a change it was Chesser who raised a hand as if to offer a caution but Gam'man caught his eye, shaking his head almost imperceptibly.

Gam'man continued, "Ms. Booth has openly wondered about our genetic or other differences. Perhaps you have even discerned nuance distinctions. To the best of our limited ability to verify this, and based on our own single visit to a Terran physician over nearly half a century on Earth, the only real difference in our make-up and yours is not physical, biological or chemical—it's extra-sensory.

"Now, I am not the one to offer an explanation as to how nearly identical life forms could develop apparently independently of the other. I can say that the only previous alien race with which Jun'orians have had contact were biologically dissimilar in the extreme, being chlorophyll-based rather than hemoglobin.

"And there is one other thing." Gam'man glanced in his countryman's direction, as if for encouragement. This provided corroboration for Ben Walker's recent suspicion that the two were really equals. Gam'man's counterpart nodded.

"Chesser and I have, over the years, ah . . . demonstrated a 'human compatibility' factor through, uh . . . 'consulting' with a number of females of your own various cultures. I will return to this statement in a few moments," said Gam'man, wanting very much to come to the point of this particular initiative, but feeling the need first to thoroughly and carefully position themselves.

"This one significant extra-sensory difference I mentioned may be as much learned as genetic. In any case I refer to the Jun'orian capacity for transcending the five basic human senses. You humans do have a sixth sense to a small degree; you have the ability to sometimes sense something not otherwise kenned through any of your five senses." Gam'man was not being patronizing, he was amazingly perceptive.

"For Jun'orians," he continued, "this extra-sensory perception has been shamelessly cultivated over eons to the point that we have severely—if not hopelessly—damaged our planetary civilization. Out of an innate and progressive individual compulsion to gain a competitive edge over business, political, and even social rivals, we long ago developed the unfortunate mental capacity to randomly detect contrary emotions. Over time these natural thoughts have come to be read as 'hostile.' As a result our populations became largely dysfunctional. Do you follow me, gentlemen?"

"To a point," replied Bascom. "While extra-sensory perception cannot be practically applied among human beings, the concept itself has limited acceptance in both the scientific and lay communities."

"Ah," responded Gam'man, "but your civilization has successfully evolved through a blunting of this latent capacity, rather than cultivation of it. Some of your philosophers—Pascal and later, Hoffer, among them—feared that if men knew what thoughts might cross others' minds it would render friendships impossible. And still, I believe it is correct to say that misunderstandings among your races, governments and in individual everyday interactions take place not so much due to people failing to communicate, but because they sense what is going on in each other's mind and . . . do not like it.

With Jun'orians, only incredibly practiced self-discipline keeps us from total chaos."

Walker posed the obvious question. "Then do we understand that you and Chesser are indeed telepaths?"

"Fortunately, Ben,"—that was Gam'man's first use of his given name—"neither of us are able to receive or transmit telepathic images with Earthlings. That has been our greatest single blessing since arriving."

"It doesn't take much imagination to fully appreciate that value, based on what you've just told us, Gam'man," said Walker. "Now, how does all this square with your current objectives?"

"The point, Ben and Flyn," said Gam'man, "is that we want permission to procreate in the 'open.'"

Walker and Bascom glanced at each other and stifled a snort.

"Openly," the alien quickly corrected himself. "Not necessarily monogamously, however." Another impolite but calculated double whuff by the insiders, a bit more muted this time.

Realizing he was being taken too literally, although suspecting that was their preference, Gam'man attempted further qualification. "I think you realize what I'm saying is that we want public recognition and acceptance for who we are. And we want to beget offspring. We want to survive as a race on your planet—or at least in a biracial form. In the process we may very well breed out this distinctly anti-social attitude possessed by Jun'orians. With such a publicly affirmed and contrite intention would we not then also contribute something to your own human race's tendency towards racial bias? Existing local, regional and national racial prejudices should seem almost petty by comparison, wouldn't you think?"

Bascom took mild issue with the surprising logic. "I'm afraid your reasoning is a bit naive, Gam'man, but I will admit there could be something to it in time."

Gam'man pressed on. "In our time on Earth, Flyn, we have witnessed a very interesting phenomenon with regard to this common bonding I spoke of earlier. Your athletic teams, your cities, your states, your countries and even your multi-national alliances tend to reduce internal tensions whenever there develops a greater threat without. If we, as living proof of an absolutely external group of a unique nature, can focus your single Earth-race on the need for compassion and support among thousands of otherwise heterogeneous groups—even if the impetus for that is somewhat superficially imposed—doesn't it logically follow that there is a decided chance for increased harmony among you?"

Gam'man was nearly finished with the single most important speech of his life. Perhaps in anyone's life over the previous nearly 2,000 years on Earth. "We do not pretend that any of this is certain to happen. It may. But in any event, Chesser and I want now to begin our new role and, frankly, to also begin acquiring some material things for our families-to-be. We have been quite alone and lonely for a very long time. You cannot imagine how arduous and emotionally telling it is to be deprived of one's family, one's culture and literally all familiar surroundings, including sounds and smells. For example, how do you think you would react to being forever deprived of anything resembling your beautiful and comforting variety of Earth birdsong? We have no hope of ever experiencing even the least of our cultural familiarities again—with one possible exception, the starting of our own families. We probably haven't a great many years left to us, Chesser and I, and we are after all of a sexual as well an entrepreneurial and acquisitive culture."

Walker took a deep breath and exhaled through a deep if compassionate frown. "Gam'man, you and Chesser surely must know that we have no authority to either grant or deny you permission for your ambitions. In fact, such authority doesn't exist on Earth so long as you are lawful.

"Now we will certainly bear witness for you once you have righted the wrong started and perpetuated by your fellow being. That is what I meant earlier when I referred to your 'survival.' Exactly how can you help us see to correcting that situation?" Walker's implied threat was meant as a challenge and that was precisely how it was interpreted by the Jun'orian pair.

61

Pulling the plug on Scipone and company would be a relatively simple task, according to the plan Chesser had devised with Walker's input. Since both Walker and Bascom were recognizable by a number of MM personnel, Chesser would pose as a service technician for a 'reported' computer malfunction in the Atlanta Mirror Magic plant.

Walker tested Chesser's confidence. "Do you really think you can pull this off?"

Chesser looked straight into Ben's eyes and with an impish look, replied, "It's no step for a dancer."

Phase One was surprisingly easy to accomplish. With Chesser's 'inspection' of six of the seven original subliminal rehab machines in the heavily staffed, but—since Sloan's death—poorly secured primary operations laboratory, he easily removed and quickly destroyed a key Earth technology-irreplaceable component from each piece of equipment.

Finished and away from the building, he phoned Walker with the 85 percent mission-accomplished news. "There was only one machine missing, Ben, and packing crates were everywhere. One supervisor volunteered the answer after I complimented him on the amount of business my firm did with MM. I learned that all special process manufacturing is being consolidated and moved to their New Jersey plant.

"He even gave me the address," chuckled Chesser, "when I mentioned we would extend correction of the computer problem to the New Jersey factory's equipment. In order to finish the job, I have booked a flight for early this afternoon to Newark International. I should be back tomorrow. I will simply advise the people there that I have been sent to correct the system-wide software glitch which originated in Atlanta, and if necessary give the supervisor's name for reference." Before Walker could protest, Chesser had hung up.

"I don't like it, Gam'man. Phase Two was for him to merely confirm the existence and location of any missing machines, then to get out so we could come up with an actionable follow-up plan.

"He did very well but Chesser does not have the experience to deal with Scipone and his cronies. Bascom and I are not exactly Simon and Simon either, but we have gained certain experience over the past year or so in dealing with these clowns. They are rarely funny."

Walker and Gam'man caught a plane bound for the New Jersey airport the same day as Chesser's, taking a hotel shuttle to where Ben's secretary had made Chesser a reservation. The registration clerk confirmed that he had earlier checked in but was not in his room presently. They took two rooms of their own to await the return of agent Chesser and ponder the situation.

Chesser was more excited than he had been at any time during the last 40 years of his Earth stay. He had not been able to sustain Gam'man's undiminished enthusiasm for their extra-Jun'orian experience, at least not since the novelty—for him—had expired.

Gam'man was an individual of vision and one who reveled in what-could-be; well, that and his active if not obsessed goal of implanting his personal Jun'orian seed within a thousand Earth maidens. Not that his interests concerning the raising of a formal family as stated to Walker and Bascom were anything other than sincere.

Chesser, too, had a need to 'scatter his bindles.' He longed for his beloved if flawed Jun'or, and for his family, though he left no mate. She had deserted him several years into his confinement, but their two offspring would both likely have provided him with grandseed by this time. Sadly, long before coming to Earth he had become estranged from his children. That very notion had come to weigh more heavily on him than the fact that he would never again see them.

Chesser's clean, crisp 'company' uniform and his assumed authoritative manner easily gained him entrance. First, he entered the factory itself, then the huge environmentally-controlled but surprisingly deserted operations room where new equipment had apparently just been positioned for imminent start-up. Neon-colored ribbons decorated the room amid several posters which read "Look Again Into Mirror Magic." He was not prepared, however, for the sight of a roomful of 30 to 40 replicated subliminal processors aligned like stock cars at the start of the *Firecracker 500.*

Panic. Chesser was familiar with social panic, but not with business crises or the life-threatening variety. He had often recalled those fleeting social or personal moments of blind panic. Like the time when he was barely into puberty and his parents had left him at home alone for a full week for the first time while they attended a cross-sector conference. Idly inspecting himself in his parents' bedroom full-length mirror one morning he suddenly gasped and fell to one knee in terror. He had noticed for the first time in his life that his scrotum had one bag hanging significantly lower than the other. That was unforgettable panic. He recalled that his thoughts then had been of having acquired such a grossly disfiguring mutation that he would never be able to broach it to his family. Thus must he be prepared to suffer in silence for life. Or, as it turned out, long enough to complete some discrete observations in the change-room of the male youth showers of the exercise center. Where had he been all his young life that he had never noticed before? What a relief for the young Chesser to note that his body's apparent deformity was the norm.

Back in real time. There stood the processors, lined up as uniformly as pecan trees in a southern Georgia orchard. Recovering from his shock he could only deduce that Mirror Magic engineers must have discovered an alternative solution for the subliminal projection technology. Perhaps they had substituted heavy duty alternating-current electricity for the more sophisticated and self-contained Jun'orian power source of the original machines. What he knew for certain was that they must still utilize the even more complex software developed by Sloann for programming the mirror sensors to accept the advertising messages. Chesser knew now it was at this place and time that he must make his mark. He immediately began work to accomplish that end.

62

On the floor above where Chesser feverishly but surreptitiously labored, Mario Scipone took a phone call from Arthur Bonnelli. Scipone had just drawn to a close preparations for this afternoon's New Jersey plant celebration over installation of the new equipment that would ultimately empower him in his drive to become the don of dons. Within seconds, Bonnelli was screaming into the speaker phone, flushed with rage, but at the same time trying to appease his already damaged heart. He manifested this paradox by gripping both ends of his Manhattan office desk simultaneously, arms outstretched and clamped like a vise grip. His voice now marshalled his message into cadence, but with only slightly less intensity.

"Mario, I asked you not to do this political thing with the mirrors. I said we could buy influence just as we always have. You insisted that it was important to test the coming expansion process. Against my own counsel I gave in. You will remember, however, that I said if you must do it, do not embarrass me."

The old man let that sink in and then continued, "Mario, I am embarrassed! We have been hounded, sued and now sabotaged in Atlanta. I curse you for your failure! I curse you but it is I who must undo what you have done. You will not embarrass me again. You are out! Out! Out! Do you hear!" Bonnelli lunged and violently swept the phone to the floor, gasping for air as he did so.

Bonnelli fell back into his padded desk chair and sat quietly, semi-recovering from his outburst. He then fastened his pained gaze on the figure seated opposite him. He spoke to Tersa Ver Meer in a calmer tone. "He has been an obedient soldier and a loyal consiglieri, but once too often he has shown the same poor judgement of the politicians we own. He has served me well and I may still have use for him, but on this, Mario was wrong. Very wrong. Trying to influence people in this strange fashion is not what we know. Unions, garbage, making book, dealing drugs, prostitution, these are the things we know. Physical threats, payoffs, extortion, hits, chemical dependency, these things we understand. Psychology and advertising—what do we know? Nothing!"

She said nothing. She didn't have to. Bonnelli was saying everything for her.

"But I went along with it because Mario wanted it. And for Mario's promise of huge profits. Now we see that my head was wrong and my gut was right. We have too many players, too many secrets, and too much risk. Something was bound to happen to bring too much heat down on us: the press, decline in business, loss of respect."

Bonnelli was nearly exhausted and what he was about to do went against the basic tenets of generations of exclusively male family leadership. He had no intentions of it being permanent, merely expedient.

"T. Ver Meer (he could not bring himself to address her by her given name. Neither was it prudent for him to openly express his disdain for her by using only her surname, so he compromised), starting now, you are in charge of a Bonnelli Family operation—Mirror Magic. I want you to immediately terminate Mario's vote-influence program but continue with everything else as before. As in the old days, I want profits, profits, profits, until we can sell out. We will continue to buy our necessary support and protection. That is not your problem."

Tersa Ver Meer would take her promotion under no illusions, but she smiled her best sneer anyway, partly for the lucky triumph over Mario Scipone and partly for the additional power she would gain. She had no one with whom to share anything, however, thus her need for a greater and greater number of 'things' never diminished. This filled the void where people would have been. The reality of her power and ascendancy, however, lay in her ability to plan for her future needs, and was thus her only perspective. She needed more insurance.

That someone had learned enough of what they were doing and had been bold enough to subsequently penetrate the Atlanta facility and actually challenge the Bonnelli organization was very disconcerting to Ver Meer. It meant she had to take immediate steps to protect this plant and the new equipment Scipone had built—the very resource that would either maintain or deny her survival.

63

Within the hour Ver Meer had hired a private car which had taken her from Manhattan to the New Jersey plant. She wasted no time in establishing her new authority, raining four-letter epithets on the befuddled security guard for his apparent hesitation in clearing her after-hours entrance. Actually, his confusion was brought on by his personal concern about advising her that—against company rules—the computer repairman was still on the premises. So he didn't bother at all.

Still infuriated and striding as quickly as her four-inch heels would allow her, she slipped slightly as she approached the main entrance to the special operations room, but instantly caught herself by the doorknob. Only then did she realize the door was unlocked. What light had shone under the windowless door suddenly darkened.

She quietly entered the room and immediately crouched, moving to one side and scanning the opposite wall which had thick glass bricks substituting for windows. They permitted a filtered version of the evening's full moon to cast a pale sheet of semi-light into the room. A slight movement caught her peripheral vision and she saw for only an instant the faint shadow of a low-profile silhouette. The saboteur! He would have to pass her on the way out. She would outlast the patience of the intruder—unless he exited the one other entrance. No, it was unlikely he had thought to clear both locks when he gained access.

She moved behind the machine nearest her, the one whose proximity to the door insured that her prey would have to come close to it in order to exit by the only available escape route. She slowly trained her .38 calibre weapon perpendicularly to that path, waiting with far more excitement than she had ever felt in an encounter with a paying personal customer. She had fired a handgun many times before, but only on firing ranges, since her methods of 'obstacle adjustment' in Phil Sloan's employ had been by other means.

The instant the amateur saboteur caused himself to be framed in the room's moon sheen, not having varied his angle of approach to the exit, she fired without hesitation. Chesser caught just enough of a glimpse of menacing shadow that the natural Jun'orian instinct to protest—rather than evade—caused the bullet to first tear through his outstretched hand and then savagely rip into his chest cavity. He was hurled backward and fell, sprawled across the floor. Chesser's life blood was draining onto a formerly forgiving alien world. The few tools from his belt holster lay scattered beside him in mute testimony to his own unselfish efforts in making good the Jun'orian pair's commitment to undo the horrible wrong of their former fellow.

Before his assailant could reach the body, however, the lights snapped on and the white-haired, veteran security guard appeared at the door, his pistol drawn. "Hold it right there!" he shouted.

"Guard, it's me, Tersa Ver Meer," she said as she stood up, her own firearm still resting in one hand, "I just shot a trespasser. He tried to kill me." The guard pressed his portable security alarm to signal the police, saying to her, "I only heard one shot, Ms. Ver Meer, and your repairman's 'weapon' looks a lot like an ordinary flashlight to me."

64

It was the shaken voice of Amanda Booth on the phone as she spoke with Ben Walker in his hotel room in Newark only an hour later. "Ben, a hospital—the St. Francis—only a few miles from where you are staying just called the office. Chesser has been shot and is in critical condition. They found a calendar card in his wallet with the Baxter Products name and phone number on it. I was still in the office when they called, worrying about all three of you.

"We're on our way, Amanda. Thanks for being there."

Gam'man stared unblinking out the side window of the taxi as the two of them were driven to the emergency entrance and entered the hospital. They waited anxiously near the operating room for some time, Walker pacing and Gam'man standing and staring out yet another window. Conversation was limited to an occasional, but unanswered irrelevance offered by Ben.

After more than two hours in the operating room, a middle-aged doctor approached them in the crowded waiting room, a fresh scrub-gown in place so as not to alarm them at the sight of the blood-drenched garment he had just removed. He walked slowly and addressed them with compassion. "Which of you is Mr. Gam'man?"

Gam'man nodded slightly, his lips drawn tightly against each other in the universal physical technique employed to resist irrepressible emotion. "I'm Dr. Weissman," he said. "I'm afraid there is nothing else we can do to save your friend, Mr. Chesser. He is still bleeding from multiple internal injuries. I now know what you must know; he is not human. He is struggling valiantly but he won't survive much longer. He uttered your name even when he should have been unconscious from anesthesia. Funny, he seemed almost immune to its effect; the worse for him. But for that reason he is conscious at this moment. I suggest you visit him immediately if you expect to do so at all."

As they entered Chesser's room the alien slowly looked up at his two best friends, his hands grasping the bed's restraining rails as if they were lifelines. He looked first at Walker, smiling weakly, "Ben . . . I . . . accomplished our mission . . . " he spoke haltingly.

Walker placed a hand on one of Chesser's, then laid his other on top of it. His eyes teared, speaking eloquently of their short-lived but fast-developed bond.

The dying Chesser turned his gaze to his countryman and his smile broadened for just an instant. They each blinked once, slowly and simultaneously, communicating much more than the elapsed time would have suggested possible. Chesser spoke clearly, more out of respect for the human ears present than of the need for Gam'man.

He took one deep breath and coughed deeply before he could speak. "Gam'man, you know I return to Jun'or uplife to rejoin our fathers. You have sustained me in life, my friend. I hope in death I will be able to sustain you. With his final breaths Chesser repeated a Jun'orian prayer: "Weep not over my body, for it will not be me. I am now, and forever will be."

Walker turned to Gam'man. "At the expense of his own life, this . . . man . . . I can use no more complimentary word to describe him, has lifted from me my obsession for avenging Jon Baxter's death. The price was too great. Chesser's attacker will not go unpunished, although somehow I feel that this would not be as important to him as it is to us."

Gam'man now spoke for the first time since they had boarded the taxi for the hospital. His simple lamentation was profound in its sadness. "I have not only lost my best friend in life, but also the final contact with my lifeform."

The body was buried as it would have been on Jun'or, privately, without even official ministration. Ben, Amanda, Flyn and Janie witnessed Gam'man sprinkle onto the earth-seated coffin a half-measure from a tiny ceramic bottle filled with the Jun'orian soil with which he had carefully dusted his pockets before their original off-world incarceration nearly 95 Earth years ago. The simple ceremony concluded with Gam'man's reading of the epitaph that would be cast onto the marker of the only known non-terrestrial grave on Earth: "P. Chesser—His nature was to keenly observe, humorously comment, compassionately judge and decisively act."

65

Three years later it was a seriously ill Arthur Bonnelli, still calling rowing cadence for a boat shipping water as fast as it could be bailed, who summoned his battlefield-appointed lieutenant, Tersa Ver Meer.

"Sit," he sighed, and then hesitated only long enough for her to take a chair. "For the last time in my life—and very likely yours, I am going to explain the facts of life, manager Ver Meer.

"It cost us more than five million dollars and some political markers we didn't want to call in to get you off on Chesser's homicide charge. If our lawyers hadn't been able to cloud things through technicalities involving the rights of an Earthling versus a freaking ET, your pretty little ass would have been bagged. We even beat Baxter Products' civil suit against Mirror Magic. Ha!" he laughed without mirth. "No hard evidence could be produced. It was back to business as usual and we have poured big money into world wide distribution of your product,"

Bonnelli continued his lecture. "Unfortunately, your Mirror Magic operation has not performed. Now, how the hell is that possible!" he shouted at her. "You've had Scipone's hijacked process working for you around the clock for more than one thousand days."

The object of his remarks stood up to argue the point, although her only defense would come in the form of the non-performing executive's eternal cliche. "I've done the best I can, given the circumstances, Mr. Bonnelli," she said. "I do not know the problem except that our distributors can no longer be counted upon to buy from us in spite of our product's extraordinary built-in advantage over the competition. It is a paradox, but it is not my fault."

She had always feared death more than life. Her motivation over the past few years had progressed from self-indulgence to simple survival. She was hardly contrite; she had simply lost her ability to continue rationalizing her acts, and as a result had come to envision severe punishment in death for her life. Fear was a terrible companion.

"Sit!" he repeated, raising his voice. "I am a dying man. No one cares one way or the other, except for the possible benefit to them as a result of my death. I have deliberately made no provision for my successors, knowing that will be my revenge against those who have failed me. But you, manager Ver Meer, I am personally taking care of."

His eyes widened and his voice quivered with perverse satisfaction. "You will die where you belong: on the streets. And you will take your post within the hour—with no bank account, no cash, no credit cards, no car, no drug supply, no apartment, and," he smiled with finality, "no one."

Tersa Ver Meer would not die of neglect, and life today would not end privately. Lynn Michelson's "Seven-Come-Eleven" television crew would be through the building's doors at the sound of the anticipated gunfire. Bonnelli's promise had not fallen short of her expectations. She rose slowly as if to take her leave, smiling faintly as she appeared about to apologize for her shortcomings.

"Mr. Bonnelli, I just want you to know that . . ." She was standing fully erect by now and in a smooth and rehearsed move suddenly withdrew from her purse a small calibre hand gun, just as quickly levelling it at Bonnelli's head, less than four feet away. In a very different tone she now crammed all of her life's abuse, tragedy and sins into the moment, completing the sentence she had just begun, . . . "You are the mother of all whores."

Bonnelli reacted to the two very nearly simultaneous actions by clutching his right hand to his heart, fearing seizure.

Ver Meer continued. "I could kill you now before you can summon a body through the door, but I want much greater satisfaction than your mere death. Reach into the desk drawer for your own gun and slowly place it on top of the desk." Her weapon was still pointed directly between Bonnelli's eyes, her finger lightly on the trigger. The perspiration began to rain from his face while she continued to set the stage.

"I am a dying woman. No one cares one way or the other, except for the possible benefit to them as a result of my death. Listen carefully, Arthur Bonnelli, and you may yet live. When I say 'one,' I want you to pick up your gun, point it at my chest, and pull the trigger. If I count to two and you haven't fired—I will."

"One!" she cried out.

Bonnelli could not make sense of it. His seasoned mind, however, dispensed with logic. Awkwardly, he picked up his gun, now wet from its owner's ordeal. He quickly raised the weapon, pointed it as directed and before she could call out another number pulled the trigger twice, but not before his would-be murderess sprung her trap.

At the instant Bonnelli raised his gun, Tersa Ver Meer wheeled 180 degrees. Her heart and lung each caught a bullet from the opposite side intended by her assailant. Even as she fell dead to the floor, her last thought was of the prosecuting attorney and the key question he would be asking of the defense, "How is it that the defendant's victim of self-defense managed to be shot in the back?"

66

Gam'man and Walker sat in the latter's office discussing the previous year's multiple obituaries, which included Arthur Bonnelli, who escaped both the Ver Meer homicide charge and his much-anticipated cardiac arrest by virtue of a cerebral hemorrhage suffered in jail while awaiting trial. Within a few weeks of Bonnelli's demise, Mario Scipone died from a rival's gunshot even as he was attempting to pick up the rotting reins of Bonnelli's organization.

"Gam'man, these 'good news' notices are anti-climactic following as they have the steady downhill slide of Mirror Magic to the point where it has become nothing more than an ordinary, legitimate, if troubled, industry supplier with new ownership. MM's fragmented board—which had become dominated by 'front' lawyers—simply had no use for a sharply declining sales-and-margin manufacturer.

"That also effectively rendered both the original and the replicated subliminal message-processing machines of no value. Baxter Products bought them for a song. I had all but one of the original machines destroyed, and that one will be for museum purposes."

"I have no real interest in that," said Gam'man, "except as it interests you." He sat with his legs crossed, more at ease and displaying considerably more enthusiasm for life than at any time Walker had seen him since Chesser's death.

Walker nodded appreciation for Gam'man's compliment and then Ben added a curious commercial. "All this industry can again offer the advertising and promotional interests, now that the Mirror Magic taint had been removed, is a vast array of imprinted, useful items which can effectively and economically deliver its message alone or in concert with any of the mass media."

Gam'man looked at him quizzically but then interjected a straightman's follow-up. "And catch and hold the interest of the emerging decade's audience through a variety of distribution methods. Ben, you have already saturated my mind on the subject of your industry."

"Of course, Gam'man, you have practically become an expert without ever having been a practitioner," acknowledged Walker. "You'll have to excuse my penchant for rehearsing lines. My friends overlook my eccentricities," he laughed.

"I'm giving an interview to my favorite television reporter this afternoon. This should hit the wire services and I want to make certain I don't omit some of the more salient plugs. She'll try to sidestep my efforts, but if she wants some final inside stuff on MM and BP she'll have to accept the commercial as well. But please excuse my business-centered indulgences, Gam'man. You said over the phone you wanted to see me about something."

"Yes. Actually, several things, Ben," he began. "First of all, I have finally made a decision to go forward with the original interest Chesser and I brought to your attention when we first visited you and Dr. Bascom in Atlanta. I am prepared to begin procreation. All I require, naturally, is a suitable partner. Perhaps you or Amanda could make some recommendations."

Walker smiled and shook his head in resignation. At least he wasn't asking his permission this time.

"The second thing, probably of more interest to you than the first, has to do with the very remarkable transformations which have taken place around the world over the past four years, since Chesser's death."

Gam'man's gestures fit his words more naturally now than they had when they first met. Amanda had coached him and it didn't take long for him to discover what he had not noticed in all his prior years on Earth—he and Chesser having spent them almost exclusively reacting to, rather than interacting with, humans.

Gam'man was at peace with himself. He had since taken to ranching in a rural Nevada-Arizona area just east of Las Vegas. By and large, he preferred the solitude and introspection that went with watching over his range cattle.

He still required a monthly run into one or other of the many available Nevada casinos. His interest remained not to accumulate money at the tables, but to test the degree to which he could influence external circumstances. For fun, and with a new and particularly cocky dealer, Gam'man relished placing an evening's winnings on one turn or fall, letting a fortune slide back to the house just as the dealer was loosening his tie and frantically signalling for his pit boss.

The casino principals all knew of Gam'man and had considered barring him, but he was more of an attraction than a liability, something of a celebrity. Nevertheless, he made them extremely nervous from the standpoint that he might one day choose to break their bank.

Walker responded to the point about world wide events. "That's a suitable and descriptive choice of words, Gam'man, 'remarkable transformations.' In fact, there has never been a more remarkable time in history. At least not one that hasn't been linked to a very definable cause and effect—such as world war, economic depression, catastrophic geologic event, assassination, or the like. And never before in terms of good news. Not to upstage your point, but just for the exercise let me list these remarkable phenomena: continued historic world democratic reforms on the heels of communism's flight, relative stabilization in the Persian Gulf states, third world enlightenment in implementing distribution of outside-supplied food and other aid for starving masses, and even a marked lessening in terrorist activities world wide.

Beyond this, some would say perhaps the single greatest impact of all has come with the lessening of the world drug problem. Now that's the biggest puzzler of all. One would think this would require a fundamental attitude adjustment involving everyone from peasant growers, power and money-based dealers, common pushers and addicted users. I wish we could attribute all of this, as well as the demise of Mirror Magic, to Chesser's efforts, but in all candor I don't see any connection."

"You are entirely correct in your observations about effects, Ben, but not about the cause," replied Gam'man. A self-assured countenance accompanied his remark. "Chesser, indeed, had everything to do with these events. As a matter of fact you even overlooked the development of the public environmental conscience and its impact on politicians and governments in this country and many others. Absolutely unprecedented, wouldn't you say?" Gam'man spoke with the conviction that comes of knowledge, which he was about to share.

"Ben, do you remember your comment some time after we first met, a remark that had to do with your early curiosity as to Mirror Magic's inordinate success and how it had led you to deliberately break and inspect a double M mirror?"

"Of course," he replied. "But I didn't learn anything from that exercise."

"That's because you didn't know what to look for," teased Gam'man.

"What are you getting at?"

"Something at once incredible and true," Gam'man began his revelation. "Chesser did much more than simply 'accomplish his mission' as he reported on his death bed. My curiosity about things was recently prompted after reflecting on the nearly simultaneous development of the many events you just listed. The ramifications have been world wide and have essentially occurred in recognizable form in the past three years. I, too, deliberately invited a little bad luck by 'breaking' a recently manufactured double M mirror and carefully disassembling it."

"Don't tell me you had a 'Magic' mirror hanging in your home, you disloyal dirtbag." Walker complimented Gam'man with the same sort of irreverence good friends shower upon one another during mutually positive moments. "Goes to show you just can't trust a 'green card' carrier," he laughed.

"If I knew someone in the gift mirror business I wouldn't have to hang a competitor's," Gam'man returned the compliment, laughing his slightly odd, but pleasing laugh. "Actually," he explained, "one of the casinos Chesser and I regularly frequented had bought thousands of them over the years, imprinted with the casino name and logo. They distributed them to businesses of every type in Las Vegas and Atlantic City, as well as to 'comped' regulars, as highly visible reminders of that particular hotel and the fun junkets themselves.

"But back to my point, Ben. I thus was able to 'read' one of that casino's mirrors given out some time after Chesser's death. Now hear this. Chesser did not neutralize the subliminal effect of the software in the New Jersey factory as we had supposed."

Walker suddenly chilled, fearing that the whole MM program was—impossibly—still in place. "I don't believe it, Gam'man. You're saying that MM was still projecting its doctored subliminal messages right up to Ver Meer's and Bonnelli's deaths?

"Hell, man, Chesser's mission was to mask the equipment's operative subliminal function, and he said he had accomplished just that! Not to mention the fact that MM's business has been downhill ever since." He couldn't be hearing this correctly. Gam'man had to be toying with him.

The alien was mastering the nuances of the language. He paused, milking everything from the moment, then smiled broadly and continued, "My trick, Ben. Forgive me. Chesser did, however, eliminate the machines' capacity to accept new messages. But not before he reprogrammed the software. I still have in my possession a prisoner-rehab tutorial ring from the few things not burned in our original escape vehicle's demise. I used it to understand the equipment's modified capabilities after having developed my suspicions.

"I discovered what Chesser had already learned and adapted prior to his second sabotage sortie to Mirror Magic; namely, that it was possible to insure that any subsequent programming attempt would only appear to be accepted. The very thing that lost us the court suit, tangible evidence, also allowed the seeds of MM's failure to be sown—causing them to unwittingly sponsor a multi-year altruistic ad effort. This shortcoming on their part was due to the same lack of any sort of visible verification of the presumed program."

"But what was the message?" asked Walker, trying to figure the enigmatic Chesser.

"As I said, I would never have suspected his benevolent interference had not the events been both prolific and timely in the wake of his death. I was also thrown off track in that he spoke with such gravity at the very moment of his cessation of life on an alien world," said Gam'man. "He couldn't tell us what he had done knowing that we could not, in good conscience, permit it. Ben, Chesser left his own epitaph—in subliminal form."

"Epitaph?" echoed Walker.

"Yes, in the form of a Mirror Magic computer virus. It has resulted in the single most effective advertisement ever communicated to man. It went thusly:

> Feed and free the masses.
> Be tolerant; teach it.
> Cleanse the body, the mind,
> And the environment.
>
> Kilroy Was Here.

"Up until you recently purchased and destroyed the machines," explained Gam'man, "Mirror Magic had relentlessly pushed both national and international distribution of their full product line. At first, their market plan was simply to continue capitalizing on their longtime leadership and market share position, then—with the unexplainable decline in their heretofore dramatic sales increases—their efforts were stepped up, intent on recapturing lost momentum. Of course that only magnified the output of the humanitarian message while their competitive advantage was totally negated."

Walker hitchhiked on the revelation. "That explains why the magic disappeared from MM as suddenly as it did. When we lost our lawsuit we thought it would be business at the same old stand for them. We couldn't figure the reversals though. With their artificial market prop removed, it became like water seeking its own level. All this thanks to Chesser and his choice chestnuts." Walker smiled, shaking his head in both relief and amazement.

Gam'man added, "I'm thinking of the quadrillions of world-enhancing advertising impressions Chesser caused to be registered with humankind over that almost four-year period—all at Mirror Magic's expense."

"True, Gam'man, and I would have to say he went a long ways towards undoing your unprincipled countryman's murderous deeds, even though Sloan was certainly not your responsibility. But even given that it was a wholesale invasion of individual privacy, I would have to classify this as the ultimate 'what's good for General Bullmoose is good for the world.'"

"A bull moose general?" questioned Gam'man. "You must be speaking idiomatically, Ben."

"Exactly. What's good for Chesser was good for the human race. But no great good lasts forever, Gam'man. Alas, there will be no new distribution of his messages. But, on the plus side of the ledger, the average use-life of a mirror is easily more than twenty years—a generation—and in those four years more than twenty million such subliminal-message mirrors have been hung or placed around the world in businesses and homes. And in public, private, institutional and governmental locations of every description. The classic-of-classics promotion, with generational pull-through. Call it a marketing success of literally historical proportions. Unfortunately, it's a classic that will never make it into the textbooks because only a handful of us know about it and no one else would believe it."

"Oh, I don't know, Ben. How else would someone explain the sudden international popularity for the name Kilroy?"

Epilogue

Within 30 minutes of Gam'man's departure Muriel Baxter-Bennett knocked lightly and entered Walker's office for their appointment. He smiled instantly, hugged her affectionately, and motioned for her to sit amid the clutter of boxes packed with books and other paraphernalia from his shelves and walls.

"Ben, first of all," said Muriel, "I want to repeat a few of the things I said to the group the other night at your going away party. These last four years since my husband and I returned to Atlanta so I could learn the business and carry on for Dad has meant everything to me. I could not possibly have done it if you hadn't patiently tutored me and in fact 'sold' me to our employees."

"Muriel, I did not 'sell' your capabilities to anyone. It was obvious from the start that you have what it takes to run Baxter Products. And besides, the third generation of Baxters is exactly what this company needs to keep morale up with the loss of Jon."

"You're far too modest," she said, quietly tearing. "If it hadn't been for your unselfish efforts, this company and perhaps many others in the industry would have suffered irreversibly. The only thing Dad could have wanted further from you is your staying, in whatever role you desired."

Muriel Baxter meant what she was saying. She was quite confident in her own abilities, but she would have gladly taken second rein to Ben Walker had he only agreed.

"I fully appreciate what you're saying, Muriel, but I am truly excited about the decision I've made. I'll be seeing you at the shows anyway, once Jun'or Presentations is underway. Amanda and I are flying to Tallahassee tomorrow to meet with the Bascoms concerning start-up details. Your own minor investment in the new company, along with that of Gene 'Nitpicker' Ellison, plus the out-of-this-world engineering and consulting expertise of one O. Gam'man, will give the Walker-Bascom management team the potential to develop as a formidable new supplier to industry distributors."

Walker had no illusions about the difficult road ahead, but he radiated enthusiasm for both the challenge and the opportunity.

"Well," said Baxter, "You should certainly have no problem with distribution, as well known as you are. You're a hero to a lot of people in the industry, you know."

"Oh, I don't know about that. I talked with Walt Manley last week and he was half-pissed over my causing him to lose more than $100,000 a year in Mirror Magic renewals!

"Seriously though, when I told him about our new venture and the flagship product we'll be introducing, he said he might even be willing to pay for a sample, and present it to a client or two—if we can deliver."

Muriel Baxter caught Walker's contagious laughter and added, "Well, may it all turn out as successfully as you deserve, Ben," she offered her hand as she was about to leave, and then cautioned him. "But remember, leave the conventional mirrors and C.P.S. to Baxter Products!"

Ben and Amanda were spending an idyllic weekend at their favorite Florida cypress-and-water retreat. Monday was to be mostly business between them and the Bascoms, but this was early Sunday. Amanda sat on the side of the bed watching a colorful, mixed bag of birds including gallinules, mallards, herons and ibis, none identifiable to her city-bred eye. Some were floaters, others waders. Some swooped down gracefully to snatch from the river/spring their selections from the breakfast buffet set only a few semi-tropical yards outside the human interlopers' second-story window. In the open-doored bathroom Ben's 'music-to-shave-by' portable tape player was throbbing with the marked beat of one of his swing favorites. This time it was Woody Herman's "Woodchoppers' Ball," aptly named for Maine guides competing in a wood-chopping contest inspired by one of the band's bass playing sidemen. Very fitting, Ben thought, considering their wooded locale, though he hardly needed any rationale for listening to his personal soul music.

Amanda's conversational voice was suddenly competing with the music. "Ben," she sighed, framed in the doorway in her familiar style, "This was such a thoughtful idea, coming here on our third wedding anniversary. But with the excitement of Jun'or Presentations," she said, positioning a little pout just so Ben could see it in one corner of the bathroom mirror, "I really thought you might overlook it."

She was also pregnant with their second child, who would, like its sibling, be bearing a middle name honoring one of two truly unique beings. That placed them only two behind the rascally Gam'man and his charming wife. He was certainly proving to be much more 'games man' than 'observer.'

Walker didn't answer immediately. He had been thinking about JP's prototype first product, developed at Gam'man's suggestion and after diligent research by both Flyn and Ben. The payoff after only a year of actual development was a true advertising hologram.

Commercial pseudo-holograms had been around the industry and on the retail market for years. Everything from acrylic key tags to magazine covers and credit cards had professed to present them. But they were really little improvement on the stereopticon (with the added production elements of foil and lasers) of more than a hundred years before, except one didn't have to view the effect through a hand-held contraption.

The Holo-Jun', as Ben had named the product, was inspired by a combination of something he had once read in an Isaac Asimov novel, a relatively unimaginative description of a 'holomirror,' and the holo-word processor he had first seen in Gam'man's Las Vegas hotel room. With the Holo-Jun', however, the user would be able to view a precise image of himself from any angle of a 360-degree perspective, in miniature—and live!

This amazing mirror-projection device sensed heat from any live body exceeding approximately 50 pounds. When the body entered an area within six feet of, and perpendicular to, the Holo-Jun's mirror face, the holographic sensor was activated. Slowly and continuously it would rotate the projected image until the source of the heat moved outside its range. A person could thus view the back of his own head, neck, clothes, etc., without moving, and without the aid of secondary mirrors.

Along with the image thus projected in this home and office marvel of personal vanity, would appear a much smaller but nevertheless continuously visible advertising logo and message, programmed on behalf of the advertiser.

Ben still had not gotten over the fact that their prototype actually worked. A true holographic advertising mirror, a three-dimensional projection from a single plane receptor. And no viewer enhancement equipment required. Well, okay, so it was a little pricey, but so what? Think of it as an incentive for special awards, performance recognition, trade show traffic, safety, service or sales promotion, VIPs, retirement, speaker gifts, dealer loaders—he couldn't think fast enough.

God, would that be uncommon influence or what? Then, in a more propagandistic mode he thought, yet more evidence for the once-disdained industry's increasingly credible claim to be the promotional medium for the 21st century.

He returned to the mirror at hand with the one sobering aspect of his new challenge. Against the objection of the others he had insisted that a small-print disclaimer accompany each Holo-Jun', which would read, "Advertising may be harmful to your free will."

"We'll put it right on the case; advertisers will love it," he had assured the dissenters.

Wiping the lather from his face with a hot wash cloth Ben realized he hadn't responded to Amanda's half-teasing question about remembering their anniversary. He caught her bright hazel-green eyes in the mirror, smiling as he fastened his gaze on her. He turned and took her in his arms, saying softly, "Amanda, love, Chesser once told me of a cherished Jun'orian phrase: 'The eyes of one in love reflect always the image of the loved one.' Have you never noticed your image mirrored by my eyes?"

I wish to thank the following promotional products industry manufacturers and decorators who graciously placed an ad in a most unlikely medium.

Stick With Us!

If it's flat, magnetic or adhesive backed and generally under a dollar, it's very often a FINN product.

From custom imprinted stick-up calendars and window decals to write-on / wipe-off magnets and boards ... FINN products take up long term residence on windows, computer monitors, refrigerators, walls, file cabinets and work stations. We help you stick around!

Your local promotional products distributor has just the idea for you!

ASI #54290

Uncommonly Present.

The Promotional Drinking Vessel

When man's earliest ancestors first began roaming the land in search of food, he very quickly made improvements on hand-cupping water for drinking.

Today's preferred drinking vessels offered by Glass America are ceramic or glass cups, mugs and tumblers, in sizes from 2 oz. to 20 oz.. At most special events and in offices everywhere, one of these highly visible promotional vessels with a colorfully decorated logo and message is almost certain to be in attendance.

Lets talk about high perceived value at the low price points in our competitive markets.

We Put America On Glass!

Dynamic Billboards from JULIE

More than thirty years ago the world discovered that, in general, people had no objection to being used as dynamic carriers for advertising and promotion. Today, they actually value wearing a graphic statement of company or message loyalty or preference via a custom-imprinted cap, jacket or shirt.

The Julie Line is a proud domestic maker and imprinter of a broad range of promotional caps (from infant to oversized adults), jackets and bags. We'll be glad to put your business logo on one of our billboards. Just ask your favorite promotional products distributor to try one on.

JULIE ASI# 63670
Uncommon wearables.

Blanket
Your
Future

LOGO
KNITS®

Give a Novel of Mystery and Intrigue to Friends and Colleagues!

ORDER FORM

YES, I want ____ copies of *Uncommon Influence* at $14.95 each, plus $3 shipping per book. (Georgia residents please include $0.90 state sales tax.) Canadian orders must be accompanied by a postal money order in U.S. funds. Allow 30 days for delivery.

My Check or Money Order for $ _________ is enclosed.

Name ________________________________ Phone _____________

Address ____

City/State/Zip ____

Please make your check payable and return to:

DCG Publishing
PO Box 767999
Roswell, GA 30076